BLACKSTONE AND
THE GREAT WAR

BLACKSTONE AND THE GREAT WAR

An Inspector Sam Blackstone Mystery

Sally Spencer

This first world edition published 2012
in Great Britain and in the USA by
SEVERN HOUSE PUBLISHERS LTD of
9–15 High Street, Sutton, Surrey, England, SM1 1DF.

British Library Cataloguing in Publication Data

Spencer, Sally.
  Blackstone and the Great War. – (The Inspector Sam
  Blackstone series)
  1. Blackstone, Sam (Fictitious character) – Fiction.
  2. Police – England – London – Fiction. 3. World War,
  1914–1918 – Campaigns – Western Front – Fiction. 4. Great
  Britain. Army – Officers – Crimes against – Fiction.
  5. Detective and mystery stories.
  I. Title II. Series
  823.9'2-dc22

ISBN-13: 978-0-7278-8123-6 (cased)

All Severn House titles are printed on acid-free paper.

Severn House Publishers support The Forest Stewardship Council [FSC],
the leading international forest certification organisation. All our titles that
are printed on Greenpeace-approved FSC-certified paper carry the FSC logo.

Typeset by Palimpsest Book Production Ltd.,
Falkirk, Stirlingshire, Scotland.
Printed and bound in Great Britain by
MPG Books Ltd., Bodmin, Cornwall.

In memory of my grandfather, Allen Rustage, one of the quiet heroes of the 'War to End All Wars'.

ONE

The troop ship docked in Calais just after darkness had fallen, and the passengers were quickly disembarked and herded, in a ragged column, towards the nearby railway station.

Once they caught sight of the train which would take them to the railhead, some of the young soldiers put on a spurt, so they would have their choice of seats, but Sam Blackstone did not follow their example. Like the old campaigner he was, he took his time, knowing that, even at this stage of the game, it was foolish to expend energy when there was no need to.

The train smelled of damp, sweat and general neglect, but considering that most newly arrived enlisted men were transported to the front line in cattle wagons, Blackstone thought, even a dilapidated third-class carriage was an unexpected luxury.

Not that unexpected luxury should be taken as a sign of things to come, he mused, as he walked along the corridor. In the eyes of the military command, ordinary soldiers *were*, and always *had been* cattle – brave, well-disciplined cattle, it was true, but cattle nonetheless. And if, on this particular occasion, they were being treated with a little more dignity than usual, that was probably because the authorities had, with typical inefficiency, failed to secure the kind of transportation that they would normally have used.

When he found a seat at the end of the train, the carriage was already occupied by seven young men.

No, not young men at all, he corrected himself, as he sat down.

They were boys!

As the train lurched, and then slowly chugged out of the station, Blackstone ran a professional policeman's eye over his travelling companions.

The boy sitting directly opposite him was a prime example of an East End hooligan, he noted. The lad was neither broad nor tall – the diet of the poor rarely fostered such growth – but he had the hard, knotted muscles of someone who had been introduced to physical labour at an early age. His head was bullet-shaped, and looked too small for his body. He had narrow eyes, a jagged scar ran down one cheek, and his teeth – already rotting – would be all but gone by the time he had reached his mid-twenties.

Blackstone had noticed the boy twice before. The first time had been at Dover, where he had been strutting up and down as if he owned the place. The second time had been on the ship, and by then the lad had lost his self-assurance and was leaning over the side, spewing his guts up. Now, on their third meeting, on dry land again, he seemed to have regained his cockiness.

'Course, the Huns have had it easy so far,' the boy was telling the lad next to him. 'Up to now, you see, they've only had to deal with *professional* soldiers, and you know what they're like, don't you?'

'No, what *are* they like, Mick?' his friend asked.

'Time servers,' the boy said confidently. 'The thing about them is, you see, they joined the army because they didn't have nothing better to do with their time, and now they've found themselves caught up in war, they're playing it safe and keeping their heads down.'

Idiot! Blackstone thought.

The boy was like so many young men who came from the Whitechapel area. He thought he was tough, and no doubt he *was* handy enough with a fist in a drunken Saturday night fight at his local boozer. But he had no idea – no real idea at all – of what war was actually like.

'Yes, you'll see,' Mick continued. 'Once the Huns find themselves up against lads with something about them – lads with a spirit of adventure – they'll all turn tail and run for home.'

There'd been eager young recruits just like him in the Afghan Campaign – Flash Harrys who weren't going to be intimidated by a little brown man who lived in a mud hut and carried an ancient rifle. Oh yes, there'd been more than enough of them – and all their arrogance had gained them had been unmarked graves, thousands of miles from home.

Mick stopped talking to his friend and turned his gaze – suddenly full of hostility – onto Blackstone.

'Have you got a problem, Grandad?' he asked aggressively.

'No problem at all,' Blackstone replied evenly.

'Don't lie to me, you old bag of bones,' the youth said. His expression changed, now more puzzled than angry – though the anger was still there. 'What are you doing on this train, anyway?' he continued. 'Why are you filling a seat with your rotting carcass when it could have been taken by a fighting hero?'

'It's a long story,' Blackstone said.

But it wasn't – it was a very short story, which hadn't even begun to be written three days earlier.

As he had walked up the long, elm-lined drive to Hartley House – an impressive ancestral pile which could probably date its origins back to the days when Good Queen Bess was still a girl – Blackstone had found himself wondering, not for the first time that day, why General Sir Michael Fortesque VC, who he had not seen for over thirty years, should have summoned him.

It was true that Fortesque and he had been close comrades in Afghanistan – or, at least, as close as an orphanage-raised sergeant and an Eton-educated captain ever could be – but the Second Afghan War was now long consigned to the history books, and it seemed unlikely that Fortesque should suddenly have felt the need to reminisce with one of the poor bloody infantry.

He had almost reached the front entrance when a footman, dressed in full livery, suddenly appeared and blocked his path.

'Yes?' the footman said, running his eyes disdainfully up and down the visitor's second hand suit.

'I have an appointment with the General,' Blackstone replied.

The footman sniffed. '*You're* the inspector from Scotland Yard?' he asked, incredulously.

'That's right.'

The other man turned the idea over in his mind for a few moments, and then seemed to decide that – however amazing it might be – Blackstone really was what he claimed.

'The servants' and tradesmen's entrance is around the side of the house,' the footman said curtly. 'Follow me.'

'I think I'd prefer to enter the house through the front door,' Blackstone told him.

The footman sniffed again. 'That's out of the question.'

'Is it?' Blackstone asked.

'Of course it is.'

'I see,' Blackstone said, then he turned smartly and began to walk back the way he had come. 'Please be so kind as to tell the General I called.'

'Where do you think you're going?' the footman demanded, in a tone which was both annoyed and incredulous.

'To the railway station,' Blackstone said, over his shoulder. 'It's where you *have to* go, if you want to catch a train.'

'But the master is *expecting* you.'

'I know.'

'Wait!' the footman shouted, and now, as Blackstone widened the distance between them, there was a note of panic in his voice.

Blackstone stopped and turned again. 'Yes?'

The footman swallowed hard.

'If you'd care to follow me, sir, I'll conduct you to the front door,' he said, forcing each word out of his mouth with considerable effort.

'That would be most kind of you,' Blackstone said graciously.

A large and ornate mirror hung in the corridor outside General Fortesque's study, and though Blackstone rarely took the opportunity to examine his own appearance, he did so now.

The man who stared back at him bore a superficial resemblance to the man he thought himself to be. Both were tall (over six feet) and had tight, sinewy bodies. Both had large noses, which could have been Middle Eastern, but weren't. Yet the man looking out of the mirror seemed older than the man who was looking into it. He seemed, in fact, to have reached that point in middle age in which he was teetering on the edge of being old.

Blackstone shook his head, as if, with that one gesture, he could also shake off his little remaining vanity. He had never expected to reach his middle fifties, he reminded himself. Nor had he particularly wanted to, because the older a man got, the longer the shadow of the workhouse became. But he *had* survived – despite Afghanistan, despite the hazards of working in the Metropolitan Police and the New York Police Department – and so, he supposed, he was stuck with life and might as well make the most out of it that he could.

The study door opened, and the butler appeared.

'Sir Michael will see you now,' he said, in the deep booming voice of an Old Testament prophet.

The room overlooked the driveway, and the General was sitting in his bath chair by the window. When the butler had turned the chair around, Blackstone could see for himself that Fortesque was a mere husk of the man he had once been.

The General raised his hand in feeble greeting, and said, 'It was good of you to come, Sergeant.'

Blackstone grinned. 'I wasn't aware I had any choice in the matter,' he said. 'If I'd refused, you'd only have contacted the Commissioner of Police, who would then have made what started out as a request into a direct order.'

The old man returned Blackstone's grin with a weak one of his own. 'Yes, as decrepit as I am, I do seem to have some influence left,' he said. 'How's life been for you since we last met, Sam?'

'I have no complaints,' Blackstone told him.

Not true! said a tiny irritating voice at the back of his mind. You *do* have regrets – and most of them concern women.

'You must be approaching retirement,' the General said.

'It's around the corner,' Blackstone agreed.

'And how will you manage, once you're no longer earning a wage?'

'I've got a bit of money put by,' Blackstone said.

But not enough – not nearly enough – because for most of his working life, half his wage had gone directly to the orphanage in which he himself had been brought up.

'I had a grandson,' the General said, changing the subject. 'He was my pride and joy.'

Blackstone, noting the past tense, said nothing.

'He was killed on the Western Front, just a few days ago,' the General continued.

Blackstone nodded gravely. 'War's always been a terrible thing, but from what I've heard, this one makes the one's we fought seem like a bit of harmless sparring,' he said. 'God alone knows how many of our young men will die on the battlefield before it's finally over.'

'Charlie *didn't* die in battle,' the General said, and there was a deep anger in his voice now. 'If he'd been cut down doing his duty, I could have borne that. It would have been hard for me, yes, yet no harder than it has been for generations of my family who have gladly made the sacrifice. But he was never given the opportunity to give his life for his country – he was murdered.'

'I'm sorry,' Blackstone said – and so he was.

'I want you to find his killer,' the General said.

'You want what!' Blackstone exclaimed.

'I want you to find his killer,' the General repeated.

'The military have police of their own.'

'So they do. And they're usually very good at their job – but that job doesn't include tracking down murderers.'

This was insane, Blackstone thought.

'I'm a civilian, now,' he protested. 'I have been for over a quarter of a century. The military would never brook my interference.'

'Of course they will, if I ask them to,' the General said, with an absolute certainty. 'Besides, you've always had a strong belief in your own self-worth, and you're unlikely to allow any man in a fancy uniform to intimidate you.'

Blackstone walked over to the window, and looked down at the spot on which he'd been standing only a few minutes earlier.

He chuckled, and said, 'I thought you might be behind it.'

'Behind what?' the General asked innocently.

'Behind the little charade when I first arrived. It was you who told the flunkey to bring me in through the servants' entrance, wasn't it?'

'Is that what you really believe?' the General asked, curiously.

'No, not when I stop to think about it,' Blackstone admitted. 'You're much too subtle for that. So you didn't tell him to treat me like a piece of offal – but you knew that he would!'

Fortesque smiled. 'I've always known how the men who served under me would react in any situation. A good commander has to – because there are no second chances in war. And Hopwood – that's my "flunkey's" name – has a very high opinion of himself, and fondly imagines that, one day, he'll be the butler at one of the finest houses in England.'

'But he won't?'

'Of course not. A butler in the making doesn't need to *act* as if he's superior – it's enough for him to *know* that he is.'

'So you arranged the little skirmish with Hopwood to see whether or not I still had fire in my belly,' Blackstone said.

'I had to be sure,' the General replied. 'Thirty years is a long time, and men change. But you haven't lost your fire,

Sam, and that's why I want you go to the Western Front as my representative.'

'I don't even know how the modern army works,' Blackstone protested.

'And that's why I want you to go to the Western Front,' the General repeated, and now his voice was so firm that, if Blackstone had closed his eyes, he could easily have imagined he was talking to a much younger man. 'I could ask your superiors to order you to go – and they would. I could offer you money – and, indeed, if you bring my grandson's murderer to justice, I will give you five thousand pounds. But I did not call you here to either threaten or bribe you.'

'No?' Blackstone asked, sceptically.

'No,' the General said. 'I asked you here so that I could plead with you – as an old comrade I would have given my life for back then – to do something which might perhaps ease an old man's suffering a little. Will you do this one thing for me, Sam?'

'I'll do it,' Blackstone agreed. 'You haven't left me much bloody choice, have you?'

The old train continued to rattle and groan. The young soldier was still staring angrily at Blackstone.

'You shouldn't be here at all,' Mick said. 'Matter of fact, when we stop again, I'm going to throw you off.'

'You should save your rage for the enemy,' Blackstone told him. 'And even then, you should have it under control.'

'Or maybe I won't even *wait* until we stop!' Mick said, infuriated by his calmness. 'Maybe I'll throw you off right now.'

'I wouldn't do that if I was you,' Blackstone advised.

'Oh wouldn't you?' Mick scoffed. 'Well, you're *not* me, are you? I'm a young man, and you're just a useless old fart.'

He stood up, and reached across for the lapels of the old fart's jacket. Blackstone grabbed his wrist, found the pressure point, and squeezed tightly.

Mick's face went white as he fought the urge to scream, but it was already a losing battle, and as Blackstone maintained the pressure and forced him to his knees, the young soldier gave a gasp of pain.

'The first thing you need to learn is never to get into a fight unless you absolutely have to,' Blackstone said. 'And the second is that if you *do* get into a fight, never underestimate your enemy.'

Mick was biting his lower lip, and searching in vain for the strength to fight back.

'I'll let you go if you promise to sit down and be quiet,' Blackstone said. '*Do* you promise?'

Mick nodded his head. 'Yes,' he said, in a wheeze.

'I'm telling you all this for your own good,' Blackstone said, as the boy returned to his seat and gingerly massaged his wrist. 'With the attitude you've got now, you won't last a day at the Front.'

But even as he spoke the words, he knew Mick probably wouldn't listen. That was the trouble with lads like him. And that was why – though they didn't even realize it – they were already walking dead men.

TWO

At a speed which would have made a lethargic snail ashamed, the train chugged through the flat French countryside.

The view from the window offered little in the way of distraction. Occasionally, there would be a gnarled old peasant leading a nag which was all skin and bone. Once in a while, the train would pass through a small station, and offer a brief glimpse of the village, battered by war, which lay beyond it. Other than that, the locomotive could have been travelling through a land which the world had quite forgotten.

This total lack of any sort of drama – this absence of anything to fire the gung-ho spirit – soon began to have an effect on the young soldiers, and their animation drained away, to be replaced by a kind of bored stupor.

That was what war was like, Blackstone thought, observing them. It could be excruciatingly painful, and it could be bowel-movingly terrifying. It could even – when you realized that there was a good chance you were not going to die that particular day – be a joyous experience, an orgasm of relief. But mostly, as these lads were starting to discover, it was mindlessly boring.

They reached the railhead – a shabby little station which,

pre-war, would have been lucky to see a dozen passengers a day – as darkness was falling. A couple of the boys stood up with obvious relief that the cramped journey was finally over, and stepped out into the corridor to stretch their legs, but a bellow from one of the sergeants posted there soon had them scurrying back to their seats.

Another half an hour passed painfully slowly before the sergeant opened the door.

'If you look out of the window, you'll see half a dozen sergeants standing on the platform holding up paraffin lamps,' he said. 'You're to muster in front of the third lamp from the end. Got that?'

'Yes, Sarge,' the young soldiers said, in unison.

The sergeant turned to Blackstone. 'You're being met,' he said. Then, out of deference to the fact that the man he was addressing was a civilian — albeit a middle-aged one in a shabby suit – he added, 'Ain't that right, *sir*?'

'That's right,' Blackstone agreed.

'Well, the best thing you can do is to try and keep out of the way until your liaison makes himself known to you,' the sergeant said.

'He'll recognize me, will he?' Blackstone asked, with a smile.

'You'll stick out like a vicar in a brothel,' the sergeant said, flatly.

Yes, I suppose I will, Blackstone thought.

The sergeant turned smartly on his heel, and left the carriage.

'I never thought it would be like this, Sid,' Mick said to his pal, then glanced quickly at Blackstone to see if he had somehow managed to cause offence.

'No, I'll bet you didn't,' the Scotland Yard man agreed.

The soldiers picked up their kit, climbed out of the carriage, and lined up in front of the third lantern from the end.

Blackstone followed, feeling odd that he should be a part of all this, and yet, strictly speaking, no part of it at all.

Once the men were in more or less orderly lines, a sergeant major who had been observing the whole spectacle blew his whistle, and the men fell silent.

'You will be marched out to the reserve trench, where you will be issued with gas masks and rations!' he barked. 'Any questions?'

'Could we please have something to drink, Sergeant Major?' one of the soldiers murmured.

'What was that, lad?' the sergeant major asked, rounding on him.

'It's . . . it's just that we haven't had anything since we left the port,' the soldier told him.

'Is that right?' the sergeant major asked. 'Well, you poor lad! That's such a touching story that I'm finding it hard to fight back the tears!'

'I only wondered . . .' the soldier said weakly.

'It's not your job to *wonder*!' the sergeant major said harshly. 'It's your job to *obey orders*.' He ran his eyes over the ranks of recruits. 'You're in the army now. You eat and drink when you're given the opportunity, and you don't whine when you're not.' He paused for a second, then added, 'Any *more* questions?'

And the silence which answered him was almost deafening.

Looking along the platform, Blackstone saw a small group of officers who had arrived on the same train, and who had been met by a young second lieutenant. The officers, he noted, were not asking for something to drink. But then they didn't need to – because an orderly, with a tray of drinks in his hand, had already satisfied that requirement.

The second lieutenant – who couldn't have been more than twenty or twenty-one – noticed Blackstone standing there, and detached himself from the group.

'Are you the chap from Scotland Yard?' he asked, brusquely.

'Yes, I'm the "chap" from Scotland Yard,' Blackstone agreed.

The lieutenant seemed outraged by the response.

'I'm the chap from Scotland Yard, *sir*!' he barked.

'Are you?' Blackstone asked, in a bemused tone. 'I thought *I* was the copper. Still, I do get confused easily, so you're probably right.'

'Now listen here, my good man . . .' the lieutenant blustered.

'And there's no need to call me "sir", even though, strictly speaking, I probably hold a higher rank in the police than you do in the army,' Blackstone interrupted him.

'I . . . I . . .' the lieutenant began.

'Are you my escort?' Blackstone asked.

'Your escort?' the lieutenant repeated, as if he could hardly believe the cheek of the man. 'You don't have an *escort*. You're to march with the men to the reserve trench, and once you get there, you're to find an officer to report to.'

Well, that certainly put him in his place, Blackstone thought.

Following the bobbing paraffin lamps which the sergeants held up in front of them, the new arrivals marched through the dark suburbs of the town and soon were out in open countryside.

For the first mile or so, they heard little but the tramp-tramp-tramp of their own boots, though occasionally one of the men would cough or whisper something to the man nearest to him. Then, as they got closer to the front, they heard a low rumbling sound – the sort of noise a great beast might make as it lay there, slowly dying.

They marched on, and the sound grew louder and angrier, and now there were sudden flashes of light exploding through the darkness.

The sergeant at the head of the column stopped, and turned around.

'Ten minutes tobacco rest!' he bawled.

Some of the young soldiers took off their packs before sitting down, but the majority simply sank awkwardly to the ground with the packs still in place.

They had already learned a second important thing about war, Blackstone thought – it wasn't just the fighting which was exhausting, it was the whole bloody business!

He was lighting up a cigarette when he heard a voice to his left say, 'I'm sorry about what happened earlier. I should never have been so bleeding rude to a man who could probably half-kill me without even breaking into a sweat.'

'You should never be so bleeding rude to anybody at all, Mick,' Blackstone said.

'You're right,' the young soldier admitted. 'But it was the way you were looking at me in that carriage that got me all upset, you see.'

'And how *was* I looking at you?'

'As if I was nothing! As if I was a piece of dog shit you'd stepped in! I've been getting that look all my life, and I'm heartily tired of it.'

'I promise you, I wasn't looking at you as if you were a piece of dog shit,' Blackstone said.

'No?' Mick said, disbelievingly.

'No,' Blackstone repeated. 'I was looking at you as if you were a bloody idiot.'

Mick chuckled. 'Oh, that's all right then,' he said, 'because, if truth be told, I'm *not* all that bright.'

'Don't underrate yourself. You're sounding brighter all he time,' Blackstone told him.

'Thanks for that, sir,' Mick said, sincerely. 'I wouldn't have thrown you off the train, even if I'd been able to. That was just me being stupid.'

'I know,' Blackstone said.

Mick hesitated before speaking again.

'Are we all right with each other, now?' he asked finally. 'I mean, are we pals?'

'We're all right with each other, certainly,' Blackstone said. 'I'd like to leave it a day or so before I decide if we're pals or not.'

'Fair enough!' Mick replied, with a cheeriness which, despite himself, Blackstone found endearing.

There was another series of booms in the distance.

'Why are they fighting at night, sir?' asked a new voice, which Blackstone recognized as belonging to Mick's friend, Sid.

'They're *not* fighting in any real sense of the word,' Blackstone said. 'They're just firing off shells.'

'But what's the point of that, if they can't even see if they're hitting their target?'

Blackstone sighed. 'Some shells *will* hit their targets – or, at least, when they're filling in their reports, they'll decide that whatever they hit *was* what they were aiming for all along. But the main point of the bombardment is not to *hit* anything – it's to wear down the enemy's nerves.'

'Doesn't seem very sporting,' Sid said dubiously.

He's been wrong to call these lads *boys*, Blackstone thought – they were more like babes-in-arms.

After they had marched for another three miles, they reached the artillery batteries which had been making all the noise.

Some of the men broke step in order to take a closer look at them, but then one of the sergeants shouted, 'What are you gawping at, you useless bleeders? This ain't August bank holiday on Hampstead Heath – keep moving.'

They were a hundred yards beyond the guns when a series of shells whizzed over their heads on their way to German-held territory, and though it was obvious that they were in no danger themselves, some of the soldiers still faltered, causing the men behind to crash into them.

Ahead of them – way ahead – they saw red flashes as the shells landed.

Sid laughed nervously. 'Well, I certainly wouldn't like to be one of them Huns tonight,' he said.

'The Germans have big guns too,' Blackstone reminded him. 'Probably more than we have.'

And almost as if they had been listening to him – waiting for his signal – the German guns answered back.

It was the whooshing noise – coming relentlessly through the air at them – that alerted the young soldiers, and they threw themselves down in a panicked confusion of knees and elbows.

Then the shell landed – not thirty yards in front of them – first thudding heavily into the earth, and then exploding.

The ground shook, and the supine men felt tiny ripples of movement running along the length of their bodies.

'Oh, sweet Jesus!' someone moaned.

'Watch out for the shell casing!' one of the sergeants called out, in a calm, authoritative voice.

There was a curious hissing sound in the air, a little like the noise a mermaid might have made when attempting to sing underwater, and then small pieces of shell casing, some no bigger than a coin, began to rain down on them.

'Right, excitement over!' the same sergeant said, after a few seconds had passed. 'You can stand up now.'

The soldiers clambered awkwardly back to their feet.

'Bloody hell, that was a close one,' Mick said shakily. 'If we'd been marching a bit faster, it would have had us.'

'I'm going to die,' said Sid, in a voice so calmly fatalistic that it chilled Blackstone's blood.

'No, you ain't,' Mick replied. 'You're looking at things arse-ways up, my old mate. That shell was a sign from heaven – it was a way of telling us that we've got a charmed life.'

It was a noble effort from someone who was obviously badly

shaken up himself, Blackstone thought, but it seemed to have little effect on Sid.

'I'll never see my twentieth birthday,' the young recruit said, his voice still eerily level. 'I know I won't.'

'Course you will!' Mick said, and now there was an edge of desperation in his words. 'Bleedin' hell, Sid, you seem to have forgotten that your birthday's only *four days away*.'

'If you manage to get back to Blighty yourself, tell Maisie I *would* have married her if I'd lived,' Sid said.

'Come on, old pal, don't be like that,' Mick pleaded.

'Tell her that she was the best thing that could ever have happened to a nobody like me,' Sid said, with sad certainty.

THREE

B lackstone followed the red-bereted MFP corporal along the reserve trench, which was half a mile behind the front line. The trench itself was roughly twelve feet deep, and perhaps ten feet wide, he calculated. It did not run in a straight line, but in a zigzag, with a blind corner every nine yards or so. Duckboards covered its earthen floor, sandbags supported its earthen walls.

And it stank – God, how it stank!

Ever the professional observer, Blackstone found himself attempting to isolate each of the individual smells which worked together to make up the putrid, disgusting whole.

There was cordite, certainly, but that was hardly surprising, given that, even in the short time he had been in the trench, he had heard the sound of at least a dozen rifle shots, fired – almost certainly pointlessly – at the enemy lines.

There was the odour of the overflowing cesspits – mere holes in the ground, covered with planks – which the men used as their latrines.

There was a hint of cigarette smoke, the chemical sting of the lime chloride laid down to prevent the spread of disease, the mouldy smell of rotting sandbags and the rank odour of men's unwashed bodies.

And occasionally, when a slight breeze blew over the trench, he thought he caught a whiff of the decaying corpses, hastily buried in shallow graves in No Man's Land.

There were private soldiers in the trench. They were a miserable, bedraggled bunch, as different to the square-jawed confident heroes of the recruiting posters as it was possible to imagine. Some were squatted down, smoking, playing cards or talking in low, hoarse whispers. Others were huddled into the small dugouts, carved from the side of the trench, trying to catch a little sleep.

The soldiers did not look up as Blackstone approached them, but he felt their eyes following him once he had passed by.

They knew why he was there, he thought – they probably weren't supposed to, but they knew right enough.

The redcap came to a halt in front of a wooden door in the back wall of the trench, rapped on the door with his fist and said, 'Visitor and escort, seeking permission to enter, sir!' in a voice which would have carried all the way across a parade ground.

There was a muffled response from inside, and the redcap opened the door and gestured to Blackstone that he should step forward.

The room that they entered was a substantial one, and a far cry from the holes in the trench in which the enlisted men did their best to get some rest. Close to the door was a table covered with a clean white cloth, on which sat a bottle of whisky and a set of crystal glasses. Beyond the table, there were a number of armchairs and a wind-up gramophone, and at the back of the dugout there were three or four beds with comfortable mattresses.

There were five officers sitting at the table, two captains and three second lieutenants.

The redcap looked first at one captain and then at the other, as if unsure of which one to address.

That was the army for you, Blackstone thought, amused at his obvious perplexity. The captain at the head of the table was probably the company commander, which, under normal circumstances, made him unquestionably the most important man in the room. But the other captain, as was evident from his badge, was a military policeman – which meant he was the redcap's boss – and that fact alone was enough to muddy the normally clear blue waters of military protocol.

'You may go, Corporal,' the company commander said.

The corporal looked relieved that the decision had been taken out of his hands. He saluted – wisely looking straight at his own captain as he did so – wheeled round, and smartly exited the dugout.

From the expression on the redcap captain's face, it was clear to Blackstone that he was not entirely pleased with the way things had panned out, but equally clear that he felt he could say nothing about it in the presence of three junior officers and a mere civilian. The junior officers themselves were pretending to have a complete lack of interest in the new arrival, though when they thought Blackstone was not looking at them, they took the opportunity to study him closely.

'So you're Blackstone, are you?' the company commander asked.

'That's right,' the policeman agreed.

'I'm Captain Carstairs,' the captain told him. 'You may stand at ease, Blackstone.'

'To do that successfully, I'd first have to have been standing at attention,' Blackstone pointed out. 'And I wasn't.'

Carstairs frowned, then turned towards the younger officers.

'I expect that you gentlemen are anxious to return to your duties,' he said.

The lieutenants nodded – recognizing an order when they heard one – and stood up.

'Goodnight, sir,' they said in unison.

'Goodnight Maude, goodnight Soames, goodnight Hatfield,' Carstairs drawled.

The three young officers crossed the dugout and walked past Blackstone. None of them looked directly at him – nor even so much as acknowledged his physical presence – but that couldn't cover up the fact that they had been bursting with curiosity when he first walked in.

'Maude, Soames and Hatfield,' Blackstone repeated silently.

He would remember those names and those faces, just in case their presence in the dugout that night had been more than just a coincidence.

'Do you have any questions you'd care to put to Blackstone, Captain Huxton?' Carstairs asked the other remaining officer.

'I most certainly do,' Huxton replied. 'You're a sergeant, aren't you, Blackstone?'

He had just about got the measure of the two men now, Blackstone decided.

Carstairs, despite his greying temples, was probably still only in his early thirties. He was the sort of man who would not find the burden of command an easy one to bear, but would do his best to fulfil the role honourably and conscientiously. As officers went, he was probably not a bad man, though, like most officers, his view of the world around him was probably as narrow as the one which could be viewed through a trench periscope.

Huxton was another matter altogether. He had a rounded face and a florid complexion, and his eyes told the story of a man who had gone through life with the firm belief that no problem was so large that it could not be solved by merely shouting loudly at it.

'Are you stone deaf, man?' Huxton demanded. 'I asked you if you were a sergeant.'

'I used to be,' Blackstone replied. 'I *used to be* a lot of things – but now I'm a police inspector.'

Captain Huxton lifted his whisky glass, and took a leisurely sip, leaving Blackstone standing there in front of the table, as if he were a guilty schoolboy who had been summoned to the headmaster's study.

Huxton smacked his lips in appreciation, put his glass down, and said, 'I hear you served in India and Afghanistan.'

'I did,' Blackstone agreed.

'Well, that must have been a long time ago now,' Huxton reflected. 'Soldiering has changed a lot since your day.'

No, it hadn't, Blackstone thought – not if these men were anything to go by. The weapons may have become more lethal, the tactics might now be very different, but the army was still the army he had known – and Carstairs and Huxton were the living proof of it.

'We've had to lower our standards since this bloody war started, and the average age of my chaps now is considerably higher than it used to be,' Huxton continued, 'but even so, you're much older than I'd normally consider acceptable.' He paused. 'And then there's the fact that all my men are corporals, while you're a sergeant.'

'Is that a problem?' Blackstone asked.

'Yes, but not an insurmountable one,' Huxton said

complacently. 'I'm sure that as soon you've learned how we go about our business in today's army, you'll fit in well enough. But one thing will have to change – and change damn quickly,' he warned, his voice hardening and his finger wagging, 'and that's your attitude. You're far too casual. I expect the proper deference from all my men – and I don't care how old you are, I expect it from you.'

'You seem to be labouring under a misapprehension,' Blackstone told him. 'I haven't been enlisted, and I won't be working for you.'

Huxton snorted in disbelief. 'Of course you'll be working for me. I'm the Assistant Provost Marshal. Who else would you be working for?'

'I won't be working for anyone,' Blackstone said. 'My investigation will be entirely independent of the army, though I may, when the need arises, ask for the assistance of a few of your men.'

'You might *ask* whatever you choose,' Huxton said, his florid face now almost lobster-red. 'But if you seriously expect me to allow any of my men to take orders from you, then . . . then you're completely off your head.' He turned to Carstairs for support. 'That's right, isn't it, George? He must be completely off his head.'

'I'm afraid it's not as simple as that,' Carstairs said.

'What!' Huxton exploded.

'Believe me, I can quite see your point, and if I were in your position, I'm sure I would feel exactly as you do,' Carstairs said. 'But the War Office communiqué leaves us very little room for manoeuvre. In fact, it states quite explicitly that we are to extend to Inspector Blackstone any assistance that he sees fit to request.'

Carstairs was enjoying this, Blackstone suddenly realized – and there was probably good reason for that.

Even in his soldiering days in India, the regular army had never regarded the military police as proper soldiers, and had resented the way their powers cut across the command structure. And the police, for their part, had felt aggrieved that regular soldiers failed to acknowledge the vital role they felt they played in holding a rabble army together.

But there was more to it than that, Blackstone told himself. Carstairs disliked Huxton on a purely *personal* level – and in that way, at least, he and the company commander had something in common.

'But . . . but the man's nothing but a retired sergeant!' Huxton protested.

'Oh no, he's much more than that,' Carstairs said, and once again, he was making little effort to disguise his pleasure at Huxton's discomfort. 'He's an inspector from Scotland Yard – as he's been at pains to point out himself – and the personal representative of General Fortesque, and while I can't insist that you cooperate with him—'

'Damn right, you can't insist!'

'—there are those who outrank both of us who *will* insist, and I would strongly advise you to cooperate willingly, rather than under compulsion.'

He could have phrased it more tactfully – and in private – Blackstone thought. But tact was not part of Carstairs' battle plan – though what that plan actually was had yet to emerge.

'I . . . I . . . don't suppose there's any harm in answering a few of the man's questions,' Huxton blustered. 'Do you *have* any questions, Blackstone?'

'As a matter of fact, I have,' Blackstone replied.

'Well, let's hear them, then.'

'I assume you've taken statements from all the men who were in the trench that night, Captain Huxton.'

'I might have done – if half of them hadn't been bloody well dead,' Huxton snarled.

'In purely military terms, Lieutenant Fortesque's death came at a rather inconvenient time,' Captain Carstairs explained.

The aim of the planned offensive is to capture the small village – scarcely more than a hamlet, but of strategic importance – which lies beyond the German lines. The young staff officers, and – of course – the enlisted men, have not been informed of this, though, if they have any sense at all, they will know it is coming.

For days, new artillery batteries have been arriving, and night trains have rumbled into St Denis station, packed with shells.

New trenches – saps – are being dug, at right angles to the front line, and heading towards the German trenches. Not only that, but some of the sap heads are being joined up to make what, in effect, is a new *front line.*

Fresh consignments of ladders – which will make climbing out of the trenches a much quicker process – are delivered.

The artillery has begun a heavier-than-usual bombardment of the German trenches, and – more importantly – of the coils and coils of wicked barbed wire which separate the two armies.

And the Royal Engineers are digging new pits in front of the trenches, which everybody knows – though nobody says – can have no purpose other than to accommodate gas cylinders.

So the soldiers understand perfectly what is about to happen – and so do the French villagers and the Germans.

'Lieutenant Fortesque was murdered less than twenty-four hours before the offensive was due to begin,' Captain Carstairs said. 'I realized immediately that the Assistant Provost Marshal needed to be called in to investigate the matter, but you were away on official business, weren't you, Geoffrey?'

'Yes,' Captain Huxton said, begrudgingly.

'I sent him a telegram immediately,' Carstairs continued, 'but it took some time to reach him, and even when it had, getting back here, in the middle of the preparations for an offensive, wasn't easy.'

In other words, the killer had chosen just the right time to strike, Blackstone thought.

'Captain Huxton arrived here late in the evening, a few hours before the men were due to go over the top,' Carstairs continued. 'He did not ask if he could question the men at that time, and I could not have permitted it even if he had.'

Huxton shot him a look of pure hatred. 'Now look here, old chap, I'm the Assistant Provost Marshal, and if I'd wanted to question them, I damn well would have done, whether or not—'

'You're perfectly correct, Geoffrey, and I apologize,' Carstairs said – though he did not sound the *least* apologetic. 'If you'd wanted to interrogate the men, you would have been quite within your rights. But you realized, even without my having to point it out to you, that questioning them just before an offensive would have been bad for morale.'

'Well, as long as that's clear,' Huxton muttered.

'What I don't understand is why the platoon wasn't questioned earlier in the day,' Blackstone said.

'For God's sake man, can't you follow even a simple

argument?' Huxton demanded. 'You've already been told I wasn't here.'

'Couldn't some of your corporals have done it?'

'*I was not here,*' Huxton said, speaking the words very slowly, perhaps in the hope that Blackstone would finally understand, 'and *because* I was not here, they did not have the authority.'

Ah yes, he'd forgotten momentarily that this was the army, Blackstone thought – they did not have the authority, and so they had done nothing.

'The offensive did not go well,' Carstairs said. 'The gas-company commander told divisional headquarters that the gas couldn't be discharged, because there was no wind, and divisional headquarters said he should discharge it anyway. So they did discharge it, and it just bloody hovered there, right in front of our bloody trench. Some of it even blew back in, so we were gassing ourselves.'

Huxton smirked. 'If I were in your shoes, I think I'd choose my words a little more carefully, old boy,' he said. 'After all, you don't want an inspector of police – who is also General Fortesque's personal representative – thinking that your chaps simply don't know their job.'

But Carstairs, caught up in a wave of genuine anger, was not about to exercise caution.

'At any rate, we did send the men over eventually, once some of the gas had cleared,' he continued, 'and it was a disaster. The shelling hadn't cut the barbed wire properly, Fritz had had plenty of time to prepare for us – if he hadn't picked up on any other clues, the gas was all the confirmation he needed – and once the men were in No Man's Land, it was like a bloody pheasant shoot.'

'Has your plodding policeman's brain managed to grasp the point, Blackstone?' Captain Huxton asked.

'What point?'

'That with over half Fortesque's platoon killed that morning, there's a very good chance that his murderer – and anyone else who might have assisted us in our investigation – is already dead.'

'So you're assuming that Fortesque was killed by one of his own platoon, are you?' Blackstone asked.

'Well, of course I am. Who else would have done it? You're surely not suggesting it was a private from one of the other platoons, are you?'

'It could have been,' Blackstone said. 'Or it could have been one of the officers.'

'It most certainly could *not* have been one of the officers!' Huxton exploded. He turned to Carstairs for support. 'Will you remind this bounder of his place – or should I?'

'At this stage of the investigation, I don't think we can afford to rule any possibility out,' Carstairs said calmly.

'What!' Huxton asked, outraged. 'Are you saying that you're willing to subscribe to the disgraceful notion that an officer could have . . . could have . . .'

'I think it's highly unlikely – but not entirely inconceivable,' Carstairs said.

Huxton stood up. 'I find it impossible to play any part in an investigation which could entertain the idea that a gentleman could be party to such an act – and I wash my hands of the whole affair,' he bellowed. 'And as for you, Carstairs,' he continued, as he strode furiously to the door, 'all I can say is that I consider you a traitor to your class.'

Once Huxton had slammed the door behind him, Carstairs sighed and said, 'You may sit if you wish, Blackstone.'

'That would have been a most welcome invitation fifteen minutes ago, but now I think I prefer to stand,' Blackstone told him.

Carstairs nodded. 'I don't suppose there'd be any point in offering you a whisky, either.'

'Not at the moment.'

'I may have pointed out to Captain Huxton the necessity of cooperating with you,' Carstairs said, 'but I certainly wouldn't want to have given you the impression that I approve of you being here and—'

'You haven't,' Blackstone told him.

'Kindly do not interrupt,' Carstairs snapped. 'I want it clearly understood that I am only giving you my support in this venture of yours because that is what I've been *ordered* to do.'

'That *is* understood,' Blackstone agreed.

'And you might make both your task and mine a little easier if, as an ex-sergeant, you showed some respect when addressing an officer,' Carstairs continued. 'For example, I'd appreciate it if you called me "sir".'

'I'm sure you would,' Blackstone agreed.

'Well, then?'

'And if the men heard me calling you "sir", what would they think?'

'They'd think it was only right and proper.'

Blackstone shook his head. 'No, they wouldn't. What they would think is that everything they told me would come straight back to you.'

'And so it should. Not that I'm expecting you to report it to me directly, of course.'

'No?'

'No – the NCO who accompanies you will file the report.'

'There won't be any NCO accompanying me,' Blackstone said.

'I'm afraid you're quite wrong about that,' Carstairs said firmly.

'None of you seem to have quite got the hang of what's going on yet, have you?' Blackstone asked 'I'm conducting a criminal investigation here. I'll go *where* I want to go, and talk to *who* I want to talk to—'

'That's out of the question.'

'—and if there are any restrictions placed on me, I'll be on the next train out of here, and *you* can explain to the General Staff why I've gone.'

'I don't like being threatened,' Carstairs growled.

'And I'm not threatening you,' Blackstone replied. 'But if I'm to find the guilty man, be he a private soldier or an officer—'

'The idea that an officer killed Lieutenant Fortesque is quite out of the question,' Carstairs said.

Blackstone grinned. 'That's not what you said to Captain Huxton,' he pointed out.

'I have since revised my position,' Carstairs told him.

Blackstone shook his head. 'No, you haven't. You were *never* prepared to consider it.'

'Are you calling me a liar?' Carstairs demanded.

'No,' Blackstone said. 'I'm calling you a *tactician*.'

'And what exactly do you mean by that?'

'You didn't want Huxton involved in this investigation, not because you think he's a fool – which he undoubtedly is – but because you'd already decided I need to be tightly controlled, and he's clearly not up to the job. That's why you were baiting him from the moment I arrived. That's why you pretended to agree with me about the possibility of the killer being an officer – because you wanted him to storm out, just as he eventually did.'

'Whatever I may have said, and for whatever reason I may have said it, my position now is quite clear,' Carstairs told Blackstone, in the growling voice of a wounded beast. 'I consider it unthinkable that one of my officers would contemplate, even for a moment, anything as dastardly as committing a murder.'

'That's not quite what you mean,' Blackstone said.

'No?'

'No. What you're actually saying is that it's unthinkable that any of the officers serving under you would contemplate killing *one of their own kind.*'

'That's the same thing, isn't it?' Carstairs asked, sounding genuinely mystified.

'Not by a mile,' Blackstone told him.

Then he reached down for the whisky bottle and poured himself a shot.

'What the devil . . .' Carstairs exclaimed.

'You did offer me a whisky earlier,' Blackstone said, looking him squarely in the eye.

'Don't push me too far,' Carstairs said.

'I'll try not to,' Blackstone promised. He took a sip of his drink. It was malt – far beyond the pocket of a humble police inspector. 'In my time, I've arrested a wide range of people, from the lowest guttersnipe in an East End flophouse to members of the aristocracy in their own stately piles. And the main lesson I've learned from making those arrests is that, given the right circumstances, anybody is capable of killing anybody.'

'That's preposterous!' Carstairs said.

'Is it?' Blackstone asked. 'When I reached for your whisky just now, wasn't there a brief moment when you wanted to kill me?'

Carstairs looked distinctly uncomfortable. 'I wouldn't put it quite as strongly as that,' he said.

'The feeling might have only lasted a split second, but *for* that split second, you *did* want me dead,' Blackstone told him. 'There's no point in denying it, because I could read it in your eyes.'

'Balderdash,' Carstairs said, unconvincingly.

'You wouldn't have reacted like that if I'd been one of your young lieutenants,' Blackstone continued. 'You'd have been annoyed, certainly. You'd have torn a strip off him, undoubtedly.

You may even have put him on some kind of punishment parade. But you wouldn't have felt the *rage*. And why did you feel it when *I* helped myself to a drink – because I'm a jumped-up ex-sergeant who refuses to even call you "sir"!'

'It's not as simple as that,' Carstairs mumbled.

'It's exactly as simple as that,' Blackstone contradicted him. 'If the circumstances are right, anyone can kill anyone. And that's why I'm here – to find out what those circumstances were.'

'I want to make one thing absolutely clear,' Carstairs said, in a tone which was both chilling and resolute. 'I love this regiment, and if you do anything which affects either the morale of the men I command or the honour of the regiment, I will kill you – and damn the consequences!'

'I'll bear that in mind,' Blackstone said.

FOUR

Soon, the sun would appear on the horizon behind the German lines, and light would begin to filter down into the trench. For the moment, however, the only illumination that Blackstone and Carstairs had was from the captain's flashlight, its beam bobbing along the trench floor in front of them – and it was like walking in a tunnel.

'If you once get lost down here, you can be wandering about for hours, trying to find your way back,' Carstairs warned.

Blackstone did not doubt it. The trench system was more complex than he would ever have imagined it could be. In addition to the reserve trenches, there were not only the fire trenches – the front line for both armies – but also the relief trenches and countless communication trenches which intersected and criss-crossed each other with bewildering regularity. It was almost like a small town, with its highways and byways, alleys and cul-de-sacs.

As the narrow communication trench joined the much wider fire trench, Carstairs came to a halt.

'The General's wasting both my time and yours, you know,' he said. 'You'll never catch your killer.'

'What makes you think that?' Blackstone wondered. 'Is it that you share Captain Huxton's conviction that he's probably already dead?'

'I try to share as little as possible with Captain Huxton,' Carstairs said disdainfully. 'But on this occasion – and more by luck than judgement – he might well be right. We lost fifty per cent of the platoon in the offensive, which means logically, that there's a fifty per cent chance the killer was amongst them. But even if he survived – and any possible witnesses survived along with him – you still have no chance of making your case.'

'And why's that?

'Let me tell you a story,' Carstairs suggested. 'I heard it from another officer, a man I'd trust with my life, so though I can't personally vouch for it, I'm sure it's true. It seems that a sanitary-man was in the area between the fire line and support trench one night, and was in the process of burying the night-soil he'd taken from the latrine when he was killed by a stray bullet. By the time he was discovered, rigor mortis had set in, and his right arm, which had been stretched out at the moment he died, was as stiff as a board. Well, I suppose the recovery party could have broken the arm, but they didn't. They brought the dead man back to the trench and laid him out on the fire line, where he was to stay until the burial party could pick him up and take him to the graveyard.' Carstairs paused. 'We do like to give the men a proper burial whenever we can, you know.'

'Now that is kind of you,' Blackstone said.

'Don't you dare ridicule me in that way!' Carstairs said, suddenly angry. 'I care about my men – I might not *like* them, but I do *care* about them. And whenever possible, I treat their bodies with the respect they deserve.'

'I'm sorry,' Blackstone said.

And so he was, because he recognized that – within his limits – the captain was both a decent man and a decent officer.

'But that's not the point I was about to make,' Carstairs continued. 'They laid the dead man on the fire step, but because his arm was sticking out, it inevitably blocked a good half of the trench. And how do you think the other men reacted to that?'

'I don't know,' Blackstone admitted.

'Most of them treated the arm as if it were a turnstile at a football ground – just brushed it aside and, as they did so, said things like, "Don't get in the way, you selfish old bugger." Some of them actually shook the dead hand, and asked him how he was getting on. They'd known the man while he was alive – they'd been his comrades, for God's sake – but now that he was dead, he was no more than a comic prop for them.'

Perhaps he was, Blackstone thought – but perhaps treating him as a comic prop was the only way they had of dealing with his death.

'Why are you telling me this?' he asked aloud.

'So that you'll understand what this war – more than any which has preceded it – has done to the common soldier. He feels no compassion – not even for his own kind. So why should he care who killed Lieutenant Fortesque? And even if he knew, why should he bother to tell you?'

They turned on to the fire trench. The platoon occupying it was lined up in strict military order, under the watchful eye of their lieutenant and sergeant.

'If an attack comes, it will either be at dawn or dusk, and that's why we're always ready at those times,' Carstairs told Blackstone.

If he'd been Captain Huxton, he might have added an oafish, 'I *know* these things, and you *don't* – and your lack of knowledge about what goes on here is yet another reason that you'll never find your killer.'

But Carstairs, being more subtle than Huxton, knew there was no need to add it, because it was obvious enough, Blackstone thought.

'None of those men will have been here the morning that Lieutenant Fortesque was murdered, will they?' the inspector asked.

'No,' Carstairs replied. 'The survivors of that platoon will have been rotated after the offensive. They're most probably in the village of St Denis.'

As they approached the platoon, the lieutenant turned and saluted.

'Anything wrong, sir?' he asked with all the anxiety of a young man who does not fear death, but lives in perpetual trepidation of doing something which does not conform to the correct military code.

'Nothing at all wrong, Toby,' Carstairs assured him. He glanced at the platoon. 'Your men are very well turned-out, under the circumstances. You're doing a splendid job.'

'Thank you, sir,' the lieutenant said, with a barely disguised sigh of relief.

Carstairs looked up at the lightening sky. 'Any minute now,' he said to the lieutenant.

'Any minute now, sir,' the lieutenant agreed.

The stillness of the air was suddenly shattered by loud explosions from both the British artillery and the German guns.

Blackstone, who had been under fire more times than he cared to remember, still found it hard to believe that anything could generate this amount of noise.

'The men call this the Morning Hate,' Carstairs said, shouting to be heard above the din. 'It normally lasts for about ten minutes.'

'And does it achieve anything?' Blackstone bawled back.

'A few lucky shots might produce some casualties, and it certainly shreds some of the weaker men's nerves – but apart from that, it doesn't achieve a damn thing!' Carstairs replied. He turned to the lieutenant, and tapped him on the shoulder. 'Could I have your periscope for a moment, Toby?'

The lieutenant handed the periscope to Carstairs, and Carstairs handed it to Blackstone.

'Why don't you take a look at the world outside, Mr Blackstone?' the captain suggested.

Blackstone raised the periscope and looked out on to No Man's Land. It was the barbed wire fence he saw first – a complex twisted tangle of wicked spikes, stretched tautly between strong posts and gleaming in the early light.

He closed his eyes for a moment, and imagined himself dashing across No Man's Land under heavy enemy fire – knowing that his only hope of salvation lay in reaching the enemy trench – and then suddenly coming up against this evil, impenetrable web of sharpened metal. There could be no despair in the whole world quite like that, he thought.

Yet that was just what had happened to Lieutenant Fortesque's platoon, the morning after he died. The big guns were supposed to have cut the wire, but they hadn't – and there was nowhere to run and nowhere to hide.

Blackstone took a deep breath, and looked beyond the fire to a meadow, glistening green as the sun caught the morning dew. There were summer flowers, too, poking up between the lush blades. But there were also holes – deep pits made by the shells which landed short of their target, and gouged up the earth.

Beyond the meadow was more barbed wire – German, this time – and beyond even that, the enemy lines.

'Seen enough?' Carstairs shouted into his ear.

'More than enough,' Blackstone told him.

'Then we'll go and look at the dugout,' the captain said.

The dugout where Lieutenant Fortesque met his death was located midway down the section of trench.

Captain Carstairs opened the door, and waved Blackstone through.

'Here you have it,' he said. 'The scene of the crime.'

The bombardment continued, but it did not seem quite as loud inside the dugout as it was outside, and when Carstairs spoke again, it was almost in his normal voice.

'When you were looking through the periscope, did you happen to notice the pits that the shells had made?' he asked.

'It would have been hard to miss them,' Blackstone replied, grimly.

'They're where the wounded crawl to die,' Carstairs said. 'There are bodies lying at the bottom of most of them. Once in a while, we get the opportunity to clear them out, but by then, the rats and the maggots have done their work, and they hardly look like men at all.'

'Why are you telling me this?' Blackstone wondered.

'I'm doing it because I want you to see the world through our eyes,' Carstairs said.

'Go on.'

'In your world, death is a significant event, but out here it's commonplace and relatively unimportant. It's not human life that we value here – it's those things that we are shedding our lives to protect that truly matter.'

'Like patriotism?' Blackstone suggested.

'Yes, like patriotism,' Carstairs agreed wearily. 'But, above all, it is honour that drives us – our own, and that of the regiment.'

Blackstone nodded, then looked around him.

This dugout was smaller than the one which served as the company headquarters, he noted, but in all other respects it was very similar. There was a rough wooden table (with two upright chairs), a wind-up gramophone, an easy chair and a camp bed.

'When we found Lieutenant Fortesque, he was sitting at the table, facing the door,' Carstairs said. 'As you probably already know, his skull was completely smashed in.'

'What direction did the attack come from?' Blackstone asked. 'Was he hit from behind – or from the front?'

'Neither from the front, nor from behind,' Captain Carstairs said. He touched the side of his own head lightly, with his right hand. 'This was where he was struck. And from the damage done, I would judge it was not one blow, but several. There were fragments of bone all over the floor.'

'Which probably led you to believe that the killer was in a state of rage,' Blackstone said.

'Naturally,' Carstairs agreed. And then something in Blackstone's tone made him reconsider his response. 'Is there any reason I shouldn't have thought that? Aren't all murderers enraged?'

'Some are,' Blackstone said, 'and some of them commit their crimes as coldly and unemotionally as if they were slicing a loaf of bread. Some walk away from their crime sickened by what they've done, and some have never felt happier. The only rule of thumb in a murder investigation is that there *is* no rule of thumb.'

'But we've already agreed that it was a particularly violent attack,' Carstairs protested. 'And if the killer wasn't enraged, why did he continue long after it must have been obvious to him that Fortesque was already dead?'

'Maybe he wanted to give the *impression* of being enraged, even though he wasn't,' Blackstone said. 'Or perhaps he actually *was* in a fury. At the moment, we've no way of knowing.' He looked around the room again. 'Have you found the murder weapon yet?'

'No, we haven't,' Carstairs said.

'Do you know if Captain Huxton's men even bothered to look for it?' Blackstone wondered.

'No, I don't know, as a matter of fact,' Carstairs admitted. 'What I *do* know is that if I'd been in his place, I wouldn't have wasted my men's time on such a pointless exercise.'

'Pointless?' Blackstone repeated quizzically.

Carstairs sighed. 'In case you haven't noticed, we're in a trench – in the middle of a bloody war,' he said. 'There's any number of things lying around that the killer *could have* used. There are hammers, there are shovels – he might even have used the butt of his rifle. Of course, you could look for something that had a bloodstain on it, but given that a German shell fell in this trench two days before the murder – blowing up three men in the process – you'd be very lucky to find something that *wasn't* bloodstained.'

'You said he might have used his rifle butt,' Blackstone mused.

'And so he might.'

Because it was an enlisted man who killed Fortesque, wasn't it, Blackstone thought. It just *had* to be an enlisted man.

'Who has access to this dugout?' he asked.

'The officer who is on duty, his servant, a visiting officer, a sergeant making a report . . .' Carstairs paused. 'That's about it.'

'Do enlisted men ever enter the dugout?'

'Of course not! The dugout is the officer's sanctum.'

'Is it possible that Lieutenant Fortesque might have summoned one of the enlisted men?'

Carstairs shook his head, almost pityingly. 'I don't know how things worked in your day, Sergeant, but in *my* army, an officer does not address the men directly, but instead communicates with them through an NCO.'

Thus avoiding the unpleasant necessity of breathing the same air as a member of the working class, Blackstone thought.

He'd been right in the assumption he'd made in the command dugout – the army hadn't changed at all.

'An officer doesn't address the men directly, yet, according to your theory, one of the enlisted men *did* enter this bunker,' he said to the captain.

Carstairs laughed at the detective's obvious stupidity.

'It would be a serious breach of regulations for a common soldier to enter the dugout without permission,' he agreed, 'but given that he had his mind set on a cowardly murder, he was probably more than willing to wave such minor considerations aside.'

'So the killer checks there's no one watching, bursts into the dugout, and kills the lieutenant,' Blackstone said.

'Exactly!' Carstairs agreed.

'Then why was the blow which killed Fortesque delivered to the side of his head?' Blackstone asked.

A frown filled Carstairs' face. 'I'm not following you.'

'Didn't you say that Fortesque was sitting in his chair, facing the door?'

'Yes, I did,' Carstairs agreed, puzzled. 'What of it?'

'I have a theory,' Blackstone explained. 'Would you mind sitting where Fortesque was sitting, so that we can test it out?'

'All right,' Carstairs agreed, walking around the table and sitting down facing the entrance.

'I won't be a moment,' Blackstone told him, opening the door and stepping out into the trench.

The bombardment had stopped, and the soldiers were squatting on the duckboards, eating the breakfasts which had been sent up from the field kitchen. Blackstone nodded to them, but only one or two nodded back. And even then, it was a cautious nod – a nod which said, 'Judging by the way you're dressed, you might just be on our side – but we're not putting any money on it.'

Blackstone turned, opened the door again, and re-entered the dugout.

'Well?' Carstairs demanded. 'Are you going to tell me about this theory of yours, or must we continue playing silly bloody games?'

'If you were facing the other way – towards the back of the dugout – you might not even have noticed I'd come in,' Blackstone said, 'but you're not facing the back of it – and neither was Fortesque.'

'So what's your point?'

'You're Fortesque, and you see an enlisted man enter your dugout without your permission. What do you do?'

'I ask him what the devil he thinks he's doing.'

'Exactly! And what does the killer say?'

'How the hell would I know?'

'Remember, this is a major breach of protocol, so Fortesque is both outraged and on his guard. If the killer wishes to blindside him in order to deliver the fatal blow, he must first calm him down. I'm right, aren't I?'

'Possibly.'

'So how does he go about doing that?'

Carstairs considered the matter.

'He makes up some excuse for being here,' he said finally.

'Like what?'

The captain shrugged. 'I don't know. Perhaps he says that there's an emergency further down the trench.'

'Wouldn't he report that to the sergeant?'

'Normally he would, but perhaps he tells Lieutenant Fortesque he can't *find* the sergeant.'

'Let's try that theory out,' Blackstone suggested. 'When I next speak, I don't want you to think about what I've said – I want you to react instinctively.'

'All right,' Carstairs agreed.

Blackstone turned away in a leisurely way, then suddenly swung round again and shouted, 'The Huns have overrun the trench, sir!'

Carstairs sprang to his feet immediately, then checked himself, and slowly sat down again.

'Do you see the point now?' Blackstone asked.

'Anything that the killer said to Fortesque would have been much more likely to get Fortesque out of the dugout than the killer in,' Captain Carstairs conceded reluctantly.

'Just so,' Blackstone agreed. 'But that didn't happen, did it? What actually happened was the killer was *allowed* to advance.'

'You don't know that for a fact,' Carstairs said stubbornly. 'The killer could well have lured Fortesque to the door, killed him there, and then put him back in the chair.'

'So Fortesque walks over to the door and turns sideways on, in order to allow the killer to hit him on the side of the head?'

'He could have been distracted. The killer says, "What's that on the wall?" Fortesque turns his head, and the killer strikes.' Carstairs smiled triumphantly. 'Your problem, Blackstone, is that you just don't think things through.'

'You said there were several blows to the head, didn't you?'

'Yes, of course, but . . .'

'I think if I'd received a sharp blow to the head, I'd probably keel over, fight back, or try to escape.'

'As would any man.'

'But Lieutenant Fortesque doesn't do any of those things. He just sits there, and allows the killer to finish off his work. Is that what you're saying?'

'Of course not! He *did* do one of those three things you mentioned.'

'Which one?'

'He keeled over.'

'And landed conveniently on his side, thus giving the killer the opportunity to continue raining blows on exactly the same spot?'

'It's possible,' Carstairs said – but it was plain from his tone that he didn't really believe that.

'I want to try something else,' Blackstone said, walking across the dugout and positioning himself at Carstairs' side. 'In a second, I'm going to grab you.'

'You're going to *what*?'

'To grab you. I realize it will be distasteful to you to be touched by a member of the lower orders, but for the purposes of this experiment you're just going to have to grit your teeth and put up with it.'

'For Christ's sake, man, just get on with it!' Carstairs growled.

Blackstone gripped Carstairs' left shoulder firmly with his left hand, and swung his right fist until it made brief contact with the right side of the captain's head. Carstairs tried to struggle free, but the fact that he was sitting down put him at a distinct disadvantage, and he had still not managed to break away when Blackstone's fist made contact for a second time.

'And remember, the more times I manage to hit you, the weaker you become,' Blackstone said.

'That's enough!' Carstairs bellowed.

Blackstone released his grip, and the captain brushed off the left-hand shoulder of his jacket, and smoothed down the right-hand side of his hair.

Carstairs was undoubtedly angry, Blackstone thought, but even in his rage, he could not dismiss the idea that what he had just endured was probably an accurate reconstruction of what had actually happened to Fortesque.

When the captain turned to look at Blackstone, his face was an emotional blank.

'Fortesque not only allowed his killer to enter the dugout, but also let himself be blindsided,' he said.

'It looks that way,' Blackstone agreed.

Carstairs shook his head in what might just possibly have been admiration.

'I appear to have underestimated you, Inspector,' he said.

'You wouldn't be the first.'

'Thanks to your efforts, I see the whole thing clearly now,' Carstairs said. 'Thanks to your efforts, we now know who the killer is.'

'We do?'

'Of course! The only person who could have killed Fortesque – because he was the only person who'd have been permitted to get into the position in which an attack was possible – was Fortesque's servant. I'll inform Captain Huxton of that immediately, and the guilty man will be under arrest within the hour – and in front of a firing squad within the week. And as for you, Inspector Blackstone, you can return to England immediately, with a letter of commendation – which I will personally sign – in your pocket.'

'Why *should* his servant have killed him?' Blackstone asked.

'I really have no idea – but, as you said, it's the only possibility.'

'I *never* said that.'

'All right, then, if it's a motive you're looking for, then how about this – the servant felt that Fortesque had insulted him, though how you insult a servant, God only knows – and wanted to get his revenge. Or perhaps this constant bombardment we've been under had turned his mind. At any rate, it doesn't matter to me *why* he killed Fortesque – it's enough to know that he did.'

'You're ignoring the other possibility,' Blackstone said firmly.

'But there *is* no other possibility,' Carstairs said, looking mystified. Then, as he realized what Blackstone was implying, his face darkened. 'I have already made it quite clear to you that I will not entertain the idea that an officer might be the killer,' he continued, angrily.

'An officer wouldn't need an excuse to enter the dugout,' Blackstone pointed out. 'He would have a right to be there, as you said yourself.'

'Once he's arrested, the servant will break down and confess – and you will look very foolish,' Carstairs said confidently.

'I've no doubt that Huxton's lads will make him confess – given the right circumstances, most men can be made to confess to almost anything,' Blackstone said, 'but that won't necessarily mean he's guilty.'

'What do you want, Blackstone?' Carstairs asked, suddenly sounding very tired. 'What do I have to do in order to make you see the truth?'

'You have to do nothing,' Blackstone told him. 'I'll get to the truth – the *real* truth – in my way and in my own time. And I'll start by questioning Fortesque's servant.'

'You will do no such thing!' Carstairs said. 'What *you* will do is catch the first available train back to Calais, and—'

'And as soon as I get back to England, I'll go and see General Fortesque and tell him that you stopped me from doing the job he personally sent me out here to do,' Blackstone interrupted him. 'And how will he take it? Do you think he will consider you've acted *honourably*?'

Rage burned in Carstairs' eyes, but slowly it became damped down by the blanket of inevitable defeat.

'General Fortesque is a great hero of mine,' he said. 'If he questioned my honour, I do not think I could live with myself.'

'I know,' Blackstone said.

Carstairs shook his head slowly from side to side. 'Very well, since you have so little sense of your own honour that you are prepared to ride on the coat-tails of a great man to get what you want, I will permit you to question the servant,' he said. 'Are you satisfied now?'

'No,' Blackstone said. 'There's something else I want.'

'Are there no limits to your demands?' Carstairs asked, exasperatedly.

'Not when I'm conducting a murder investigation, no,' Blackstone said simply.

'Then what more *do* you want?'

'I'd like to see Lieutenant Fortesque's body.'

'That's not possible,' Carstairs said.

And then he laughed, as if he'd realized he'd just scored a small triumph, which did, at least, do *something* to mitigate his larger defeat.

'Why isn't it possible?' Blackstone asked. 'Give me a couple of men with spades, and I'll—'

'Do you think that he was buried here in France, like a common soldier?' Carstairs said scornfully.

'Wasn't he?'

'He most certainly was not. The lieutenant's body has been

shipped back to England, where, with all due and appropriate ceremony, he will be laid to rest with his ancestors, in the family vault.'

Of course he would, Blackstone thought, because even in death there was one law for the rich and another for the poor.

FIVE

T he village of St Denis was perched at the apex of a small hill, some four miles behind the British lines. An old stone church stood at its centre – its spire straining upwards, as if it wished to pierce the sky – and the houses and shops were clustered around it. Seen from a distance, across the sunny summer meadows, it was as pretty a village as any which had ever graced a picture postcard.

It must have been a quiet, peaceful place a few years earlier, Blackstone thought – a sleepy hamlet which fully accepted that there was a whole wide world beyond its own narrow boundaries, but had no real interest in knowing any more about that world than was strictly necessary. But those days were gone forever. The simple innocence, in which the village had once been snugly packed, had been roughly ripped from it by the great iron fist of war - and the place would never be the same again.

He was less than half a mile from the village when he first noticed the rows of low grey tents pitched in a field at the foot of the hill. As he drew closer, he could see the soldiers, too. Some were being endlessly paraded up and down, in full battledress. Others, under the screamed encouragement of their NCOs, were charging sacks of sand, and stabbing them with their bayonets.

So even here, there was no respite from the war, Blackstone thought. Even here, where the weary and disillusioned men should have been able to snatch a little rest, they were being put through pointless drills which would be of no use to them at all, once they came under the deadly scything action of hot machine-gun fire.

Shaking his head, Blackstone slowly walked up the steep cobbled street which led to the church. The houses he passed were all half-timbered, and several of their lower floors had been converted into quaint business premises – a bakery, a butcher's, a pharmacy, a doctor's surgery, and a modest cafe – though all of them were now empty.

Several of the houses had all but been destroyed by shells fired in earlier battles, and even those that remained standing were pockmarked with bullet holes. And there were no civilians to be seen – no pretty girls, no gnarled peasants, no crafty shopkeepers – just men in khaki uniforms who wandered aimlessly, finally free of their pointless duties for a while, but with no avenues open to them to really enjoy that freedom.

At the top of the street he reached a square, with the church on one side of it, and the *mairie* – which was now flying the Union Flag instead of the Tricolour – directly opposite.

But it was not the *mairie* – nor the church – which immediately captured his attention. Instead, his gaze was drawn to the two-wheeled cart at the centre of the square – next to the village fountain – and to the soldier who seemed to have almost become a part of it.

The cart, known in military parlance as a limber, had been designed for moving heavy artillery, and so its wheels were over six feet high. And it was against one of these wheels that the man had been spreadeagled, his wrists tied to two of the upper spokes, his ankles to two of the lower ones.

'Drunk and disorderly?' Blackstone asked, as he approached the man.

'That's right,' the soldier agreed, and he grinned sheepishly, though he was obviously in some discomfort. 'Still, there's worse things than Field Punishment Number One, ain't there? Hanging here's not so bad, once you get used to it – and they could have made the case for having me shot, if they'd been of a mind to – so I've no complaints. And they'll be cutting me down in a few hours.'

'And tying you up again tomorrow morning,' Blackstone said.

'That's the way it goes,' the soldier said philosophically, and if he'd had sufficient freedom of movement to shrug, he would probably have done just that. 'Twenty-eight days, they gave me. I did three days before we went down to the front line, and I've done another six since we got back here. So, if they don't send us into the trenches again, I've got another –' he did a quick calculation – 'another nineteen to do. Course, if they *do* send us back – and I get killed – the army will just have to whistle for the rest of the punishment.'

There was a part of Blackstone that admired the man for his spirit of endurance, and part of him that was furious at the soldier's casual acceptance of the brutality meted out to him. But there was no point in expressing either of these emotions – because this was not *his* army or *his* war.

'Can I get you anything?' he asked.

The soldier grinned again. 'A pint of best London bitter would be much appreciated,' he said, 'but I'll settle for a drink of water from the fountain.'

'Get away from that man!' screamed a voice behind them, and turning around, Blackstone saw a redcap corporal standing in the doorway of the *mairie*.

Blackstone laid his carpet bag on the ground, walked across to the fountain, scooped up some water in his cupped hands, and returned to the man on the wheel.

'Didn't you hear me?' the redcap bawled as he strode furiously across the square. 'I told you to get away from that man!'

Blackstone held his hands up, and the man on the wheel drank greedily.

The redcap had drawn level with them now.

'Can't you understand the King's English, you ignorant bloody Frog?' he demanded. 'You shouldn't even be here in this village – let alone be making contact with the prisoner!'

He gave Blackstone a rough push, and seemed surprised when the other man held his ground.

'Now listen,' he continued, raising his fist threateningly, 'if you don't do what I say, you could get hurt.'

Blackstone balled up his own fists.

'Touch me again, and I'll break your nose,' he promised.

Perhaps it was his tone of calm confidence that caused the redcap to lower his arm, or perhaps it was simply the fact that he realized he was dealing with a fellow countryman.

'You're English!' he said.

'You're as sharp as a needle aren't you?' Blackstone asked.

The redcap frowned. 'You're not that copper from New Scotland Yard, are you?' he asked, incredulously.

'Yes.'

'I expected somebody a bit smarter-looking.'

'If you were expecting me, I assume that makes you the welcoming committee,' Blackstone said.

The redcap's frown deepened. 'I'm Corporal Johnson, the bloke what's been ordered to show you your billet, but you ain't welcome in any shape or form,' he said. 'The MFP are the law out here on the Western Front, an' we don't like no civilian coming in and telling us how to do our job.'

Blackstone ran his eyes quickly up and down the other man. Johnson was around twenty-three or twenty-four, he guessed. He was of average height and had the sort of face which would not stand out in even a small crowd. His eyes suggested steadiness, but no great intelligence. He was someone you could put in charge of any routine task with confidence – but if you were expecting any leaps of imagination from him, you were almost bound to be disappointed.

'Did you hear what I said,' the corporal repeated. 'We don't want no civilians coming in and telling us how to do our job.'

'You do *know* that your superiors are trying to pin Lieutenant Fortesque's murder on one of your own people, don't you?' Blackstone asked.

'One of my own people?' the corporal repeated, as if Blackstone had suddenly switched to a foreign language. 'What do you mean by that?'

'They want to put the blame on someone from the ranks.'

'And how are they *my own people*? I'm no common soldier – I'm a corporal,' Johnson said, tapping his stripes with two fingers, in case Blackstone hadn't noticed them. 'These mean that I'm a non-commissioned *officer.*'

'And your old man – or is it your uncle? – is a porter at Billingsgate Fish Market,' Blackstone said.

Johnson looked thunderstruck.

'Who told you . . . how did you know . . . ?' he began.

I know because your accent gives you away, Blackstone thought – because there are just a few nuances in it that pin you down to Billingsgate, and if that's where you're from, it would be a bloody miracle if somebody in your family *didn't* work in what's possibly the biggest fish market in the world.

'Having been given the right to sew two stripes on your sleeve doesn't cut you off from the lads you grew up with – not unless you let it,' he said.

But Johnson had stopped listening to him, and was clearly turning over in his mind something he'd heard – but not fully understood – earlier.

'Hang on,' he said finally. 'If you think they want to *pin* the murder on one of the enlisted men, then that means that you *don't* think it was an enlisted man that did it.'

'I knew you'd get there in the end,' Blackstone said.

Johnson's brow furrowed again, as if so much thinking was starting to hurt his brain.

'But if it wasn't one of the men who killed Lieutenant Fortesque, then it has to be . . . it has to be . . .'

'There's a good chance it was one of the officers,' Blackstone supplied.

'But it can't be!' Johnson protested.

'Why not?'

'Because . . . because they're all gentlemen.'

It was terribly sad when a man chose to betray his own class in return for a few scraps from his master's table, Blackstone thought.

But it was more than sad when the man accepted the mythology that the master used to justify his own privilege.

In fact, it was bloody tragic.

'I'd like you to show me to my billet,' he said.

'It's this way,' Johnson said sullenly, turning to cross the square.

'My bag, man!' Blackstone barked in his best sergeant's voice. 'Pick up my bag!'

Johnson turned again, confused.

'Uh . . . sorry, sir,' he said, bending down to pick up the bag.

And that made Blackstone feel sadder still – but at least it seemed to have amused the man strapped to the wheel.

They passed a smithy – its forge stone-cold, its anvil silent – and a dress shop inhabited solely by lonely naked mannequins.

They turned a corner, and saw at least two dozen soldiers lined up impatiently outside an otherwise nondescript house.

'That's the local knocking shop,' Johnson said.

Blackstone smiled. 'Really?' he asked. 'If you hadn't told me, I'd never have guessed.'

'Three pox-ridden whores servicing the whole bloody army,'

Johnson continued. 'None of them ever last more than a couple of weeks, and they must have insides like an infantryman's boot to be there for even that long, because sometimes they work round the clock.'

'Have you ever taken the opportunity to visit the place yourself?' Blackstone asked casually.

'Me? Go in there? No!' Johnson said vehemently. 'Like I told you, I'm a non-commissioned officer.'

And once more, he could not resist the temptation to touch his stripes.

'Never been there yourself,' Blackstone mused. 'Yet you still know there are *three* prostitutes inside. I suppose that's because you've inspected the place as part of your official duties.'

'That's right,' Johnson agreed – far too eagerly.

'Or could it be that when there's a troop rotation going on – when you know there's no chance there'll be any enlisted men there – you take the opportunity to slip in yourself?'

Johnson sniffed. 'Most of them *are* pox-ridden whores,' he said, 'but there's just a few – now and again – who are very nice girls.'

The house in which Blackstone had been assigned his billet was at the end of a steep cobbled street, almost at the point at which the village petered out. None of the houses close to it showed any signs of habitation, and he thought it was more than likely that this one had been chosen because it was as far away from the officers' billets as it was geographically possible to be.

Blackstone's room was furnished with a camp bed, two army blankets, an oil lamp, an enamel bowl and jug, a table and two rickety chairs.

'It ain't up to the standard of the Ritz – but then neither are you,' Corporal Johnson said.

'Just put my bag on the bed,' Blackstone told him.

Johnson looked down at the carpet bag in his left hand, and a puzzled expression came to his face – as if he were suddenly asking himself how the hell it had ever got there in the first place. Then he dropped the bag on to the floor, and a cloud of dust flew into the air.

'Are all the surviving members of Lieutenant Fortesque's platoon in St Denis?' Blackstone asked.

'As far as I know, they are,' Johnson replied, indifferently.

'I need to talk to them,' Blackstone told him. 'I'd like them brought here within the hour.'

'Would you now?' Johnson asked. 'Well, it can't be done – not without Captain Huxton's permission. And he doesn't like making hasty decisions. Sometimes, he'll think about them for days.'

'In other words, he'll block me any way he can,' Blackstone said.

'We'll *all* block you any way we can,' Johnson replied. 'I told you before, we don't want you here.'

'You are aware that I'm the personal representative of General Fortesque, aren't you?' Blackstone asked.

'I did hear something about that.'

'And that if I have to send a telegram to the General, there'll be consequences.'

Johnson chuckled. 'The General's not as powerful as you might think,' he said. 'Captain Carstairs will jump through hoops for him – because they're from the same regiment. But Captain Huxton works for the Provost Marshal's office, and he's not quite so easily bullied. He might have to give way in the end, but he can stall for days, if he has to.'

'Ah, I see!' Blackstone said, as if he'd suddenly realized there'd been a misunderstanding. 'You thought the telegram that I'd send would be about Captain Huxton.'

'Wouldn't it?'

'No, it would be about *you*.'

'Me?'

'That's right. I'll say that you haven't been cooperating with me, and ask him to use his influence in the War Office to have you transferred from the redcaps to something a little less pleasant – say, the sanitary engineers.'

'You wouldn't!' Johnson gasped.

'I would,' Blackstone countered. 'And do you seriously think that there's anybody in the War Office who's prepared to stand up to a general, just to save an insignificant little corporal from spending the rest of the war shovelling shit out of cesspits?'

'I . . . what if the captain finds out?' Johnson asked worriedly.

'He won't find out,' Blackstone assured him. 'He's the kind of man who couldn't find his own arsehole, even if you gave him a map.'

'But if he *does* find out,' Johnson persisted, 'you will tell him I had no choice in the matter, won't you? You'll say that you *ordered* me to bring the men to you?'

'I'll tell him I held a gun at your head, if that's what you want,' Blackstone replied.

SIX

S itting at the table in his new billet, Blackstone heard the sound of heavy footfalls in the corridor outside. Then the door was flung open, and Corporal Johnson entered the room, followed by two other redcaps, who had another man – a private – sandwiched between them.

The prisoner – and a prisoner he undoubtedly was – was small and thin, and was wearing a uniform which hung on him like sacking. His eyes were as large as a wild deer's, but betrayed no great depth or intelligence. And he had what seemed to be a permanent twitch in his cheek, though – given the circumstances that he found himself in – that was only to be expected.

'Private Blenkinsop,' Corporal Johnson announced in a loud military bawl. Then, in a much lower – and much angrier – tone, he added, 'You've been playing me for the complete bloody fool, haven't you, Mr Blackstone?'

'Have I?' Blackstone asked.

'Bloody right you have! When we were talking earlier, you said the top brass were trying to pin the murder on somebody from the ranks.'

'Yes, I did,' Blackstone agreed.

'And then you gave me all kinds of guff about not betraying my own kind – when all the time, you already knew that the killer *was* a Tommy, the lieutenant's servant, Private Blenkinsop.'

'I *didn't* know Blenkinsop was the killer at the time,' Blackstone said. 'As a matter of fact, I don't know it *now*.'

'Then why did you tell Captain Carstairs that Blenkinsop should be arrested?' Johnson asked, now more puzzled than angry.

'I didn't.'

'But in the dispatch he sent to me, he said—'

'I never killed the lieutenant,' Blenkinsop sobbed. 'I'll swear on a stack of Bibles that I didn't!'

Johnson wheeled round, and slapped the prisoner across the face.

'Shut up, you murderous little bastard!' he screamed, and was just about to hit the man a second time when Blackstone said, 'Corporal Johnson!' in a commanding voice.

Johnson swung round again, and came to attention. Then, realizing what he'd done, he relaxed his body and said sulkily, 'What is it now?'

'You will never hit a suspect in my presence again,' Blackstone told him. 'Is that understood?'

'But surely, you yourself must have—' Johnson began.

'Never!' Blackstone interrupted him. 'I asked you if it was understood – and I'm still waiting for an answer.'

'I suppose so,' Johnson replied.

Blackstone nodded. 'Very well, you can go now.'

'You want us to take the prisoner straight back to the lock-up?' Johnson asked, confused. 'But we've only just . . .'

'*You* can go – Blenkinsop *stays*,' Blackstone told him.

'I can't have that,' Johnson protested.

'The war might last another two or three years,' Blackstone pointed out. 'You could end up having to clean out an awful lot of shit out of an awful lot of cesspits in that time.'

Johnson sniffed – as if the smell of the excreta were already beginning to seep into his nostrils.

'I . . . I . . .' he said weakly.

'Go now – and come back in half an hour,' Blackstone said.

Johnson still stood there, weighing his fear of Captain Huxton's displeasure against the future that Blackstone was threatening him with.

'Have you got a gun, Inspector?' he asked, to buy himself time.

'Now why would I need a gun?' Blackstone wondered. 'You won't cause me any trouble, will you, Blenkinsop?'

'I didn't do it,' the private moaned, hardly aware he was being spoken to. 'I swear I didn't do it.'

Johnson was still wavering.

'Cesspits, Corporal Johnson,' Blackstone said.

'Half an hour?' Johnson asked, defeatedly.

'Half an hour,' Blackstone agreed.

Johnson nodded to the other two corporals and they released their grip on their prisoner, turned smartly, and walked to the door. Denied their support, Blenkinsop seemed on the point of crumpling into a heap on the floor.

'I didn't do it,' he said. 'I didn't. Honest, I didn't!'

'Why don't you sit down?' Blackstone suggested softly.

Blenkinsop tottered uncertainly over to the second chair, which was facing Blackstone's own, and collapsed into it.

A good soldier-servant, Blackstone knew from his own observations, had to be perceptive and sensitive, industrious, efficient and sanguine. If his officer's appearance fell below the accepted standard, then both the servant and the officer were deemed to have failed – the former for turning out his master in an improper manner, and the latter for displaying a lack of judgement by selecting a servant who was clearly not up to the job. Thus, when ex-soldier-servants chose to go into service in some of the grander civilian households – and many of them did – it was no surprise that they rose rapidly up the hierarchy of domestic service, and often even attained the exalted position of butler.

Blenkinsop, in complete contrast to the usual type, was clearly *not* a good soldier-servant and none of the great houses would have considered him for a moment – even as the assistant bootboy.

'How long have you been Lieutenant Fortesque's servant?' Blackstone asked the quivering wreck.

'Three . . . three months,' Blenkinsop told him.

'What happened to his previous servant?'

'He was hit by a bit of shrapnel in the trench, and given his papers back to Blighty.'

'I see,' Blackstone said. 'And why do you think that Lieutenant Fortesque chose you to replace him?'

'I don't know.'

'You have no idea at all?'

'None.'

'And you didn't ask him why he'd chosen you?'

'No. I . . . I didn't think to.'

Of course he hadn't thought to. Men like Blenkinsop didn't wonder why things happened – they just reacted to them.

'Do you remember the day he selected you?' Blackstone asked.

'Yes.'

'How did he do it? Did your sergeant tell you to report to the lieutenant's dugout?'

'No.'

Blackstone sighed. Blenkinsop was hard work – but at least he seemed willing to give honest answers, as long as he was led to them.

'So where were you when he told you that you'd been selected?'

'I was by the cesspit.'

'By the cesspit!'

'Yes, you see, I . . . I'd got into a fight with some of the other lads in the trench.'

'*You* got into a *fight*?' Blackstone asked, disbelievingly.

Blenkinsop shrugged. 'Well, it wasn't so much a fight as that some of the other lads was ragging me.'

Of course they were, Blackstone thought.

Blenkinsop was a natural victim – the sort of man that other men will automatically take their own frustrations out on.

'Go on,' Blackstone said.

'Lieutenant Fortesque caught them at it. He got very angry, and said they shouldn't be forcing any of their comrades' heads into the cesspit, but if they had to do it to somebody, they shouldn't choose *his* servant. And, like I said, I didn't even know he'd chosen me as his servant at the time.'

Of course you didn't, Blackstone thought. And if it hadn't been for the bullying, he probably never *would* have chosen you.

'What was the lieutenant like to work for?' he asked aloud.

Blenkinsop shrugged again. 'He got cross with me, sometimes. I don't blame him – I tried as hard as I could, but I wasn't very good.'

'Did he even threaten to replace you?'

Blenkinsop shook his head. 'He used to say, "You're bloody useless, Blenkinsop. I'd be better off with employing a baboon to do your job – but if I threw you out now, you wouldn't last a day." Then he'd pick up his boots and start cleaning them himself.'

'Tell me about the days leading up to his murder,' Blackstone said.

'We were in the trench,' Blenkinsop replied, as if he couldn't understand why the question was even being asked.

Blackstone sighed again. 'Did anything unusual happen?'

'How do you mean?'

'Did something happen that stuck in your mind?' Blackstone asked – with more hope than expectation. 'Something that wasn't quite normal?'

Blenkinsop thought about it hard and long.

'Well, there was that argument he had with the other officers in his dugout, if that's what you mean,' he said, finally.

'What argument?'

There are two reasons why an unexpected visit of the three lieutenants to the dugout makes Blenkinsop nervous. The first reason is that officers always *make him nervous – even the ones he only knows by sight, and who have never got their sergeants to shout at him. The second reason is the hard and unyielding expression on the faces of the three young men as they look at Lieutenant Fortesque.*

One of the officers glares at Blenkinsop's clumsy attempt to salute, then says, 'Get out, you snivelling little bastard!'

Blenkinsop knows this is not protocol – that the only person who is supposed to order him about is Lieutenant Fortesque himself – but he still finds himself scurrying for the door like a frightened rabbit.

Once out in the trench, he doesn't know what to do. He suspects the officer intended him to get well away from the doorway, but he is reluctant to go too far from the dugout in case one of his tormentors spots him and something unpleasant happens. So he stays where he is, trembling at the thought of the officer's wrath, but comforting himself with the knowledge that if it gets too bad, Lieutenant Fortesque will step in and rescue him.

At first, all he can hear from inside the dugout is a low murmuring, but then one of the voices is raised – and that voice belongs to Lieutenant Fortesque.

'It was wrong – I can see now that it was wrong – and I'm going to come clean about it,' he says.

'Now you really don't want to act too hastily, do you, Charles?' says a second voice, and Blenkinsop thinks that while the speaker is undoubtedly angry – and perhaps even threatening – he also sounds rather worried.

'You can't talk me out of it,' Fortesque tells him. 'The chances

are, I'll be killed in the offensive tomorrow – but if I'm not, I'll take that as a sign that I should stand up like a man and confess.'

'Have you thought about the consequences?' asks the second voice.

'I have.'

'They'll strip you of your commission.'

'They might do worse than that – they may send me to jail. But it doesn't matter – I'm still going to do what's right.'

'And what about us?' the other man demands. 'Have you thought about that? It will ruin us, too.'

'I know,' Lieutenant Fortesque says, 'and I'm very sorry for that. If I could find some way to spare you all, while doing the right thing myself, I would. But there is no way.'

'What happened after that?' Blackstone asked.

'I don't know,' Blenkinsop said. 'The sergeant spotted me standing there, told me I was an idle little bleeder, and ordered me to go to the reserve trench and fetch the rum ration.'

'Were the three officers still there when you got back?'

'No, they'd gone.'

'And how did Lieutenant Fortesque seem?'

'He was sitting at his table with his head in his hands. I asked him if there was anything I could do for him, and he said there was nothing *anybody* could do. I think . . . I think he knew he was going to be murdered.'

'But you say that *you* didn't kill him?'

'No, I . . . he was kind to me. He even . . .'

'He even what?'

'He asked me once if I'd ever . . . you know . . .'

'No, I don't know.'

'If I'd ever been with a woman.'

'And what did you say?'

'That I hadn't. Then he asked me if I'd ever wanted to, and I told him that of course I'd wanted to, but when I'd asked women if they would, they'd only laughed at me. So he said that there were some women who wouldn't laugh at me – who'd let me do it to them as many times as I wanted to, as long as I had the money.'

'Prostitutes,' Blackstone said.

'That's right,' Blenkinsop agreed. 'And he said that even though

I had a cushy number, what with being his servant, there was still a chance I'd get killed by a stray bullet or a grenade, and no man should have to die a virgin. So the next time we came to this village, he gave one of the corporals some money, and told him to take me to the brothel.'

'He didn't come with you himself?'

Blenkinsop laughed at Blackstone's obvious ignorance. 'Officers don't go to the same brothels as the men. They don't do it to whores who've already had it done to them fifty times that day. What officers do is go to Paris, and sleep with ladies who smell of perfume and are dressed in silk from head to foot.'

'What I don't see is why, if you hardly ever left the dugout, you weren't there when Lieutenant Fortesque was killed,' Blackstone said.

'Oh, that was because he'd sent me on an errand,' Blenkinsop told him.

It was half an hour, to the second, when Corporal Johnson and the other two redcaps returned.

'We've come for the prisoner,' Johnson said – as though that wasn't already obvious.

'Take him outside,' Blackstone said to the other two redcaps. 'But I don't want him locking up yet.'

'If you don't mind—' Johnson began.

'But I *do* mind,' Blackstone interrupted. 'I mind very strongly. And once the other three are outside, Corporal Johnson, you and I are going to have another one of our cosy little chats – at the end of which, even someone like you should be able to see why I mind.'

Johnson nodded to the other two redcaps, who grabbed Blenkinsop and frogmarched him out of the room.

Blackstone waited until they'd closed the door behind them, then said, 'Tell me, Corporal Johnson, before you arrested Blenkinsop, did you bother to check out his alibi?'

'He didn't give me one,' Johnson said, as if that were all the defence he needed. 'He just kept babbling on about how he hadn't killed the lieutenant.'

'So he didn't give you one – and you didn't think – even for a moment – to ask him if he *had* one?'

'There was no need to, was there?' Johnson replied. 'Captain Carstairs' note made it quite clear that he was the guilty man.'

What was the matter with these people? Blackstone wondered – although he already knew the answer.

'Blenkinsop claims that Lieutenant Fortesque stayed up all night, drinking whisky,' he said.

'Officers do that kind of thing,' Johnson said. 'It's because they're gentlemen, you see.'

'Though if an ordinary man did it, you'd just call him a drunk – and lash him to the wheel in the town square,' Blackstone pointed out.

'It's not the same thing at all,' Johnson said stubbornly.

'How is it different?'

'I can't explain it – it just is.'

Because the officers *said* it was, Blackstone thought.

'Blenkinsop also says that, as a result of spending all night "being a gentleman", Lieutenant Fortesque had drained his bottle by an hour before dawn,' he continued.

'That's possible.'

'And that the lieutenant ordered him to go and get another bottle from the quartermaster's office in the reserve trench.'

'Well, he would say that, wouldn't he? A man who's worried about being shot will say anything.'

'Yes, he will – and sometimes, it will even be the truth.'

'What do you mean?'

'Blenkinsop says he can produce witnesses who will support his claim. He says that when he left for the reserve trench, there were several other privates near the dugout, and they can testify that Lieutenant Fortesque was standing in the doorway, alive and well.'

'I don't see—' Johnson began.

'You mean, you don't *want* to see,' Blackstone interrupted him. 'Blenkinsop further claims it took him about twenty minutes to reach the reserve trench. That would be about right, wouldn't it?'

'More or less,' Johnson said reluctantly.

'And that when he did reach the reserve trench, the supplies still hadn't arrived, and he had to wait until they did. All of which meant that by the time he returned to the dugout, Lieutenant Fortesque's body had already been discovered. Have you got all that clearly in your mind, Corporal Johnson? When Blenkinsop left, Fortesque was alive – and when Blenkinsop returned, Fortesque was dead.'

'He could have doubled back,' Johnson said.

'Would there have been time?'

'I don't know.'

'Then bloody well find out!'

'He was the only enlisted man who could have got close enough to Lieutenant Fortesque . . .' Johnson muttered, mantra-like.

'Did you question Blenkinsop shortly after the lieutenant's body was discovered?'

'Yes.'

'Where?'

'In the trench, of course. Just outside the dugout.'

'And was he holding a whisky bottle in his hand?'

'I can't remember.'

'Oh come on!' Blackstone said, exasperatedly.

'I was investigating the murder of an officer. A whisky bottle's not something you notice at times like that.'

'Well, here's something you *will have* noticed,' Blackstone said. 'Was the front of his uniform soaked with blood?'

'No, but . . .'

'You did *see* Lieutenant Fortesque's injuries for yourself, didn't you, Corporal Johnson?'

'Well, yes . . . I . . .'

'And was it at all possible for the man who inflicted them *not* to have been covered in blood?'

'Well, no – but he could have changed into another uniform.'

'The army must have altered a great deal since my day,' Blackstone said, 'because, back then, enlisted men didn't have spare uniforms they *could* simply change into.'

'They don't now,' Johnson said worriedly.

'But officers do, don't they?'

'I don't know.'

'Let me ask you that question again,' Blackstone said menacingly. 'Do officers have spare uniforms?'

'Some of them might,' Johnson conceded.

'I want you to examine Blenkinsop's alibi carefully,' Blackstone said. 'And if it checks out – and it *will* check out, because he hasn't got the imagination to have invented it – I want you to release him. Is that clear?'

'It's clear,' Johnson said, dejectedly.

'Are the other men I wanted to talk to still waiting outside?'

'Yes.'

'Then send one of them in.'

The private who took Blenkinsop's place in the chair opposite Blackstone was called Hicks. He was about twenty-two or twenty-three, and had intelligent eyes.

'What did you do before you joined up?' Blackstone asked.

'I was a cooper,' Hicks said. 'I followed my old man into the trade. And between us, sir, we made the best beer barrels in the whole of London. You could always tell if you were drinking your bitter out of one of our barrels – somehow, it just tasted better.'

Blackstone smiled at the young soldier's obvious enthusiasm for the work that the war had robbed him of, but before he went any further, he wanted to make sure that Hicks was as steady as he seemed to be.

'Have you ever been in any trouble with the police?' he asked.

Hicks grinned. 'Have I ever been in trouble with the police?' he repeated. 'With a dad like mine to answer to? You've got to be joking, sir.'

'He's a bit of a hard case, is he?'

'Not really,' Hicks said seriously. 'As a matter of fact, he never raised a hand to me when I was growing up – not even once. But if I'd ever done anything to bring the coppers round our house, he'd have thrashed me within an inch of my life – and I'd have deserved it!'

Blackstone nodded.

Hicks was just the kind of witness every policeman dreamed of – law-abiding, sober, and hard-working.

'I want to ask you what happened in the trench the morning Lieutenant Fortesque was killed,' he said.

'All right,' Hicks replied.

But already, his free and open attitude was starting to evaporate, and a note of caution was creeping into his voice.

'Blenkinsop says that the lieutenant sent him off for a bottle of whisky about an hour before dawn,' Blackstone said.

'That's right, he did,' Hicks agreed, relaxing a little.

'You saw him yourself, did you?'

'I certainly did. As clear as I'm seeing you now. And I can

go even further than that – I heard what the lieutenant said to him.'

'And what *did* he say to him?'

'He said, "Quick as you can, Blenkinsop. I really need that drink".'

'Did you see anybody enter the dugout after Blenkinsop had left?' Blackstone asked.

Hicks' eyes suddenly went blank.

'No, I didn't,' he said in a wooden voice.

'Nobody at all?' Blackstone persisted.

'Not a soul.'

'So the lieutenant bashed his *own* brains in, did he?'

'I don't know.'

Blackstone sighed. 'What sort of officer was Lieutenant Charles Fortesque?' he asked.

'A good one,' Hicks replied, without hesitation. 'One of the best. Nobody wants to charge into the jaws of hell, but if you have to do it, then you want a bloke like Lieutenant Fortesque leading you.'

'And yet – despite your obvious admiration for him – you don't want to see his killer brought to justice?' Blackstone asked.

Hicks looked guiltily at the table. 'If I thought I could help you, sir, then I would,' he muttered.

'You *can* help me,' Blackstone said. 'All you need to do is tell me who you saw going into the dugout.'

'What if the person I saw was an officer?' Hicks asked.

'What if it was?'

'They're never going to charge an officer with the murder, are they? You could have a watertight case against him, and he'd still get away with it, because his kind always will.'

'Give me his name,' Blackstone said.

'But what would happen to the poor bloke who fingered him?' Hicks continued, ignoring him. 'Well, that's a different matter entirely, isn't it? He'd be a marked man.'

'No one need ever know you'd told me,' Blackstone assured him.

'They'd find out,' Hicks said fatalistically. 'Somehow, they always seem to find out.'

'Just give me the name,' Blackstone coaxed.

'There was no officer, except for Lieutenant Fortesque, in the trench that night,' Hicks said firmly. 'Or if there was, I certainly didn't see him.'

With minor variations, Blackstone got the same story from the rest of the platoon. Most of the men had seen Blenkinsop leave, and several of them had heard his exchange with Lieutenant Fortesque. But none of them had seen anyone – least of all an officer – enter the dugout after Blenkinsop had left.

Blackstone lit up a cigarette, and wondered what to do next.

Well, he finally decided, after a couple of puffs, if the men who were treated like monkeys weren't saying anything, then maybe it was time he went and talked to the men who thought they were the organ grinders.

SEVEN

As he got closer to the bottom of the hill, Blackstone was not at all surprised to hear the familiar sound of leather striking willow, nor the restrained clapping which followed it.

This was, after all, a beautifully warm and gentle summer day – the sort of day the English talked about with such pride that they might almost believe they invented it.

And what else would the inhabitants of villages all over England do on a day like this, but flock to the village green, drink warm beer and watch a game so imbued with complexities and nuances that it had become the most Byzantine of English institutions?

Of course, this *wasn't* England. It didn't even *look* like England. And when the breeze blew in the right direction, it was possible to hear the boom of guns engaged in a bloody and tragic conflict. But such minor considerations had no effect on the Englishmen playing cricket on the edge of St Denis. They were doing what Englishmen always did when they were abroad – completely ignoring the fact that this was a foreign land, and carrying on as usual.

Blackstone reached the temporary pitch, and surveyed the

scene. The batsmen and the bowlers, he noted, were all dressed in immaculate cricket whites. The fielders, in contrast, wore mud-stained khaki.

So it didn't necessarily have to be viewed as *just* a cricket match, Blackstone told himself. If he were of a mind to – and at that moment he was – he could take it as a symbol of a society in which the rich and privileged had all the fun, and the poor and dispossessed ran themselves ragged making that possible.

He walked over to one of the rich and privileged, a blond-haired, sharp-featured man who, having been recently bowled out, was sitting on a camp stool – his soldier-servant standing in constant attendance behind him – and sipping at what looked like pink gin.

It was obvious that the officer was fully aware of his approach, but it was not until Blackstone was right at his side that he took his eyes off the cricket match, and looked up.

He smiled sardonically, through thin lips.

'I was wondering how long it would take you to get round to paying us a visit, Inspector Blackstone,' he said.

'And why is that, Lieutenant Maude?' Blackstone asked.

'Because, unlike many of my friends, *I* don't necessarily equate being lower class with being stupid.'

'Could I ask you to explain that?' Blackstone asked.

'Certainly,' Maude said easily. 'The last time we met was in the company headquarters dugout in the reserve trench, was it not?'

'It was.'

'At the time, you probably didn't give such a brief encounter even a moment's thought,' Maude said.

Oh, but I did, Blackstone reminded himself. Even then, I sensed that something wasn't quite right.

'And why should you have?' Maude continued. 'After all, the army is so full of arrogant young officers like Soames, Hatfield and I that you couldn't spit without hitting one of them. Is that correct?'

'It's correct.'

Maude smiled. 'Which part of my statement are you agreeing with?' he asked. 'That there are so many of us? Or that we're young and arrogant?'

'Both parts,' Blackstone said, flatly.

'I would have expected no less of you,' Maude replied. He paused, to take a sip of his pink gin. 'Where was I? Ah yes! You thought no more about us until you learned – as you were bound to do – that we were here in St Denis. And then the wheels started to turn in your brain, which I'm sure, incidentally, is a very fine one – given its obvious limitations. "If they're here now, what were they doing in the trenches last night?" you asked yourself. "They can't have been on active duty, can they?" And that thought led to another – that if we were not on duty *last* night, the chances were that we *had* been on duty the morning Charlie Fortesque was murdered. Am I following the way your mind was working?'

'Perfectly. And *were* you in the trenches on the morning Lieutenant Fortesque was murdered?'

'We were. Though we were not all on the front line.'

'No?'

'No. Fortesque and Soames were on duty in the fire trench, but Hatfield and I were in the reserve trench.' Maude took another sip of his drink. 'But to continue – the next stage in your mental process was to ask yourself *why* we were in the command dugout last night, and you reached the inevitable conclusion that we knew you were due to arrive, and were there to get your measure.'

'And is it a false conclusion?'

'Not at all. That's *precisely* why we were there.'

'You'll have to tell me more,' Blackstone said.

'I won't *have to* tell you anything,' Maude shot back at him, with a sudden flash of anger. 'You should not think, Inspector Blackstone, that because I have a healthy respect for your obvious intelligence, that is enough to make me consider you anything like my equal.'

On the pitch, Soames took a spirited swipe at the ball, and sent it hurtling towards the boundary.

'Well done, Roger!' Maude called out. He turned his attention back to Blackstone. 'I *will* tell you why we were there, Mr Blackstone – but only because I feel inclined to,' he said, in a much softer tone than the one he had used earlier. 'Roger Soames has an uncle who, purely for his own amusement, works in New Scotland Yard. Roger's uncle might, I suppose, even be called a colleague of yours – although, of course, he's much higher up the ladder than you are.'

'Assistant Commissioner Soames,' Blackstone said.

'The very man,' Maude agreed. 'At any rate, we thought it might be interesting to ask Roger's Uncle Arthur all about you.'

Blackstone said nothing.

'Aren't you curious to learn what he told us?' Maude asked.

'Why should I be interested in what a dilettante assistant commissioner has to say about me?' Blackstone wondered.

'Dilettante!' Maude repeated, with obvious delight. 'That's a big word for a humble policeman like yourself.'

'Yes, isn't it?' Blackstone agreed. 'For a humble policeman, I probably know enough big words to keep you amused for hours. "Marmalade" – that's another one. But I'm still not particularly interested in AC Soames' opinion of me.'

'I think I'll tell you what he said, anyway,' Maude replied, sounding a little disappointed. 'He said you have a reputation for being something of an agitator – possibly even one with Bolshevik leanings.'

'I have no interest in politics,' Blackstone said.

'Perhaps not, at least in specific terms,' Maude agreed easily. 'But your record shows that you do seem to take a great deal of pleasure in pulling down your betters from their pedestals.'

'If a man's guilty of a crime, I don't care what his background is,' Blackstone said stonily.

'That's probably true,' Maude conceded. 'But you do *prefer* it if he's high-born, don't you?'

'No, I don't,' Blackstone said – though he realized he did not sound entirely convincing, even to himself.

'At any rate, we reached the conclusion that, given your prejudices, there was a greater chance you'd suspect an officer than there was that you'd suspect an enlisted man. Were we right?'

'You're right, but you're also wrong,' Blackstone told him. 'I came here with a completely open mind, but the more I learn, the more I'm inclined to think that Lieutenant Fortesque was killed by an officer.'

'Well, there you are, then,' Maude replied. 'Suppose I gave you my word – as an officer and a gentleman – that Charlie Fortesque was not murdered by any officer in this regiment. Would you believe me?'

'No – but that wouldn't be based on any particular prejudice against you. The reason I'd refuse to accept your word is that unless you'd actually seen the murder yourself, you'd have no basis for giving it.'

'Ah, now you're being tactful,' Maude said, with some amusement. 'And that really doesn't sit well with you, you know.'

'All right,' Blackstone said. 'I wouldn't believe you because I think there's something that's much more important to you than your word as a gentleman – something even more important than seeing that your friend gets the justice he deserves.'

'And what might that be?' Maude asked interestedly.

'Preserving the status quo,' Blackstone said. 'If you thought, for example, that your mate Roger Soames had killed Lieutenant Fortesque, you wouldn't tell me about it, because that would mean admitting to one of the lower orders that a gentleman is capable of such a horrendous crime. Far better, from your point of view, to let Fortesque's murder go unavenged.'

'What a cynical view you do seem to have of us,' Maude said. 'I could take great offence at that, you know.'

'Yes, you could,' Blackstone agreed. 'But it wouldn't do you any good – and I might quite enjoy it.'

There was a loud cry of 'Howzat!' in the background, and Blackstone turned to see Lieutenant Soames flinging his bat down furiously on the ground.

'Well bowled, sir!' Maude shouted.

He held out his glass, and his servant took it from him. He clapped briefly, then held out his hand again, and retrieved the pink gin.

'Well, that's our team all out, but I suppose we can't complain – we've had a good run,' he said to Blackstone.

One of the enlisted fielders was already retrieving the bat from where Soames had flung it, while Soames himself – with Hatfield, his batting partner – walked slowly away from the wicket.

'Roger's just spotted you,' Maude drawled. 'Now we should see some fireworks.'

Blackstone examined the two men as they approached. Soames was large and beefy – a natural for the rougher sports in which brawn, rather than brain, was at a premium.

Hatfield was taller and slimmer, and carried himself without either the intellectual assurance of Maude or the physical assurance of Soames.

He was the weakest link in the chain – the runt of the litter – Blackstone quickly decided.

Soames scowled at Blackstone, then turned to Maude.

'What's that man doing here?' he demanded.

Instead of answering directly, Maude turned to watch the batsmen from the opposing team walking on to the pitch.

'You knocked up a good score, Roger,' he said, after a few moments, 'but that may not necessarily be to our advantage. The other side are the underdogs now, and that might just give them the push they need to best us.' He swivelled to face Blackstone. 'What do you think, Inspector?'

'I'd never underrate an underdog,' Blackstone said.

'I asked you what this man was doing here, William,' Lieutenant Soames said impatiently.

'Mr Blackstone?' Maude replied, as if fielding a question he'd never expected to be asked. 'Oh, he's here because he suspects one – or all – of us of killing Charlie Fortesque.'

'He does what!' Soames demanded, outraged.

'I have got that right, haven't I, Mr Blackstone?' Maude asked. 'You *do* suspect us, don't you?'

'There are certainly some questions I'd like to ask you,' Blackstone responded.

'Now look here, my man, I've had just about enough of your damned impertinence!' Soames said.

'Quiet, Roger,' Maude said. 'You may not be interested in hearing what questions Mr Blackstone wishes to ask but, for my part, I find the whole matter quite intriguing.' He turned to Blackstone again. 'You may speak now,'

'You can't imagine how grateful I am for your permission,' Blackstone said. 'Why don't we start by you telling me what the argument was about?'

'Argument!' Soames said to Maude. 'I really don't know what the devil he's talking about.'

'The day before Fortesque was murdered, three officers – I assume you three – went to see him in his dugout. Fortesque told you that he was going to make a clean breast of things, and one of you told him that that would ruin you all.'

'Never happened!' Soames said dismissively.

'I take it you got this information from that sniffling little weed who served as Charlie's servant,' Maude said.

'Doesn't matter where I got it from,' Blackstone told him. 'We all know that's what did actually occur.'

'Let's assume for a moment that you're right,' Maude said,

with the smile back on his lips. 'What do *you* think that conversation he overheard could possibly have been about?'

'My best guess is that you'd all been involved in something illegal, and that Fortesque was about to confess to it,' Blackstone admitted.

'We might have been embezzling the mess funds, for example?' Maude suggested.

'That's one possibility,' Blackstone agreed.

'Now why would we want to do that?' Maude asked. 'You look like a man who will have studied his history, so you must surely know that our ancestors stole such unimaginable amounts from their starving peasantry that our prosperity is assured until the end of time.'

'I knew a lord when I was soldiering in India—' Blackstone began.

'Knew him, did you?' Soames scoffed. 'Great friend of yours, was he? Used to wash your socks together?'

'I knew *of* him,' Blackstone corrected himself. 'He ran a string of polo ponies and, when he was sure someone was watching, he lit his cigars with Indian bank notes. But the money didn't come from his family, as yours does. It came from the brothels that he owned – brothels which employed girls as young as twelve.'

'I'm surprised, once you learned how he was "exploiting" the poor niggers, that you let him get away with it,' Soames said mockingly.

'I didn't,' Blackstone told him.

There was a moment of awkward silence.

Then Maude laughed and said, 'That really is a *most* amusing little anecdote, Inspector Blackstone, but you shouldn't let it lead you into believing that we all need to run brothels in order to live in the style to which we've quite rightly become accustomed.'

'No?' Blackstone asked.

'No,' Maude said. 'Soames' family, for example, owns half of Berkshire. Isn't that right, Roger?'

'Wouldn't say it was quite half,' Soames replied.

'While my own people control considerable tracts of the wilds of Yorkshire – a place I've never visited in the past and have no intention of visiting in the future,' Maude continued. 'And as for

Hatfield here – well, it's true that his grandfather earned his money in *trade*, but he made *so* very much from it that we're more than willing to forgive him.'

Maude was treating this whole encounter as a game, while Soames regarded it as an assault on everything he held dear, Blackstone thought. But Hatfield was neither amused nor enraged – merely uncomfortable.

'So just what *was* it that Fortesque could have done which might have ruined you?' he asked the three lieutenants.

'Nothing at all,' Maude said calmly. 'Charlie Fortesque's servant – who ranks on the evolutionary scale slightly below pond scum – heard what was merely amusing banter between friends, and got completely the wrong idea. I'd be more than willing to tell you what the joke was, if I could remember it – but it was so inconsequential that it's gone completely out of my mind.'

'You're lying, of course,' Blackstone said.

'Damn your impudence!' Soames exploded. 'Fifty years ago – civilian or no civilian – I could have had you horsewhipped for saying that.'

'Not fifty years ago, Roger – much closer to a hundred,' Maude said, still amused. 'But you're quite right, there was certainly a time when you could have had Mr Blackstone horsewhipped – and if you had, I, for one, would gladly have paid money to see it.'

He had gone *almost* as far as he could with this particular interrogation, Blackstone decided, but he still had one last shot to fire.

He turned to face the weakest link in the chain.

'You've said absolutely nothing, so far, Lieutenant Hatfield,' he pointed out. 'I wonder why that is?'

Hatfield opened his mouth wide, but the only words which came out were, 'I . . . I . . .'

'Benjamin prefers, quite rightly, to let the senior members of our little group do the talking,' Maude said.

'And the senior members of the group would be you and Lieutenant Soames, would they?' Blackstone asked.

'Oh yes,' Maude agreed. 'By several centuries, at least.'

There was a loud cry of 'Howzat' from the field.

'The innings has only just started, and the opposition is already one wicket down,' Maude said. 'It would appear that, in this case at least, the underdog is being much less successful than he might have hoped.' He paused for a moment. 'You will bear that in mind, won't you, Mr Blackstone?'

'If the underdog *always* won, he wouldn't be the underdog any more,' Blackstone countered. 'But the fact that he's still *called* the underdog indicates that next time he just might come through.'

'I have no idea what the damn fellow's talking about,' Soames said, to no one in particular.

'No, you wouldn't have,' Blackstone agreed. 'But you understand what I'm saying, don't you, Lieutenant Maude?'

'Indeed I do,' Maude said. 'In fact, I think it can safely be said that, as a result of this brief meeting, we each understand the other.'

The new batsman was walking on to the field to a smattering of half-hearted applause.

Blackstone turned to go, then swivelled round on his heel.

'When you do want to talk to me, Lieutenant Hatfield, I shouldn't be hard to find,' he said.

And then, as the bowler vanquished the new batsman with his first ball, he turned again, and walked away.

EIGHT

Blackstone sat at the table in his billet, deep in thought, and occasionally sipping from the bottle of French beer – the only beer available in the NCOs' mess – which he held in his hand.

He had never investigated a case quite like this one before, he mused. And what made it so unique was that he was almost certain he knew who the murderer was – or, at least, that he could pin it down to one of three possible suspects – but he had absolutely *no* idea of what the motive could possibly be.

He had almost completely dismissed the idea that Fortesque had been killed to prevent him revealing the details of a racket they had all been involved in, because that simply did not square with the characters of the three young men he had talked to at the cricket match.

For openers, Hatfield was too earnest to become involved in anything shady, and Soames was too stupid. As for Maude, it would be beneath his dignity – and his intellectual pride – to do anything which could as easily be done by a *common* man. And then there was Fortesque – the fourth member of the group – who, Blackstone hoped, had inherited at least a little of his grandfather's integrity.

Besides, it was hard to think of any kind of racket they could become involved with in the bleak, muddy trenches.

A gambling debt, then, he asked himself, taking a drag on a French cigarette which, to his taste, was only slightly better than dried camel dung.

It was true that many officers had been destroyed by gambling, but gambling was, by its very nature, a solitary activity, and Blenkinsop had distinctly heard one of the lieutenants say that if Fortesque came clean, it would ruin *them all*.

A woman?

Back in England, perhaps, the love of a woman might lead to a crime of passion. But there were no women within a hundred miles who these young men might feel strongly about. And even if they *did* visit fancy whores in some of the better brothels in Paris – women covered in perfume and silk, according to Blenkinsop – no man kills his friend over a whore.

The stumbling block, from whatever angle he examined the problem, was always the same three little words – *ruin them all*.

This was one investigation that he could not handle alone, he decided – and the help he needed would have to come from both sides of the Channel.

England was no problem.

There, he could rely on Dr Ellie Carr, the brilliant forensic scientist who was his sometime-lover. She had helped him find the solution to seemingly unsolvable crimes before, and if anyone could pluck a vital clue from the dead body of Lieutenant Charles Fortesque, it was Ellie.

There, he could draw on the strange and idiosyncratic talents of Detective Sergeant Archie Patterson – a man with a huge attic of a brain, crammed full of information which others would long ago have discarded, but he had carefully stored in case, one day, it just might come in useful.

Getting any help in France was a completely different story.

In France, he was hemmed in from all sides by invisible walls – walls which had been erected by the officers who would *not* help him and the enlisted men who didn't dare to – and try as he might, he could think of no way of breaking those walls down.

The knock on the door took him by surprise, and the surprise deepened when the door swung open and he saw who his visitor was.

'Good afternoon, Captain Carstairs,' he said. 'I wasn't expecting you, but now you're here, do please take a seat.'

Carstairs sat down in the chair opposite him – the chair from which Privates Blenkinsop and Hicks had so recently told their tales.

'I'll come straight to the point,' he said. 'I'm sorry to inform you that I've had complaints about your recent conduct from some of my young officers.'

This was a Captain Carstairs he'd not seen before, Blackstone thought.

This new Carstairs was much softer spoken, and even sounded a little apologetic. And his face mirrored his voice – the expression on it one of a neighbour who feels he must complain about the noise, but doesn't really want to cause a fuss. But it was all a disguise, because underneath the bland reasonableness, Blackstone could sense a bubbling rage.

'Can I offer you a beer?' the policeman asked his guest, playing the same game. 'I'm afraid I can't offer you a glass – I wasn't issued with any – but if you wouldn't mind drinking out of the bottle . . .'

'You did hear what I just said, didn't you?' Carstairs asked, the disguise slipping a little.

'Yes, you said you've had complaints about me from some of your officers. But was that what you really meant?'

'I don't understand.'

'Didn't you really mean that you've had complaints from *one* of your young officers – Lieutenant Soames?'

Because it *had* to be Soames, didn't it, Blackstone thought.

Lieutenant Maude would never have complained, because that would have been as good as admitting that he'd let a common man like Blackstone rattle him. And – for the moment at least – that was an admission he was not prepared to make, even to himself.

As for Hatfield, he would have been too frightened about rocking the boat to have complained without first getting Maude's permission.

'Is it only Lieutenant Soames you have a low opinion of – or do you feel contempt for all my young officers, Inspector?' Carstairs asked, with what seemed like genuine curiosity.

'I don't hold them in contempt,' Blackstone said. 'I may not like them very much – though I suspect I *might* have liked Charlie Fortesque if I'd ever met him – but I accept that that's not entirely their fault. They can't help having been brought up to privilege, any more than I could have helped being brought up in an orphanage. And I *do* admire their obvious courage.'

'Roger Soames has courage – and to spare,' Carstairs said.

'No, he doesn't,' Blackstone contradicted him. 'The others show their courage – as most men do – in the way they fight to control their own fear. Lieutenant Soames, on the other hand, has neither the intelligence nor the imagination to even know what fear is.'

'Do you suspect him of killing Fortesque, Mr Blackstone?' Carstairs asked bluntly.

'Do you seriously expect me to answer that question, Captain Carstairs?' Blackstone countered.

'No, I suppose not,' Carstairs replied, 'although your evasion answers it well enough for me. But you're wrong. Soames could never have done it.'

'Of course he couldn't – because he's an *officer*!'

'I'm prepared to concede that the murderer could be an officer,' Carstairs said.

'You don't believe that for a second,' Blackstone told him.

'No, I don't *believe* it, but suppose that, for the sake of putting forward an argument, I was willing to concede it as a *possibility*,' Carstairs said. 'Would *you* then be willing to listen to that argument?'

Blackstone shrugged. 'Why not?'

'If an officer did, in fact, kill Fortesque, then I am sure that officer would not have been Soames, because, despite your opinion of him, I know him to be both courageous and thoroughly decent.'

'Those are just words,' Blackstone said.

'Then let me give you a concrete example of what I'm talking about,' Carstairs said. 'The night before young Fortesque was killed, Roger Soames led a patrol out into No Man's Land—'

'Why would he have led out a patrol *at night*?' Blackstone wondered. 'What would be the point of that? What could it possibly achieve?'

'Isn't it obvious?'

'Not to me.'

'It is a matter of regimental pride that during the hours of darkness, it is we – and not Fritz – who hold the area.'

'Was that the only reason he was there?' Blackstone asked incredulously. 'Was there no tactical advantage to it?'

'There could have been a tactical advantage,' Carstairs said, as if that were a minor point, barely worth consideration. 'It was always possible, I suppose, that the patrol might have got close enough to the German trenches to hear something useful. That has happened in the past. But as I said, the main objective of the exercise was to have control of the area.'

'That's insane,' Blackstone said.

Carstairs looked disapproving. 'I would have thought, as an ex-soldier yourself, that you might have had at least some sense of the honour of your regiment,' he said.

'I do,' Blackstone replied. 'I just don't see how crawling around in the dirt is supposed to enhance it.'

Carstairs shook his head again, as if he had reached the conclusion that Blackstone was a hopeless case, and would never truly grasp what the concept of honour meant.

'At any rate – and for whatever reason – the patrol was out in No Man's Land when Fritz spotted it, and opened fire,' he continued. 'One of the two privates with Soames was killed instantly, and the other was wounded in the shoulder. The wounded private was too weak to move under his own steam, and if Soames had decided to leave him to his fate, no one would have blamed him. But Roger didn't do that. While still under heavy enemy fire, he managed to drag the private back to our trenches.'

'And that's how the honour of the regiment is served, is it?' Blackstone asked. 'One man was killed, and another was wounded – and all for *nothing*!'

Carstairs frowned. 'I'm afraid you're quite missing the point of what I'm telling you.'

'So what *is* the point?' Blackstone wondered.

'That when he found himself under fire, Lieutenant Soames behaved courageously. And that is not even the end of the story. Once he was back in the trenches – and despite having undergone an experience which would have, at least temporarily, shattered many men – Soames resumed his normal duties. In fact, he was the one who discovered Lieutenant Fortesque's body.'

The last time Carstairs had discussed this matter, he had talked in terms of how *we* found the body.

But there hadn't been any 'we' at all – it had been bloody Lieutenant Roger Soames.

'Why didn't you tell me before that it was Soames who discovered him?' Blackstone demanded.

'I didn't see the need,' Carstairs replied. 'Does it actually matter who first came across him?'

'Yes,' Blackstone said, 'it bloody well does!'

'You're completely missing the point again,' Carstairs said. 'By insisting on dwelling on minor details, you're failing to see the wider picture.'

'Then, by all means, paint the wider picture for me,' Blackstone told him.

'It was just before dawn when Soames discovered Fortesque's body, and dawn – as you have recently learned – is one of the times when we are most likely to be attacked by the enemy. When Roger Soames emerged from the dugout – having just seen his best friend's battered corpse – Fortesque's sergeant already had the platoon at stand-to. So tell me, Inspector Blackstone, what would you have done in that situation?'

The question caught Blackstone off-guard.

'I don't know,' he admitted.

'Exactly!' Carstairs replied, with a hint of triumph in his voice. 'You don't know now – and you wouldn't have known then. But Soames knew! He understood, you see, that the last thing that the enlisted men needed to be told at that critical moment was that their officer had been murdered. So Soames *didn't* tell them. Instead, he took over Fortesque's duties, and it was only when the men had been stood down again that he reported what he had discovered. Have you finally grasped the point, Inspector Blackstone? Soames found his best friend – someone he went to school with – murdered, but he still managed to put his duty above personal considerations.'

'That's certainly one way of looking at it,' Blackstone said.

'If there is another, I would dearly like to hear it,' Carstairs told him.

'No, you wouldn't,' Blackstone said.

'In fact, I insist on hearing it,' Carstairs said forcefully.

'All right,' Blackstone agreed. 'Soames goes to Fortesque's dugout, and, for reasons we don't yet understand, kills him.'

'Were it not for the fact that you are questioning the integrity of one of my officers, I would find that suggestion almost comical,' Carstairs said.

'If he reports the death immediately, it will be obvious to everyone that Fortesque has just died,' Blackstone continued, ignoring the comment. 'On the other hand, if he can postpone it for an hour or so, it will be much more difficult to calculate the time of death.'

Carstairs stood up.

'I could have had you brought to me by the redcaps, but instead I came to see you,' he said.

'That's true,' Blackstone agreed.

'I did it that way so we could meet on your own territory, where you wouldn't feel quite so threatened. I thought that here, you would see reason. But you're not interested in seeing reason, are you?' Carstairs asked, his voice flooded with both anger and disappointment. 'You're so eaten up with bitter prejudice that the only thing you care about is bringing down one of your betters – a finer man than you could ever hope to be.'

'If Soames didn't kill Fortesque, then he's safe enough,' Blackstone said. 'If he *did* kill him, then I won't rest until he's swinging from the end of a rope.'

'From this moment onwards, you will not talk to any of my officers without my express permission – and then only in my presence,' Carstairs said firmly. 'If you disobey this order, I will ask Captain Huxton to have you placed under arrest and escorted back to England by the redcaps.'

'The War Office will overrule you,' Blackstone pointed out.

'It might well – in time,' Carstairs agreed, 'and possibly, in a week or two, you will be back here in France. But when a soldier is holding off the enemy, he does not ask himself what the

long-term result of the action will be, he merely performs his
duty as he sees it at that moment.'

Blackstone's sudden laugh echoed round the room.

'It's all a big bluff, isn't it?' he asked. 'A career soldier like
you wouldn't dare to cross General Fortesque. It would look too
bad on your record.'

'You're right, I *am* a career soldier,' Carstairs admitted. 'I was
born a career soldier. Even as a child, I dreamed of serving my
country honourably – and I have, both in India and East Africa
– of becoming a high-ranking officer, and of finally retiring, with
my memories of my service, to live the life of a modest country
gentleman.'

'And are you seriously trying to tell me that you'd risk all that
just to get me out of the way?' Blackstone asked sceptically.

'That is the third time you've completely missed the point,'
Carstairs told him. 'Becoming a colonel – or perhaps even a
general – is no longer a possibility. I'm fighting in a war
which I will not survive. I am already one of the walking
dead.'

'You might survive it,' Blackstone said. 'Somebody has to.'

Carstairs shook his head. 'You're wrong,' he said. 'My death
may come sooner, or it may come later – but it will come. But
until it comes, I intend to do my duty as I see it. The men depend
on their officers, and their officers depend on me – and I will
not betray them.'

'I'm sorry I laughed at you,' Blackstone said sincerely. 'It was
very wrong of me, because though we may disagree on most
things, I do respect you for the way you stand up for things that
you believe in.'

'And perhaps, under other circumstances, I might respect
you,' Carstairs replied. 'But, under *these* circumstances, you
are nothing but a cancer, trying to destroy all that is finest and
most noble about my country – and I simply will not let that
happen.'

There was no more to say – no more that *could* be said – and
they both knew it.

Blackstone sat perfectly still, staring at the wall. It was several
minutes since Captain Carstairs had left, and in that time he had
scarcely moved a muscle.

Was there a chance that the captain was right and that he was wrong? he agonized.

Was it possible that he was seeing everything through eyes blinded by prejudice – that his vision of the world, though for entirely different reasons, was just as narrow as that of the officers?

If so, then perhaps Soames really was the valiant, honourable man that Carstairs thought him to be.

If so, then perhaps one officer *was* incapable of killing another – whatever the provocation – because of the way he had been brought up.

Perhaps it was all true, and he himself, a poor orphan boy, simply didn't *understand*!

He shook his head, angry with himself.

He had always relied on his own judgement, he thought. And this judgement of his was not something that he had inherited easily from proud, privileged parents, nor had beaten into him at an expensive public school. It belonged to no one but himself, and was based solely on what he had seen and what he had experienced. And he *had to* believe it – because it was the only thing he had.

Feeling a little better, he took a sip of his beer, and decided he could quite get used to it.

He placed the bottle back on the table, and began to consider the implications of Carstairs' threat.

If he tried to speak to any of the officers, he would be sent straight back to England, the captain had said – and he had meant it.

'And why exactly should that bother you, Sam?' he asked himself.

He had never wanted to be sent to France in the first place, and now he was there, he saw the virtual impossibility of ever solving the murder.

So why not just give in now? Why not ensure his rapid return to England by defying Carstairs' orders?

No one on the other side of the Channel – not even his bitterest enemies in the Yard – would find any reason to blame him, because he would just have been doing his job.

'You could be out of here within the hour, Sam,' he said.

But even as he was speaking the words, he knew it was not

going to happen, because he had never walked away from a challenge in his life, and because he felt he still owed something to old General Fortesque.

'So if you are staying, how in God's name are you going to get around the restrictions?' he mused. 'And more to the point, where the bloody hell are you going to find an assistant from?'

NINE

The building was both large and impressive, at least by St Denis standards. It stood at the edge of the village, and had the words Bureau de Poste picked out in brickwork over the main entrance. It was not a post office any longer. The locals who might have once required its services were gone, and when the British Army had taken over the village, the place had become its telegraphy office.

There was only one man inside when Blackstone entered the building, a sergeant with a round, open face.

He looked up. 'You must be that policeman from Scotland Yard,' he said. 'Inspector Blackstone, isn't it?'

'You're very well informed,' Blackstone replied.

'My name's Winfield,' the sergeant said. 'Well informed? Of course I'm well informed – I'm the *telegrapher*. And I know more than just your name, Inspector Blackstone,' he added with a grin, 'I know that you're not exactly the most popular Englishman in France at the moment – especially with Captain Carstairs.'

'He's been telegraphing London about me, has he?' Blackstone asked.

'Twice today,' Winfield confirmed. 'Of course, I can't tell you what he's actually said about you—'

'I don't think you need to,' Blackstone interrupted him. 'I'd like to send a telegraph myself, if that's all right.'

'You're supposed to have official authorization to send telegraphs,' Sergeant Winfield said.

'I have,' Blackstone replied, laying a piece of paper on his desk.

The sergeant scanned it, then whistled softly.

'It says here that I'm commanded by the War Office to give you unlimited use of this facility.'

'I know.'

'You must have friends in very high places.' Winfield grinned again. 'Is it genuine, this document – or just a clever fake?'

'It's genuine,' Blackstone assured him.

'Not that I care – one way or the other,' Winfield told him. 'I'd probably have sent your telegraphs anyway, even without authorization. I like coppers, you see – my dad was one – it's only the army I can't bloody stand.'

'You're *in* the army,' Blackstone pointed out, with a smile.

'Yes, I am, and I'm still only a bloody sergeant. Turned my request for a commission down, didn't they, the poncy buggers. Well, screw them!'

'About the telegraph,' Blackstone said, bringing him back to the point. 'I'm sorry, but it's rather a long one.'

'How long?' Winfield asked.

Blackstone told him.

'You call that *long*?' the sergeant asked, tapping his finger on the desk as if he were already transmitting the telegraph. 'That's nothing to a man like me. I once had a contest with the three other operators, to see which of us could transmit the complete works of Shakespeare the faster. Real cocky buggers, they were – thought they'd walk all over me.'

'I take it they didn't,' Blackstone said.

'You've got that right,' Winfield replied. 'By the time they admitted defeat, I was well into *Macbeth*, and they were all still stuck on *The Taming of the Shrew*. It was an outright massacre.'

'So I'm lucky to have you, rather than one of them,' Blackstone suggested.

'Bloody right, you are,' Winfield agreed.

The afternoon shadows had lengthened in St Denis. The cricket match was long since over, and the soldier on punishment duty in the square had finally been taken off the wheel and allowed to hobble back to his tent, where he would rest his aching limbs until the next day's long punishment began.

Other than that, not much had really changed in the village since Blackstone had arrived in the early morning. There were still soldiers being put through pointless drills on the temporary parade ground; still soldiers queuing up outside the brothel, hoping to be doing a little drilling themselves; and still soldiers – having neither any duties to perform nor any money in their pockets – wandering aimlessly along the village streets like the lost souls they actually were.

And then Blackstone suddenly saw a soldier who was doing none of these things. This soldier was sitting on the edge of the fountain next to the limber, and cupping his head in his hands.

'Are you all right, Mick?' he asked.

The boy slowly raised his head, and looked up at Blackstone through reddened eyes.

'You didn't tell me you was a copper, did you, Mr Blackstone?' he said accusingly.

'I would have done if you'd asked,' Blackstone replied, 'but somehow it never came up in the conversation.'

Mick forced a grin to his saddened face.

'No, I don't suppose it did,' he agreed. 'In that railway carriage, you were too busy forcing me to my knees, and later on I was too busy apologizing for being such a bloody idiot.' He paused for a moment. 'Anyway, I never told you I was a hooligan, neither – but then you wouldn't have had to be an inspector from Scotland Yard to work that out, would you?'

'Why have you been crying, Mick?' Blackstone asked.

'I haven't!' the young soldier said vehemently. 'I'm a hard case, me – and hard cases don't never yowl, whatever happens to them.'

'Why have you been crying?' Blackstone repeated firmly.

''Cos, underneath it all, I'm not a hard case at all – I'm nothing but a big soft girl,' Mick said. 'You remember my best mate, Sid Worthington, don't you, Mr Blackstone?'

'Of course I do.'

'He told us that he wasn't never going to see his twentieth birthday, didn't he?'

'Yes.'

'Well, he was right.'

'How did it happen?' Blackstone asked.

'They split us up,' Mick said. 'We thought we'd go through the whole war together, like the mates we've always been, but the moment we arrived here, they split us up.'

'Go on.'

'The platoon that Sid was posted to was serving on the front line. He'd only been there for about half an hour when the Huns fired a mortar into his trench and blew half his bleeding leg off.' Mick sniffled. 'Would it . . . would it have killed him straight off?'

'Yes,' Blackstone said – because there was always a *chance* it might have done.

'That's something, then,' Mick said. 'I wouldn't like to think of him suffering a lot.'

'It's rotten luck that your friend died that way, but this is going to be a long war, and, for your own survival, you simply can't afford to let it drag you down,' Blackstone warned him.

'It's not just Sid's death that's getting to me – though that's bad enough,' Mick said.

'Then what else is it?'

Mick's face contorted, as he struggled to find the right words to express himself.

'Did you ever see that recruitment poster?' he asked finally.

'Which recruitment poster?' Blackstone asked. 'There've been so many different ones since this bloody war started.'

'The one that I'm thinking of had this soldier right in the centre of it. He'd got his bayonet fixed on the end of his rifle, and he was going over the top.'

'Yes, I know that one,' Blackstone said.

'There was this streaked red and green sky behind him.' Mick paused. 'I said maybe that was because the sky in France *was* red and green, and everybody laughed at me. But how was I supposed to have known – one way or the other – when I'd never been outside London?'

'You couldn't have known,' Blackstone said soothingly.

'Anyway, it turns out that the sky over here is just as blue as the sky back home, so they were right to laugh at me, weren't they?'

'It's never right to laugh at other people,' Blackstone told him.

'So what I still don't understand is why they made the sky in that poster red and green?' Mick persisted.

It was all to do with group psychology, Blackstone thought.

The propagandists at the Ministry of War had read the works of
Gustave le Bon, and knew those were just the colours they needed
to use in order to manipulate the emotions of undereducated,
unsophisticated lads like Mick.

But even if he could have explained that to Mick, it
would only have made the young man feel even more
inadequate.

'Maybe, when they came to make the poster, they'd run out
of blue paint,' he suggested.

'Could be,' Mick said, agreeing easily – and making Blackstone
feel just a little bit guilty. 'Yes, that might well be it. They soon
ran out of a lot of things once the war started. Anyway, I was
telling you about the poster, wasn't I?'

'You were.'

'This soldier was standing against a green and red sky, but he
was all in black – his uniform and everything. He was a sort of
. . . a sort of . . .'

'Silhouette,' Blackstone supplied.

'That's the word,' Mick said, 'a silhouette. All black 'cept for
his bayonet, which was shining white. So, *because* he was all
black, you couldn't see what his face looked like. But you didn't
need to! And do you know why?'

'Because you already *knew* what it looked like,' Blackstone
guessed.

'Because you already knew,' Mick agreed. 'You'd seen his
face in the mirror every morning. Do you understand what I'm
saying?'

'I understand,' Blackstone said softly.

'But the more you thought about it, the more you realized
that *this* you was a *different* you. This *you* wasn't heartily sick
of the life he was leading. He didn't have to get blind drunk
on a Saturday night, just to stop himself from thinking that
the week ahead was going to be just as miserable as the week
that had just finished. He was excited! He wasn't just living
– he was alive!' Mick paused. 'Am I talking like an idiot
again?'

'Far from it,' Blackstone said. 'Tell me more.'

'It took you into another world,' Mick continued. 'Looking
up at it, you knew that if there'd been more pictures – if it had
been a comic, instead of just a poster – you'd have seen this new

you kill half a dozen big nasty Huns, and then be back in the trenches in time for tea.'

Blackstone merely nodded.

'But when you get out here, you find it ain't like that at all,' Mick said miserably.

Detective Sergeant Archie Patterson ran his hands thoughtfully over his ever-expanding stomach, and then looked through the window of his office in New Scotland Yard at the traffic passing below on the Victoria Embankment.

When he'd first entered this office, in 1896, he'd been a fresh-faced – but even then, slightly overweight – young man, and the traffic below the window had been almost exclusively horse-drawn.

Back then, the arrival of a motor vehicle – which hadn't even been *called* a motor vehicle at the time, but had been referred to as a horseless carriage – had drawn interest from the adults and produced a positive frenzy of excitement from some of the children.

Now it was the horse-drawn vehicles which were the rarity, and the motor vehicles which were king. And though he hated to admit it – as any forward-looking man who enjoyed poking gentle fun at his boss's dislike of progress would – he did rather miss the horses.

He turned away from the window and contemplated the wall. Things were very quiet – unnaturally quiet – with Sam Blackstone away, he thought.

Or had he got that the wrong way around, he wondered? Was *this* the natural state of things – the way that everyone wanted and expected them to be – and was it only when Sam started stirring things up that they became *unnatural*?

Ask any of the top brass in the Yard their opinion of Blackstone, and they would say he was ill-disciplined, disorganized, and a liability who they should have got rid of years ago.

But he was still there, wasn't he?

Because whatever they might say – and however much they might complain – they knew that when there was an investigation that had baffled every other inspector in the Met, the ill-disciplined, disorganized liability would find a way to get to the bottom of it.

Patterson twiddled his thumbs in a clockwise direction for a while, and then, for the sake of a little variety, twiddled them anti-clockwise. He should be enjoying this respite from being run ragged by Sam, he told himself, but the fact was that he was bored.

There was a knock on the door, and one of the clerical officers entered the room.

'I've got a telegram here from your boss, Sergeant,' he said. 'It's come all the way from France.'

'Well, it would have to have done, since that's where he is at the moment,' Patterson replied. 'What does he say – that the weather's lovely and he wishes I was there?'

The clerical officer grinned. 'Funnily enough, he doesn't mention the weather at all – nor even his desire for your delightful company – but he's got a great deal to say about other things.'

He produced the telegram with a flourish.

'Bloody hell fire, that must be at least five hundred words long,' Patterson said.

'Six hundred and forty-eight,' the clerical officer replied. 'I counted them personally.'

'Well, it's nice to know you've been making good use of your time,' Patterson said.

'Will there be anything else you require, Sergeant?' the clerical officer asked.

'I shouldn't think so,' Patterson replied. 'It seems to me this telegram will be *quite* enough.'

'I've been talking to some of the lads in my platoon,' Mick said, as he and Blackstone walked around the village. 'One of them – a bloke called Hicks – was telling me about this offensive they took part in the other day.'

'Hicks!' Blackstone exclaimed. 'Are you in Lieutenant Fortesque's platoon? I mean – are you in the platoon that *was* commanded by Lieutenant Fortesque,' he corrected himself immediately.

'Is he the officer who got himself murdered?' Mick asked.

'That's right.'

'Then I am in what was his platoon, only the officer's called Lieutenant Sampson now.'

'I'm sorry,' Blackstone said. 'I interrupted you. You were telling me what Hicks told you.'

'That's right,' Mick agreed. 'They had trouble with the gas that had been set off, because it had blown back on them. Hicks said, "That's one way to get us to shift out of the trench – bloody gas us," but I think he was joking.'

'I do, too,' Blackstone said.

'Anyway, when the gas had cleared, they went over the top, but Fritz . . .' Mick paused. 'They don't call them the Huns out here on the front, they call them Fritz.'

'I know,' Blackstone said.

'Fritz was ready for them. Hicks said they'd not gone more than a few yards before two of his best mates were cut down by machine-gun fire. He said that if somebody on the left flank hadn't knocked out the German machine-gunner, he'd probably have been dead himself. Anyway, they did manage to capture a section of the enemy trench, but they only held it for a few hours before Fritz took it back. So what was the point of it all?'

'There wasn't any point,' Blackstone said gravely.

'Hicks says his mates died for *nothing*. He says the only reason we're out here at all – and he's talking about the German lads, as well as ours – is to use up the enemy's bullets.'

'I wish I could tell you that I thought he was wrong,' Blackstone said.

'And we're stuck with it, ain't we?' Mick asked. 'If you run away and they catch you, they shoot you for desertion. If you wound yourself so you can't fight any more, they lock you up – and from what I've heard, that's sometimes *worse* than being shot.'

'I've heard that, too,' Blackstone said.

'Do you know what some lads do when they can't take it any more?' Mick asked. 'They kill themselves! They take one sock off, lie on the ground, put the barrel of the rifle in their mouths, and pull the trigger with their big toe.'

'It's not always as bad as that,' Blackstone said softly.

'It's not dying that gets to me,' Mick said. 'It's the futility of it all.' He paused again, uncertain. 'That's the right word, isn't it, Mr Blackstone? Futility?'

'It's exactly the right word.'

'You heard me talking on the train, didn't you? I might have seemed loud-mouthed and ignorant to you – bloody hell, looking back on it, I seem loud-mouthed and ignorant to *me* – but for the first time in my lousy life, I thought I had a purpose. And after less than a day here, that purpose has gone – and I'm left with this big empty hole inside me.'

'I could give you a purpose,' Blackstone said. 'Not a grand purpose – like becoming a hero in the defence of your country – but a purpose of sorts.'

'A purpose of sorts,' Mick repeated. 'What do you mean?'

'You could help me catch a murderer,' Blackstone said.

The first time Patterson read through the telegram, he did so at a gallop. The second time he was slower, repeating each word to himself in a soft whisper.

It was, by its very nature, an abbreviated form of communication, but he had worked with Blackstone long enough to be able to convert the terse language into what his boss would actually have said if he'd been standing there in the room.

He finished his second reading, and put the telegram to one side.

'There's no rest for the wicked, is there, Archie?' he asked himself happily, as he reached for the phone.

'Switchboard,' said a voice at the other end of the line.

'And which of our ladies do I have the privilege of speaking to on this fine afternoon?' Patterson asked.

'It's me, Victoria,' replied the operator.

'I hoped it would be,' Patterson told her. 'Though all the girls *are* lovely, you are by far the cleverest and most charming – which is why you're my favourite, by a mile.'

'I won't do it,' the operator said flatly.

'Won't do what?'

'Whenever you flannel like this, it's because you want me to break a rule,' Victoria said. 'And I won't do it.'

'Nothing could be further from my thoughts than asking you to betray the sacred operator's oath,' Patterson protested. 'I merely want you to make a trunk call to a General Fortesque.'

'And that's it?' Victoria asked suspiciously.

'That's it,' Patterson confirmed.

'It seems a simple enough request,' Victoria said. 'Even an operator who wasn't so clever and charming could handle that.'

'But not half as well as you,' Patterson assured her. 'Oh, there is one thing,' he added, as an afterthought.

'And what's that?' Victoria asked, the suspicion back in her voice.

'Generals are important people, you know, and when they talk, they like it to be with other important people.'

'Yes?'

'So when you get through, perhaps it might be best if you said *Chief Superintendent* Patterson wants to talk to him.'

'Will that get me into trouble?' Victoria asked.

'Of course not,' Patterson said.

'You're sure about that, are you?'

'And even if it does, I promise you I'll find a way to talk you *out* of trouble again.'

There was an audible sigh on the other end of the line, then Victoria said, 'There are some men who are love's young dream – so dashingly handsome that you'd lie down in front of a train if they asked you to. But, to be honest with you, Archie, you're really not one of them.'

Patterson chuckled. 'You really can be very hurtful, when you want to be,' he said.

'You're a podgy little man – and even if I did set my sights on you, I'd be wasting my time, because you absolutely adore your wife and kids.'

'Very true,' Patterson agreed.

'So why is it,' Victoria asked, sounding genuinely puzzled, 'that when you ask me to do something distinctly dodgy for you – something I *know* I should steer well clear of – I always end up doing it anyway?'

'It's a gift I have,' Patterson said – and offered up a silent prayer that it was a gift he would never lose.

TEN

It was at night, under the cover of darkness, that much of the real business of running a war – the nuts and bolts of logistics – took place.

It was then that supplies – the cases of bullets for the machine guns, the jugs of rum for the enlisted men, the bottles of malt whisky for the officers – were delivered to the trenches. It was then that the soldiers – the muscle-and-bone cannon fodder – were moved in and out of the killing zone.

It was also at night-time that foolhardy young officers like Lieutenant Roger Soames could claim that they were in possession of No Man's Land, by the simple expedient of crawling around it – like snakes – on their bellies. And it was then when more senior officers, like Captain Carstairs, could tell themselves complacently that though they might have lost a man in the process of establishing that claim, they had at least showed Fritz a thing or two.

For the enlisted men, night-time meant sentry duty – two hours standing on the fire step, two hours off it – with the prospect of death by firing squad if they allowed their exhausted bodies to doze off. It meant huddling in a small hole carved out of the side of the trench like a rat – and sometimes in the company of a rat – in an effort to grab a little rest. It was a time to reflect that however miserable your living conditions might be, it was still better than being dead – and to acknowledge that, once the dawn light came, Death might well choose to single you out for the touch of his bloody, bony finger.

Night-time was the most horrendous time in the world while it lasted. And then daytime came – and that could be even worse.

Blackstone stood at the edge of the village of St Denis, watching the company marching off to the trenches, with Lieutenants Maude and Soames in the lead.

As they passed by him, Soames favoured him with a scowl, and Maude gave him a smile which seemed to say, 'You might be the smartest policeman in the world – but you'll never get to the bottom of this murder.'

Only a few days earlier, Lieutenant Charlie Fortesque would have been part of a march much like this one – placing one heavy foot in front of the other, as he made the journey which would lead him to his death.

Fortesque would have been wrestling furiously with his troubled conscience as he marched, but what would have been the expression on *his* face? Blackstone wondered.

Uncertainty, he thought.

Guilt!

By the time his platoon had reached the trench that they would be occupying, the decision had probably already been made. And as he entered his dugout, he may well have experienced that certain lightness of spirit which comes from knowing that – whatever the consequences – you are about to do what is right.

But he had then made his fatal mistake. Out of consideration for them, he had told his fellow officers – the men he thought were his friends – what he had decided to do.

And that had sealed his fate!

'But what exactly *was it* that he'd done wrong?' Blackstone said aloud, as he walked up the sharply inclined street towards the village square. 'What was it that he needed to cleanse himself of?'

You're talking to yourself, Sam, said a voice somewhere in the back of his head.

Well, who else in this Godforsaken place *is there* to talk to? asked a second voice defensively.

You do whatever you want to do, but you might just end up talking yourself into a padded cell, warned the first voice.

I'll take the chance, countered the second.

'Stop it – both of you!' Blackstone told the voices, and then realized that he was speaking aloud again.

He had reached the square, and paused by the limber. He reached out with his hand, and felt one of its huge wheels.

Suppose it was not there in the morning, he thought.

Suppose that when the redcaps brought Private . . . Private . . .

He realized that though he had great sympathy for the man's plight – and was angry about what he was being made to endure – he did not even know his name.

Call him 'Smith' then.

Suppose that when the redcaps brought Private Smith to the square, there was no limber to strap the poor bastard to.

If he could just get the limber to the edge of the square – which would not be easy, but just might be possible – it would roll down the hill and be gone forever, he thought.

And in the morning, the redcaps would run around like headless chickens for a while, and then contact Captain Huxton, who, this being the army, would have to write a report – probably in triplicate – explaining why he needed a *new* limber.

The whole thing would take days, and in the meantime, Private Smith would get a little respite from all the pain and humiliation.

It was as Blackstone caught himself giggling at the thought of the redcaps' panicked faces that it occurred to him that he might be drunk.

What else would explain the action he'd just been contemplating? Who but a drunk would ever have come up with such a wild and fantastic plan?

And yet he was sure he'd had no more than two beers that day.

It was exhaustion – not drink – which was having this effect on him, he suddenly realized.

He had not slept since he left London, and that was over two days earlier. He needed to go back to his billet and grab some rest – before he *really* did something stupid!

The man stood in the shadows at the edge of the square, watching Blackstone examining the wheel of the limber.

Why was the detective doing that, he wondered?

Why hadn't he gone straight back to his billet – as the plan dictated that he should?

It had all seemed so simple and straightforward when they'd been discussing it earlier.

'When do I start following him?' the man had asked.

'When he's finished watching the company march out of the village,' the other had replied.

'He might not be there.'

'He will be.'

'How can you be so sure?'

'I can be sure because I understand him. He's at least as much an actor as he is a policeman, and he won't be able to resist the opportunity of showing us that he knows everything.'

Panic!

'He *doesn't* know everything, does he?'

'Of course he doesn't – in point of fact, he's on the wrong track entirely – but he *thinks* he knows.' The other had paused for a moment. 'Once he's sure we've all left, he'll go back to his billet.'

'He might not.'

'He will. He has nowhere else to go. And anyway, he'll want to catch up on his sleep.'

'Do I follow him all the way back to the billet?'

'No, he'd be bound to notice that. Just stay with him long enough to make sure that's actually where he's going—'

'You said that was where he would *definitely* be going. You said he had nowhere *else* to go!'

'—and then give him time to get into bed and fall asleep.'

But Blackstone *hadn't* gone straight back to his billet.

Instead, he was just standing there next to the limber, pressing his hand against its large wheel, almost as though he were thinking about moving it.

'I need help,' the man told himself. 'I can't do this alone.'

And then he let out a gasp of relief as the detective abandoned the limber and started to walk towards the street which led to his billet.

Blackstone lit the oil lamp first, and a cigarette which he promised himself would be his last of the day.

If he only knew what Charlie Fortesque had done that was so wrong, then he'd also know why the young man had been killed, he mused.

And if he knew that, he would also know – with absolute certainty – who the murderer was.

He walked over to the window, and looked out at the street. There was only a pale moon overhead, and the cobblestones the street was made up of were barely distinguishable from each other.

He was glad the moon was so weak that night, because there were no shutters on his window – though, from the evidence of the iron hooks embedded in the walls, there once had been.

He wondered what had happened to the shutters, and guessed they had most likely been taken down and used for firewood. It seemed a waste that something which had probably been painstakingly crafted, by a man who had spent years learning his trade, should meet such an inglorious end, but then war *was* wasteful – war was about nothing *other* than waste – and he certainly did not begrudge the poor soul who had removed them the little warmth it would have brought him and his family.

He was surprised though, when he reached for the catch to close the window, to find that that was missing, too. Why, he wondered, would anyone have gone to the effort of removing something which, once removed, could have been of so little practical use.

He moved the oil lamp closer to what was the stump of the catch. It had been sawn through, probably with a hacksaw blade, and since the ragged edge still glinted, it was likely to have been done fairly recently.

He took out his cigarette packet, placed the remaining two cigarettes in his pocket, and doubled the packet over. Next, he closed the windows, and jammed the cardboard packing under the edge of one of them.

'That should hold them well enough,' he thought, as he crossed the room towards his bed.

And then, as if eager to point out his folly, a sudden gust of wind from the street sent the two windows banging open before he had even had time to remove his jacket.

He thought about going back to the window, and making a better job of wedging it shut, but there didn't seem to be much point. If some passing girl wanted to climb through the window, throw herself on the bed, and ravage him, then she was more than welcome. And if some passing thief thought his lucky day had come, then he was in for a disappointment, since – apart from a second-hand suit, a shaving kit and some faded underwear – there was nothing much to steal.

Blackstone stripped down to his long johns, blew out the lantern, and climbed into bed.

ELEVEN

The town was dead. The streets were empty.

The enlisted men were all in their tents, playing cards, seeking silent self-relief under their blankets, or turning fitfully in a sleep which was filled with dreams of destruction.

The officers were in their billets, drinking whisky and telling each other – with varying degrees of conviction – that they were damn lucky to have a war come along just now, so they could show their true mettle.

And the whores lay still and sore in their beds, calculating how much money they had made that day – and how many more brutal embraces they would have to endure before they could afford to get the hell out of this place.

The man made his way along the same street which Blackstone had gone down half an hour earlier.

He was breathing heavily, and recognized that this was a result not of exertion, but of fear.

But why should he be afraid now, he asked himself?

He had been as brave under fire as most of his comrades. He could contemplate the possibility – the probability – of his own death on the battlefield without undue terror.

So what made this so different?

He wondered if it was because – despite the assurances he'd been given – there was a part of him which considered this to be a dishonourable act.

Yet how *could it* be dishonourable? Hadn't they all agreed it was necessary – that even if it brought his own disgrace, he would be acting for the general good?

He drew level with Blackstone's billet, and gasped at what he saw. He had known the windows would not be locked – that had been taken care of earlier in the day – but he had not expected them to be wide open.

What did it mean? How should he interpret it? Was he being led into a trap, or had fortune chosen to smile kindly on him?

He had been carrying his weapon in his fist, but now he stuck it into his webbing, to give himself a free hand.

He had only to step through the window, and he would be seconds away from completing his mission.

He was dreading what lay ahead, but at least, he consoled himself, it would soon be over.

They have made camp at the end of a long and punishing day's march in the Hindu Kush. Sergeant Blackstone posts sentries around the perimeter, tells his corporal to wake him up in two hours, then takes out his blanket and settles down gratefully in front of the fire.

He falls asleep immediately. It is a deep sleep, free from dreams of both his mother's slow death in the East End slum they shared, and the horrors he has witnessed during his time in Afghanistan. It is so calm and peaceful that he might almost be dead.

But though his mind has almost completely closed down, there is one tiny part of it – allied with his senses – which is sentry duty, and it is this small part which alerts him to the smell.

It is the odour of a man – and a man whose habits and diet are totally alien to his own.

Later, he will learn that the sentries he posted are all dead, but for now, as he slowly reaches under his blanket for his bayonet, all he knows is that there is an intruder in the camp.

The same breeze – which had treated Blackstone's cigarette packet wedge with such disdain earlier – wafted over his sleeping form now, and brought with it a reminder of that night in the Hindu Kush.

But this was *not* Afghanistan, he told himself, suddenly wide awake – and the smell of nervous sweat which was filling his nostrils emanated not from the body of a Tajiki tribesman, but from a man born much closer to home.

He could just make out a vague shape by the window – which must have been the intruder's entry point. He wondered what weapon his attacker – and he had no doubt this man had come to attack him – would use.

Not a gun! If he'd had a gun, he would have opened fire by now, spraying the bed with bullets. If he'd had a gun, it would already be all over.

A knife, then? Or perhaps a club?

But he could not use either of them effectively unless he had enough light to see what he was doing.

He would have brought a flashlight with him. He would have his weapon in one hand, and his flashlight in the other. And that was good, because he would have two things to think about, instead of just one.

If I was in his place, Blackstone thought, I would get as close to the bed as I could, then I would lift my weapon high in the air, and switch on the flashlight – aiming it at my victim's eyes. And the second that the flashlight found its target, I would swing the weapon with all the force I could muster.

The attacker – still no more than a malevolent black shape – slowly and carefully crossed the room.

Blackstone began counting to himself.

One . . . two . . . three . . .

At seven, he calculated, the attacker would switch on the flashlight, at eight he would swing his weapon, and at nine there would be a dull thud as bones cracked and brains turned to mush.

Four . . . five . . .

The intruder had now reached the foot of the bed, and was coming around the side.

Six!

The beam of light cut through the darkness, hitting Blackstone squarely in the eyes.

Too soon – far too soon – Blackstone thought, as a bright yellow ball bounced up and down in front of his eyes.

The intruder had panicked, and switched on the flashlight before he was in the right position to launch his attack. And yet his very incompetence was working to his advantage.

Blackstone twisted his body round, and lashed out blindly with his legs. He felt the soles of his feet make contact with the other man's chest, and heard – though he could not see – his assailant catapult backwards, and crash heavily against the wall.

Pain shot though his left ankle – which had taken most of the impact from the kick – and the yellow ball still bounced before his eyes. But he knew that he had to follow through quickly, whatever state he was in – had to hope that the eyes would clear and the ankle would hold him.

The ankle betrayed him – giving way the moment he put any

weight on it. He tried to compensate, shifting his weight to the other foot, but he had already lost his balance, and fell clumsily on to his attacker.

The assailant screamed, then wiggled out from underneath and crawled on his hands and knees towards the open window.

Blackstone made a grab at the fleeing man's leg, but the man was already out of reach.

The attacker struggled awkwardly to his feet, half-jumped, half-fell, through the window, and landed heavily in the street outside.

Blackstone's ankle issued dire warnings of what would happen if he attempted to follow, and knowing it would be pointless to attempt to defy it, he was forced to just lie there, and listen as the intruder hobbled clumsily up the road.

'Bugger it!' he said – and wondered if he could reach his cigarettes.

Five minutes had passed since the attacker had fled. For the first two minutes, Blackstone had lain where he had fallen, massaging his ankle. For the next two, he walked cautiously up and down the room, ignoring the pain and ordering the ankle to behave itself.

On the fifth minute he lit the oil lamp, and got his first look at the weapon which the attacker had been carrying. It was a tent mallet, heavy enough to drive metal stakes into frozen ground, and therefore more than adequate for the task of rendering him dead.

If the intruder had stayed – instead of running – there was every chance he would have prevailed in their struggle, Blackstone told himself.

An East End bully-boy, used to this kind of fighting, would have known that instinctively, but this man was not a professional thug, and so had lost his head at the first signs that things were not going exactly to plan.

Blackstone continued to walk up and down the room. He would have a slight limp in the morning, he guessed, but – with any luck – he should hardly be noticing his ankle by the afternoon.

'They wanted you out of action, Sam, which means you must be getting somewhere in this case, even if you don't realize it yourself,' he said, as he hobbled. 'That's good. That's *very* good.'

He paused for a second.

'But I wish they'd found some other way to send you that message, because, really, Sam, you're getting too old for this kind of thing,' he continued.

He was talking to himself again, he noted – but after what had just happened, a padded cell was starting to sound like an appealing prospect.

TWELVE

The train was slow – very, very slow – and the driver – for some perverse reason of his own – had insisted on stopping at every little country station en route, so that by the time it finally pulled into Hadley Compton, Archie Patterson had almost given up hope of ever reaching his destination.

Yet as annoying as the train had been, he watched it pull out of the station with some regret. It was, after all, his only real link to civilization, and seeing it go was suddenly like saying goodbye to an old and trusted friend.

There was only one other person on the platform – a porter with sleepy eyes and a ragged moustache.

'Where can I get a taxi?' Patterson asked him, speaking slowly, since he believed that was what you had to do, if you wished these country people to understand you.

'A taxi?' the porter repeated, as incredulously as if Patterson had just requested a blue and pink spotted elephant which was fluent in French. 'Whatever would youm want a taxi for?'

'I want to go somewhere,' Patterson said patiently.

'Where?'

'Hartley Manor.'

'That be no more than a mile from here,' the porter told him. 'Youm can walk it easy.'

'I'd prefer to take a cab,' Patterson said firmly.

'Ned Tottington's got a taxi,' the porter said. 'Him don't use it much, on account of him can't see too good – but him got one.'

'And where can I find Mr Tottington?'

'Siddington Derby.'

Patterson sighed. 'I'm afraid I don't know what you mean by that.'

'Him live in Siddington Derby,' the porter said, pointing vaguely out of the station. 'It be five miles that way.'

'And how do I get there?' Patterson asked. 'No, don't tell me, let me guess – I have to walk.'

'That's right,' the porter agreed.

Patterson left the station, and found himself plunged into a perfect bucolic scene. Birds were singing in the trees which lined the lane, with what seemed to him to be excessive cheerfulness. Cows stood munching away with slow contentment, in fields of unbelievably green grass. Insects chirped, butterflies fluttered, and bees buzzed – and it all made Patterson feel slightly uneasy.

The pace of the countryside was altogether too leisurely for his liking – he found the purity of the air unnatural, and the softness of the sounds grating. He had only been away from London for a couple of hours, but already he was yearning for the hustle and bustle and the soot-clogged atmosphere. And though he considered himself a fair-minded man – one who could see all sides of the question – he was finding it hard to imagine why *anybody* would choose of their own free will to live anywhere but in the big city.

He walked on, glancing over his shoulder occasionally for any signs of homicidal yokels wielding pitchforks or wild snorting bulls bent on his destruction. The railway porter's idea of a mile seemed to be greatly at variance with his own, he realized, and it was three-quarters of an hour before he reached the ornamental gates of Hartley Manor.

'Bloody countryside!' he said to himself, in disgust.

This wasn't the easiest job Sam had ever given him, he thought, as he approached the manor. For a start, General Fortesque probably wouldn't like the fact that he was there under what – strictly speaking – could be called false pretences. Nor would he care for some of the questions that needed to be put to him.

So whatever way he looked at it, the whole business could turn out to be distinctly sticky.

'You'll cope all right, Archie,' he told himself cheerfully.

'You're a jolly fat man – and everybody *always* trusts a jolly fat man, don't they?'

Once the butler had gone into the study to announce his arrival, Patterson took the opportunity to examine himself in the full-length mirror in the corridor, as he supposed everyone waiting there must do.

If the face grinning back at him was anything to go by, he was not displeased by what he saw. So perhaps he *was* a little too heavy, he thought, but his clothes fitted his rotund shape perfectly, and if he were inconsiderate enough to lose any weight, it would mean his poor wife staying up, night after night, altering them. Besides, losing weight would probably involve exercise, and while it was all very well for people to say – as they often did – that exercise never harmed anyone, his aching feet were witness to the fact that that was patently untrue.

The butler reappeared in the doorway.

'The General will see you now,' he said, before turning again and announcing – in a most unconvinced voice – 'Chief Superintendent Archibald Patterson.'

Patterson stepped into the study, and caught his first sight of the General.

The old man was sitting in a bath chair, and a heavy blanket covered his knees. He was frail – very frail – and though he was still clinging on to life, it seemed as if he was only doing it by his fingertips.

'Yes, it is almost a miracle that I'm still breathing,' the General said, reading Patterson's expression. 'Please be seated.'

'It's very kind of you to spare me the time,' Patterson said, taking the proffered seat.

The General's eyes scanned his visitor with a critical eye.

'I was expecting to be receiving a chief superintendent,' he said, 'and to be perfectly honest with you, you don't look like one.'

'That's because I'm not,' Patterson admitted. 'I'm *Sergeant* Patterson, Sam Blackstone's assistant.'

'Then why did you lie about your rank over the phone?'

'I did it to cut through the red tape. From what Sam's told me about you, I didn't think you'd mind.'

'And if I *do* mind? What if I inform your superiors of the deception?'

'Then you'd be landing me – and also a sweet young police telephonist called Victoria – in a great deal of trouble.'

'I should be sorry about the girl – but whatever happened to her would really be *your* fault,' the General said.

'Of course, we both know you're *not* going to inform my superiors, don't we?' Patterson asked.

'Do we? And why is that?'

'Because if I'm in trouble, I can't help Sam any more. And without my help, it's more than likely that his investigation into your grandson's death will grind to a halt.'

'You have a great deal of self-confidence – and not a little nerve,' Fortesque said.

'Thank you, sir.'

'Don't assume I was handing you a compliment,' the General told him. 'You said on the telephone – in your role as *Chief Superintendent* Patterson – that you wished to ask me some questions.'

'I do,' Patterson agreed, 'but before we get on to them, I'd like to ask you if you'll give your permission for your grandson's body to be examined by the police surgeon.'

The General's eyes watered.

'That's not possible,' he said mournfully.

Well, it was never going to be easy to get him to agree to something like that, Patterson thought.

'I can assure you that the body would be treated with the utmost respect,' he ploughed on, 'and that the examination might well provide us with a valuable clue to your grandson's murderer.'

'I've no doubt his body would be treated with respect,' the General replied. 'Sam Blackstone would make certain of that – but it's still not possible, because I don't *have* my grandson's remains.'

'But I was led to believe that he had been shipped back to England for interment in the family vault.'

'Yes, that was certainly the intention. But the coffin never got here. The last time its presence was officially on record, it was in Calais – and no one knows where it is now.'

'But that's awful!' Patterson said.

'It's devastating,' Fortesque corrected him. 'Devastating – but

not entirely surprising. I have fought in more wars than I care
to remember, and in all of them I have seen calm military order
on the surface – and chaos beneath it. And where there is chaos,
things go wrong.'

'Is there any chance the coffin will eventually turn up?'

'I have asked the army commander in Calais to do all he can
to find the poor boy, but I do not have high expectations of
success.' The General took a wheezing breath. 'You said you had
some questions you wanted to put to me.'

'Yes, sir. I'd like to ask you about three of your grandson's
friends – Lieutenants Soames, Hatfield and Maude.'

For a few moments the old man was silent, then he said, 'I
am correct in assuming that you're not merely Sam Blackstone's
assistant, but his right-hand man – someone he relies on
completely?'

Patterson shrugged his beefy shoulders. 'That's what he
tells me.'

'In that case, he must see a great deal in you which is not
apparent to the naked eye,' the General said.

Patterson grinned. 'I'm being tested, aren't I?'

'Are you?' Fortesque asked, non-committally.

'I think so. I've just asked a question about a charmed circle
to which you belong – and I so obviously don't – and that rang
alarm bells.'

'Go on,' Fortesque encouraged.

'It's not the done thing for someone like you to talk about
your own class to anyone who is not a member of it. In fact, it's
tantamount to being an act of treason, and you'd never normally
even consider it. However, these are *not* normal circumstances,
so you're prepared to make an exception – but first you need to
make sure I'm worthy of your trust. Hence the test.'

'Let us say you're right, and it is a test,' the General conceded.
'What do you think would be the correct way for you to respond
to my comment?'

'To your *insult*, you mean,' Patterson corrected him. 'It was
more of an insult than a comment, wasn't it?'

'To my insult, then,' the General agreed.

'There isn't *one* correct way to respond,' Patterson said, 'but
there are several incorrect ways. If, for example, I stormed out,
I would clearly not be the kind of person you wished to confide

in. Equally, if I pretended not to notice – or even worse, accepted the insult in good part – you would have no confidence in me at all.'

The General smiled weakly. 'Good,' he said. 'Now tell me more about Sam Blackstone.'

'Is this still part of the test?'

'You know it is.'

'I admire him more than any other man I've ever met,' Patterson said seriously. 'He's got more brains than the whole of the Yard's top brass combined. He's loyal, fair-minded and fearless.'

'And if he'd been born into a more privileged position in society – as I was, and the three lieutenants were – he would have been prime minister by now?' the General suggested.

'No,' Patterson said. 'There'd have been no chance of that.'

'Why not?'

'Because Sam does what he thinks is right, and if other people choose to follow his lead, that's fine with him. But if they don't choose to follow, he doesn't give a hang. And that's not the kind of attitude which will help you towards becoming a prime minister – or a general, for that matter.'

Fortesque nodded. 'You've almost convinced me of your suitability. Just tell me one more thing about him which shows that you're as good a judge of character as I am, and I think I'll be able to trust you.'

'I'm more than content with my life,' Patterson said. 'I've got my skinny little wife and my three chubby little kids, and that's all I want.'

'Whereas Blackstone . . . ?'

'Whereas Sam simply won't settle for contentment. He wants total and complete happiness or nothing.'

'And has he found that happiness?' the General asked quizzically.

'Of course not!' Patterson said. 'No man ever has, and no man ever will. And Sam's not a fool – he knows that better than anyone. But if he can't be happy, then at least he wants to be *useful* – he wants to ease a few burdens and see a little more fairness in the world. I think that's why he's a policeman.'

'You're a remarkable young man,' the General said.

Patterson grinned again. 'With all due respect to you, General,

you know that's not true,' he said. 'I'm no more than a reasonably competent middle-aged man,' he said.

'So you are,' the General agreed. 'Help me to my feet, please,
Sergeant. My old bones are having one of their better days, and
I would rather like to take a small turn around the gardens.'

THIRTEEN

When Blackstone had started out from St Denis that
morning, his ankle had hurt like the devil, but the
closer he got to the front line, the more the pain had
seemed to ease, and now that he was in the communications
trench, it was hardly bothering him at all.

The trench was just deep enough to ensure that a German
sniper wouldn't take the top off his head as he walked along it,
just wide enough for him to be able to touch both sides of it
with his outstretched arms, and though – when men or materiel
were being moved – it could be as crowded as Piccadilly Circus
at noon, he now had it all to himself.

He had just stopped to light a cigarette when the explosion
came. The sound was muffled – no louder than he might have
made by dropping a book on the floor – but from the way in which
the walls of the trench shook, it was clear to him that if he'd been
much closer, the noise would have been ear-shattering.

He could have turned around then – could have avoided the
horror which he was almost certain would lie ahead – but his
life had never been about running away, and after taking a puff
of his cigarette, he continued his journey.

He reached the end of the communication trench, and stepped
into a modern version of hell.

The shell had landed squarely in the fire trench, gouging a
huge hole in the back wall, destroying some of the heavy sandbags, and sending others flying. Huge boulders of clayey earth
were strewn on the duckboards, as if flung there by an angry
giant, and the stretcher parties were having to struggle around
them in order to get the groaning, wounded men to the nearest
dressing station.

The whole trench stank of cordite and blood. A number of men who had been far enough away from the explosion to avoid injury sat on the ground, their faces blank, their minds disengaged. Others had manic grins on their faces, and one – a blond-haired boy with a thin pale face – was sobbing uncontrollably.

A bloodied corpse lay in Blackstone's path, its face a mishmash of muscle and bone, and its right arm missing. He stepped around it, wishing there was something he could do – and knowing there wasn't.

Further down the trench, a sergeant blew his whistle loudly.

'Come on, you lads, snap out of it!' he bellowed. 'That was unlucky, I'll grant you – but we can't leave the trench like this.'

Slowly, the men rose to their feet, and made their way towards where the sergeant was standing.

'That's it, lads,' the sergeant shouted encouragingly. 'Look lively, and we'll soon have it fixed.'

Like zombies, the men reached for the picks and shovels they would need to repair the trench.

The sergeant saw Blackstone looking at him.

'It happens!' he said aggressively, as if he had read criticism in the other man's expression. 'It bloody happens, whether we like it or not – and we just have to bloody carry on!'

Blackstone nodded, agreeing silently that, yes, it did happen, and, yes, they just had to bloody carry on.

He turned slightly, and saw the missing arm of the dead soldier, lying lonely on top of a wall of sandbags. He wondered if, amid this chaos, it would eventually be buried with his owner.

'You're in the way!' the sergeant screamed at him. 'Get out of the bloody way!'

Blackstone eased himself past the soldiers with their shovels, and their angry sergeant with his whistle. He wanted to tell them all that he understood their pain and their fear, but he knew that he didn't – knew that he was only a visitor to this war which had become the centre of their existence.

He turned the corner, and entered another world. In this section of the trench, the men were following their normal routine – filling sacks with sand, stacking the sandbags against the wall of the trench, and repairing the duckboards, all with a calm, steady work rhythm.

Did they know about the tragedy which had occurred in the next section? Blackstone wondered.

Of course they did! They could not have failed to hear the boom, and were well enough aware of what damage an exploding shell could do.

But since it hadn't happened to them, it was none of their business. If it didn't touch their own struggle for survival, it could be ignored – *must* be ignored, if they were to avoid going mad.

He spotted the man he'd come to see standing at the entrance to his dugout, and looking towards the other end of the trench.

Even from that angle – and at that distance – it was obvious that Hatfield was not in command of himself, let alone anyone else, he thought.

Blackstone had known a number of officers like Hatfield during his service in India – weak men who, because they had been born into privilege, felt it was their duty to serve their country in the army. They had been quite wrong, of course – they would have better served their country by staying *out* of the army, and letting men who knew what they were doing take charge – but there had been no telling them that then, and there was no telling them that now.

'Good morning, Lieutenant!' Blackstone called out.

The words made Hatfield turn around, perhaps more quickly than he had intended to, and a wince of pain crossed his face.

'Terrible mess in the next section of trench,' Blackstone said. 'There's blood everywhere – and if the field gun had been pointed a fraction of a degree to the left when it was fired, that could have been you.'

'It will be me,' Hatfield replied. 'Sooner or later, it's *bound* to be me.'

'You're probably right,' Blackstone agreed cheerfully. 'There are some blokes who are both unlucky in love *and* unlucky at cards – and you do seem to be one of them. But if I was a betting man, I'd put my money on *Lieutenant Maude* surviving the war without a scratch – because he's the kind of man who always does.'

'Perhaps he is,' Hatfield said flatly.

'You are rather forgetting your manners, aren't you?' Blackstone asked.

'My manners?' Hatfield repeated, mystified.

'You never asked me how I was feeling this morning, which is really rather rude.'

Most other men in his position would have damned Blackstone for his impertinence, but Hatfield, after an uncomfortable silence of perhaps twenty seconds, forced himself to say, 'So how *are* you feeling this morning?'

'To tell you the truth, I'm getting a bit of gyp from this left ankle of mine,' Blackstone said. 'And how are *you* feeling, Lieutenant Hatfield?'

'I'm . . . uh . . . fine,' Hatfield replied, refusing to meet Blackstone's eye.

'Really? When I saw you turn around just then, you looked a little stiff to me. A touch of the rheumatics, is it? That's an old man's affliction, you know. I should have thought a boy of your age would have been fighting fit.'

'I *am* fighting fit,' Hatfield said, with an uncharacteristic burst of pride.

'I'm certainly relieved to hear that,' Blackstone said. 'But, as pleasant as it's been talking about health matters with you, that's not at all why I came here today, is it?'

Hatfield should have said nothing – he *knew* he should have said nothing – but once again, after a few moments of awkward silence, he felt compelled to speak.

'So why did you come here?'

'I came to bring you a present,' Blackstone said.

'A present?'

'Well, it's not really a present, I suppose. It's more a case of my returning your property to you.'

'My property?'

'You really should get out of the habit of repeating everything I say, you know,' Blackstone advised. 'It makes you sound like you're not your own man at all.' Then he reached into his pocket, took out the tent peg mallet, and held it out to the lieutenant. 'This *is* yours, isn't it?'

Hatfield folded his arms across his chest – and winced again.

'I've never seen it before in my life,' he said unconvincingly.

'You've never seen a mallet before?' Blackstone asked, in mock-surprise.

'Well, of course I've seen a mallet before, but . . .'

'But not this one?'

'That's right.'

'Now that is interesting,' Blackstone mused. 'Myself, I can't tell one mallet from another, but without even really looking at it, you're sure you've never seen this particular mallet before.'

'I have no more to say to you, Inspector,' Hatfield told him, turning towards the dugout.

'But I have a great deal more to say to you,' Blackstone replied, putting a restraining hand on the other man's shoulder. 'I watched Lieutenants Soames and Maude lead their men out of St Denis last night, but I didn't see you. Now why was that?'

'None of your business,' Hatfield said sulkily.

But he did not brush Blackstone's hand away with contempt, as Maude would have done. Nor did he take a swing at the policeman, which would probably have been Soames' instinctive reaction.

'We both know you stayed behind in the village so that you could pay me an unexpected visit in the middle of the night,' Blackstone said, 'and we both know that if you stripped off your jacket and shirt now, we'd find a big bruise on your chest that I made with my foot.'

'That's not true!' Hatfield protested.

'Well, it should be easy enough to prove, one way or the other. Are you willing to show me your chest?'

'No!'

'I thought not,' Blackstone replied. He frowned. 'Do you know what's puzzling me?'

Hatfield – having at last learned the value of silence – said nothing.

'It's puzzling me why Maude sent *you* to do his dirty work for him,' Blackstone said.

'He didn't . . .'

'He needed to send somebody, of course. I understand that. I was getting far too close to the murderers for comfort. But you'd have thought he'd have sent someone who could do a *proper* job, wouldn't you?'

'I have no idea what you're talking about.'

'Of course you have! You know that I know that it was you who attacked me, and I know that you know it.' Blackstone paused again. 'You could have finished me off when I was on the ground – Soames would have done, if he'd been in your place

– but instead you ran away like a frightened rabbit, which, when you think about it, was awfully bad form.'

'I didn't . . .' Hatfield began.

'So am I right in assuming that you *don't* want your mallet back?' Blackstone interrupted him.

'It's *not* my mallet!'

'Is it the same one you used to kill Lieutenant Fortesque?' Blackstone asked, as if the other man had never spoken. 'Oh, I was forgetting, you *didn't* kill Fortesque – that *was* Lieutenant Soames.'

Hatfield looked almost as if he was about to burst into tears.

'If only you knew what damage you were doing by being here, you'd put an end to this investigation of yours immediately,' he said.

'Damage?' Blackstone repeated, mystified. 'What damage are you talking about?'

'You have no idea of what reputations you might destroy, have you?' demanded Hatfield, drawing on reserves of spirit that probably even he had not known he possessed. 'You don't know what pain you'll be causing to some very fine people back home. You can't even begin to imagine the effect you might have on the war effort, right here in these trenches.'

'Perhaps you're right,' Blackstone agreed. 'But if you explained those things to me, I *would* understand, wouldn't I?'

'I . . . I can't explain,' said Hatfield, clearly drained by his previous effort.

And when he dove for the protective cover of his dugout, Blackstone did not try to stop him.

The two men had been walking slowly around the gardens of Hartley Manor for over a quarter of an hour, with General Fortesque leaning heavily on Patterson's arm for support. So far, not a word had been spoken, but the silence was not an awkward one – at least for the sergeant.

The gardens quite took Patterson's breath away. They were simply magnificent, he thought – like the best parts of the best London parks, only much better.

There were perfectly flat and manicured lawns. There were box hedges trimmed into weird and wonderful shapes. There were greenhouses growing fruits and flowers which the shoppers at Southwark's New Cut Market would – at best – have treated as oddities, and – at worse – would have regarded with extreme suspicion.

And there were peacocks – there were actually bloody honest-to-God peacocks – the colourful males strutting around with puffed out chests and tail feathers spread, the drab females waiting stoically for the ravaging which would come at the end of the display.

Now this was nature as it *should* be, he told himself – not wild and uncontrolled, but neat, tidy and organized.

Finally, they reached a series of ornamental fountains, and the General said, 'I'm rather tired. I think I'd like to sit down now.'

'Of course,' Patterson agreed, helping the old man gently down on to a marble bench.

The General sighed. 'Does anyone ever *really* think they'll end up old?' he asked.

'Not in the part of London where I come from,' Patterson replied. 'But then, they're mostly right not to think it – because by the time they *would have* been old, they're already a long time dead.'

'Are you rebuking an old man for his self-pity?' the General asked sharply.

'No, sir, I'm simply stating a fact,' Patterson replied.

'Yes, I suppose you are,' the General said, reflectively. 'Why do you want to know about those three young lieutenants?' he continued, suddenly switching tack.

'Because they may be pertinent to our enquiries,' Patterson said, in his official voice.

'In other words, you're not going to tell me.'

'That's right, sir.'

The General nodded.

'They were all three at Eton with Charlie. Two of them – Maude and Soames – attended a number of my house parties, but Hatfield was never invited, for some reason, so all I can tell you about him is that his grandfather was a brewer who eventually bought himself a title.'

Patterson chuckled. 'You sound as if you disapprove,' he said.

'Why would I disapprove?' the General asked. 'If a tradesman wants to spend a fortune to gain the ermine robes, then good luck to him. After all, it will probably impress his friends – and it's not as if he's fooling anyone who really matters.'

'Tell me about the other two,' Patterson suggested.

'I'm not quite sure what it is you want me to say,' Fortesque replied. 'They are both – in their own ways – fine young men.'

'In their own ways?' Patterson asked, pouncing on the qualification.

'What I mean by that is that if I was still on active service, I would have no hesitation in having them on my staff. They both love their country and would die for it without a second thought – and a commander can ask no more than that from his officers. However, I cannot say that I actually *like* either of them.'

'Why is that?'

'William Maude is something of an intellectual. I expect that, if he survives the war, he will go up to Cambridge and do quite brilliantly.'

'And what's wrong with that?'

'Nothing at all. We need our deep thinkers, just as much as we need our men of action. But, in my opinion, Maude values his intellect just a little *too* highly. He's a little like a cat that has caught a mouse.'

'I beg your pardon, sir.'

'He plays games with other people's minds, for the same reason that a cat plays with its prey – for his own cruel amusement. No doubt it's all very clever, but it does not sit well with me.'

'And Soames?'

'Roger Soames is quite a different case. He's a big strapping lad, which you would have thought would give him all the confidence in the world, but he used to follow Charlie around like a devoted puppy.'

And yet, according to Blackstone's telegram, he was the one most likely to have murdered Lieutenant Fortesque, Patterson thought.

'You sound as if you disapprove of his devotion,' he said aloud.

'It was more that I felt sorry for the boy,' the General confessed. 'We all have our heroes – we wouldn't be human if we didn't – but it seems to me that the heroes we choose should be an inspiration to us, someone who we might strive to be like ourselves one day. And much as I loved my young Charlie, he was still only a boy, who had yet to make his mark on the world.'

Perhaps that was the key to the whole investigation, Patterson thought. Perhaps Fortesque had been Soames' hero, and when he had failed to live up to the image of him that was burned into his friend's mind, Soames had felt so betrayed that he had killed him.

But that still didn't explain how Hatfield and Maude had become part of the conspiracy – if, indeed, there had been a conspiracy at all.

An old gardener shuffled slowly past, pushing a wheelbarrow with evident signs of effort.

'How are all the daffodils doing, Danvers?' General Fortesque called after him.

'They're doing fine, sir,' the other old man called back.

Fortesque shook his head sadly, as if what he had just heard merely confirmed what he already knew.

'There have been no daffodils for the last four months,' he said. 'That man used to be the best head gardener in the county. I've lost count of the number of prizes he's won me. Now I have to employ two extra men to undo the damage he does to my gardens. I should have pensioned him off years ago, but I knew it would break his heart, and I simply couldn't bring myself to do it. And now, of course, I don't suppose I'll *ever* be able to do it, however bad he gets.'

'Why's that?' Patterson asked.

'I'm not the only one who's lost a grandson,' Fortesque said. 'Danvers' grandson bought it in France, just a few hours before Charlie was murdered.' He paused for a moment. 'As I told you, I was devastated when I learned they'd lost Charlie's body, but now I've come to realize that, in a curious way, I was also relieved.'

'Oh!' Patterson said, non-committally.

'You see, it didn't seem quite right to me that my own grandson should be brought back for burial, while Danvers' grandson – who was also a soldier – languished in a shallow grave in No Man's Land.' Fortesque smiled. 'After my remarks about Hatfield's grandfather, I've surprised you, haven't I?'

'Yes, I think you have,' Patterson admitted.

'I've surprised myself,' the General said. 'Whoever would have thought that an old dinosaur like me would speak about my grandson's body and my gardener's grandson's body in the same breath – almost as if they were of equal importance. It seems so modern – so democratic.' He sighed. 'But then I suppose we're all going to have to get used to a lot more democracy once this war is over.'

FOURTEEN

Sergeant Winfield beamed with both pleasure and anticipation when he saw Blackstone enter the telegraphy office.

'You've had a reply from that Sergeant Patterson of yours,' he said. 'Now there's a man who really knows how to write a telegraph. He says more in twenty words than most people manage to say in a hundred. And damn intriguing words, they are, too.'

'Could I see the—' Blackstone began.

But Winfield was in full flow, and was not about to be interrupted. 'I like to imagine what the writer looks like when I'm taking the message down,' he said, 'and I see your sergeant as a tall, pale, handsome man, a bit like a poet, with flowing black hair. I'm right about him, aren't I?'

'It's certainly a quite remarkable description – and one I'm sure he'd be very happy with,' Blackstone said, picturing Patterson's expanding girth and thinning ginger hair. 'Do you think that I could possibly see my telegraph now, Sergeant Winfield?'

'Of course you could,' Winfield said, reaching on to the desk and handing it to him.

The message was a short one, but very much to-the-point.

Body+went+missing+in+Calais+stop+Bloody+funny+business
if+you+ask+me+stop+More+on+the+three+musketeers+to+
follow+stop+Archie+stop+end

'See what I mean,' Winfield said, tap-tapping away on his desk with his index finger. 'Is that intriguing or what?'

It was intriguing, Blackstone thought. And Archie Patterson was quite right – even allowing for the fact that there was a war going on, it *was* still a bloody funny business.

'I need to speak to the redcaps in Calais,' he told the sergeant.

'To check up on your missing body, no doubt,' Winfield said.

'That's right,' Blackstone agreed. 'Is there a phone here?'

'Well, there is – and there isn't,' the sergeant replied. 'We've still got the connection from the old post office days, but it's not in use.'

'I see,' Blackstone said. 'Well, in that case—'

'Now if you were a captain or a major, I'd look at you with a straight face and tell you it was a technical impossibility to reconnect it,' the sergeant said, 'but since you're neither of those unpleasant beasts, I'll stick a few wires together and see what happens.'

It took twenty minutes – and a great deal of electrical sparking – before Winfield was able to contact an operator, and another ten minutes before Blackstone heard a scratchy voice at the other end of the line say, 'Provost Marshal's Office, Corporal Baker speaking.'

'This is Inspector Blackstone, of New Scotland Yard,' Blackstone said. 'I wonder if you could help me with—'

'Good Lord! Inspector Blackstone! Fancy hearing from you, sir!' the military policeman interrupted.

'Do I know you?' Blackstone asked.

'I should say you do, sir. I'm Corporal *Bob* Baker – though in happier times, I was *PC* Bob Baker, a member of the finest police force in the world.'

'The East India Docks!' Blackstone exclaimed.

'The East India Docks!' Baker agreed.

It is late one night in June 1911.

Blackstone is hot on the trail of a prostitute-slasher who leaves notes next to his victims signed 'The New Ripper'.

But this man is no icy Jack. On two different occasions, he has vomited close to the scene of his grisly crime.

Ellie Carr says this combination of violence and revulsion is indicative of a certain serious type of psychological disorder with a long Latin name, and believes he probably can't help himself.

Blackstone doesn't care about that – his sympathy is with the victims, and any disorder the killer might be suffering from will soon be cured by the hangman's rope.

He is crossing the dock, heading for the merchant ship on which he has been warned the murderer is attempting to stow away, when he hears the police whistle blowing.

It is not a normal measured blast, it is a frantic, panicked plea for help, and, without even thinking about it, he turns and sprints towards the distress call.

By the time he gets there, Bob Baker is already on the ground, bleeding copiously from a wound in his side, and the two drunken Lascar sailors, who are standing over him with evil-looking knives in their hands, are just about to finish him off.

Blackstone drops the first sailor before the man even knows he's there, but overcoming the second one – who is both a better fighter and forewarned – is trickier, and by the time he goes down, Blackstone is bleeding too.

'You saved my life that night,' Baker's scratchy voice said.

'I only did what any officer would have done for any other officer,' Blackstone replied awkwardly.

'If it hadn't been for you, I'd have been a goner for sure,' Baker persisted. 'So if there's anything I can do for you now – and I do mean anything at all – you only have to ask.'

'That's good to know,' Blackstone said. 'And, as it happens, Bob, you might be able to help me. I'm out at the front line at the moment, investigating a murder, and—'

'Where exactly on the front line are you?' Baker interrupted, suddenly sounding much less enthusiastic and considerably more wary.

'It's a little place called St Denis,' Blackstone replied.

'Ah,' Baker said, 'so the murder you're investigating is Lieutenant Fortesque's, is it?'

'That's right,' Blackstone agreed. 'It appears that his body went missing in Calais, and I was wondering if you could fill me in on the circumstances surrounding the disappearance.'

'I'm not sure . . . I don't think . . .' Baker began.

And then he fell silent.

Blackstone slowly counted to ten, then, sensing that Baker was about to hang up, he said, 'Are you still there, Bob?'

'I'm still here,' Baker replied. 'Is it . . . is it really important to your investigation to know what happened to the body?'

'I can't say for certain – but it may be.'

Another silence.

'I'm in your debt, Inspector, but there's only so far I dare go,' Baker said, finally.

'If there's anything you can do for me – and you do mean anything – then I only have to ask,' Blackstone quoted back at him.

'We need to talk, sir,' Baker said.

'We *are* talking,' Blackstone pointed out.

'But not over the telephone,' Baker said firmly.

The soldier sitting on the collapsed wall close to Blackstone's billet was doing his best to assume the nonchalant air of a man who had nowhere in particular to go, and so had decided that where he was now was as good a place as any.

He didn't even come close to pulling the deception off. Instead, he resembled a puppy which had heard its master's key turn in the door, and is almost wetting itself in anticipation.

It was too soon – far too soon – for Mick to be making a report, Blackstone thought. He hadn't had nearly enough time to have done the spadework necessary to come up with anything useful.

But you can't come straight out and tell him that, can you, Sam? he asked himself.

It would be *cruel* to tell him. It would quite destroy the new self-assurance which Mick had found in his role as a police inspector's unofficial assistant. It would douse the enthusiasm which was so obviously bubbling up inside him.

No, he couldn't tell him. Instead, he would listen to what Mick had to say, express great interest, and then gently suggest that he might find something even more relevant if he followed a slightly different line of inquiry.

Blackstone glanced up and down the street to check they weren't being observed, then signalled that Mick should follow him into his billet.

The moment they were inside, Mick lit up a cigarette – and then started talking at nineteen to the dozen.

'Cor blimey, but it's a different world out here from what it is in England, ain't it, Mr Blackstone?' he asked.

'Yes,' Blackstone agreed. 'It certainly is.'

'It changes people, you know. I met a couple of blokes I used to knock around with down on the Old Kent Road. Well, they've been over here for a few months, and they're not the same blokes I knew at all.'

'They wouldn't be,' Blackstone said.

'We're about the same age, them and me,' Mick continued to babble, 'but, you know, they seem a lot older than me now.'

'It's the war,' Blackstone told him.

'Everything's different,' Mick marvelled. 'Even the bull! I'll give you a for instance. You know that Lieutenant Fortesque of yours?'

'Yes.'

'Well, he caught a few of the lads trying to stuff another lad's head in the cesspit. Not to drown him in shit, you understand – they'd never have done that – it was just like, playing a trick on him.'

'I know about that,' Blackstone said. 'His name was Blenkinsop.'

But Mick was too intent on telling his story to let the fact that Blackstone had already heard it deter him.

'Anyway, if an officer had caught them at that in England, all the lads would have been on a charge – no question about it. But Fortesque just told them they shouldn't treat any of their comrades like that, specially one that was going to be his new servant. Well, you could have knocked them over with a feather when he said that, 'cos they thought he'd been planning to give the job to another of the lads, who was called Danvers.'

'Tough on Danvers,' Blackstone said.

'Tougher than you might think,' Mick said. 'Danvers was transferred to another platoon, and was shot in No Man's Land a few days later. And if he'd been Fortesque's servant, you see, he wouldn't even have been out there.'

It was just as he'd suspected when he'd first seen Mick sitting on the wall, Blackstone thought. All that the young soldier had managed to collect so far was gossip.

But he was not entirely displeased, because Archie Patterson – who was one of the best coppers he'd ever worked with – was a perpetual collector of gossip and, just once in a while, it turned out to be useful.

Mick took a drag on his cigarette.

'Anyway, when the lads told me how this Lieutenant Fortesque had handled things, I thought they were doing it to show me how soft he was, and how much they despised him for it,' he continued. 'But that wasn't what they were telling me at all.'

'No?'

'Not at all. Quite the opposite. First of all, they said he seemed so disappointed in them that they'd felt ashamed of what they'd done. But they also said he showed them his hand in a mitten.' Mick paused. 'I haven't got that quite right, have I?'

Blackstone smiled. 'He showed them that inside his velvet glove there was an iron fist?' he suggested.

'That's right,' Mick agreed. 'What they meant was that he'd made it quite clear to them that if they ever tried anything like that again, they'd be in the glasshouse before their feet could touch the ground. They went away respecting him for the way he'd handled things – and from that moment, they said, they'd have followed him to hell and back, if he'd asked them to.'

Blackstone nodded.

If he'd been in those privates' place, he'd probably have felt the same, he thought – because a good officer, in his experience, was one who played things strictly by the rule book when it coincided with his own judgement, and tossed that same rule book over his shoulder when it didn't.

'That Lieutenant Hatfield's a different kettle of fish altogether,' Mick continued. 'The lads have got nothing but contempt for him.'

'Why's that?' Blackstone asked – suddenly interested.

'Because he's a bully – because he picks on the lads for no reason at all,' Mick said.

Blackstone frowned. Hatfield had his weaknesses – plenty of them – but he would never have marked the man down as a bully.

'Did Lieutenant Hatfield do something specific to earn this reputation?' he asked.

'Yer wot?' Mick replied, mystified.

'Why do the men think he's a bully?'

'Well, for a start, the day before your Lieutenant Fortesque was murdered, Hatfield put a couple of lads on a charge when he must have really known they'd done nothing wrong.'

Privates Clay and Jones are sitting in the trench. Jones is writing a letter at Clay's dictation, because though Clay is by no means a stupid man, writing is not one of his strong points.

'Tell her that when I get home on leave, I'll take her out dancing, if that's what she wants,' Clay says.

'Sounds a bit flat, that,' Jones tells him.

'So what do you think I could say?'

'How about, "When I come home to your loving arms, my darling, I'll take you dancing and whisk you off your feet." Doesn't that sound better?'

'It does,' Clay replies happily. 'You're a bit of a poet on the sly, ain't you, Jonesey?'

Absorbed in their task, neither hears the officer approaching, and it is only when Hatfield bellows, 'Sergeant!' that they even realize he is there.

The sergeant strides up the trench. 'Sir!'

'These men have just insulted me, Sergeant,' Hatfield says.

'Have you just insulted the officer?' the sergeant demands.

'No, Sarge,' Clay protests. 'We didn't say nothing to him. We was just talking to each other.'

'Does he take me for a complete fool?' Hatfield demands – and though he is trying to sound angry, it is not really convincing. 'He called me a useless bastard. I heard him distinctly.'

'I never . . .' Clay begins.

'Is he calling me a liar now?' Hatfield interrupts.

'Are you calling the officer a liar now?' the sergeant demands.

'No, Sarge,' Clay says, 'but I never . . .'

'I want both these men putting on a charge,' Hatfield says. 'They'll pay dearly for insulting me – I can promise them that.'

'Lieutenant Hatfield had them brought to the lock-up here in St Denis,' Mick said. 'And the funny thing is, they weren't even his own men – they were from Lieutenant Fortesque's platoon.'

Strange that Hatfield should have done that, Blackstone thought.

It did not reflect well on an officer when an enlisted man dared to insult him, which was why some of the weaker officers would pretend not to hear – yet he had chosen to make a big issue out of it.

'Were they charged?' he asked.

'No, that was the strange thing,' Mick said. 'The next morning they were released, and told to report to Lieutenant Maude.'

'You're sure that was who they were told to report to?'

Blackstone asked. 'It wasn't to Lieutenant Hatfield, who'd had them arrested, was it? Or Lieutenant Fortesque, who was their platoon commander?'

'It was Maude,' Mick said firmly. 'I mean, think about it, Mr Blackstone, Lieutenant Hatfield couldn't have seen them, could he – because that would have been like admitting he'd been wrong to put them on a charge.'

'True,' Blackstone agreed.

'And as for Lieutenant Fortesque,' Mick continued, 'well, he was dead by then.'

'Of course he was,' Blackstone said. 'Carry on.'

Maude is sitting at the table in his dugout, a glass of whisky in his hand, when the sergeant marches Jones and Clay in.

'Lieutenant Hatfield has been thinking over the incident which occurred yesterday, and has decided he may have misheard what you said,' he tells the two privates.

'Honest, sir, I would never have—' Clay says.

'Shut your mouth, Private Clay!' the sergeant screams.

'Since there now appears to be some element of doubt, Lieutenant Hatfield is willing to drop the charges against you,' Maude continues, with a smile that could almost, but for its cold edges, have been considered benevolent. 'Now that is good news, isn't it?'

Jones and Clay say nothing.

'Answer the officer!' the sergeant bellows.

'Yes, sir,' Jones and Clay mumble in unison.

'I can't hear you!' Maude says harshly.

'Yes, sir,' the two men repeat, louder this time.

Maude nods his head.

'You've been lucky on this occasion,' he tells Jones and Clay. 'Very lucky. You are to return to your normal duties immediately, and, if I were you, I would take the first opportunity I got to thank Lieutenant Hatfield – through his sergeant, of course – for your release.'

Maude's sergeant looks at the lieutenant, and when Maude nods, he says, 'Dismissed.'

Jones and Clay salute, and then execute a smart military turn.

'Just a second!' Maude says. 'Haven't you forgotten something?'

Jones feels his heart sink. He has already spent one night in the lock-up, and he does not want to endure another.

'Thank you, sir,' he says, hoping that is what was expected.

'Thank you?' Maude repeats, mystified. 'What are you thanking me for?'

Oh God, what does he want *me to say, Jones thinks desperately. Oh God, oh God, oh God . . .*

'For . . . for taking the time to talk to us like this' he says finally. 'For explaining things.'

Maude scowls. 'I'm your superior, not your kindly Uncle Fred,' he says. 'I neither expect, nor want, your thanks.'

'Then I'm sorry, sir, but if it's not that, I don't know what . . .'

'I asked you if you had forgotten anything. Well, have you?'

'No, sir, I don't think so,' says Jones, in a complete panic now. 'At least I can't—'

Maude raises his hand to silence him, then points with his index finger to the corner of the room.

'Your rifle, man! Your bloody rifle!'

Jones feels an enormous sense of relief.

His rifle!

Of course!

The redcaps had relieved them of their rifles when they were arrested, and now both weapons are propped up in the corner.

'Your rifle is your best and only true friend, Private Jones,' Maude says. 'It should be such a part of you that you feel incomplete without it.'

'I'm sorry, sir, but what with all the worry—'

Maude raises his hand to silence him again.

'Collect your weapon and leave,' he says.

Hatfield's putting the two men on a charge in the first place had been a mistake, Blackstone thought, but withdrawing the charges was a bigger one – because there were only two possible conclusions that his superiors can draw from this.

The first conclusion was that Hatfield was publicly admitting that he'd been wrong – a fatal error on the part of an officer.

The second was even worse – that he had been so weak that his men had bullied him into backing down.

And whichever interpretation they chose to put on it, Hatfield had seriously damaged his career.

But perhaps having the two privates arrested had been nothing more than a small part of a bigger plan, in which Hatfield's own military advancement was of no importance, Blackstone thought – a plan, formulated by Maude, of course! – which had come to fruition with the murder of Lieutenant Fortesque.

He closed his eyes, and tried to picture what might have happened shortly before Hatfield made his accusation.

Jones and Clay respect Lieutenant Fortesque – and even like him, as much as an enlisted man is ever allowed to like an officer – but they are still nervous about being summoned to his dugout without a sergeant in attendance.

Fortesque seems nervous himself.

'I think of you men as my comrades,' he says. 'I would die to protect you, if that was necessary.'

You are not supposed to nod in the presence of an officer, but Jones and Clay can't help themselves, because what Fortesque had just said is quite true.

'I have reason to believe my life is in danger,' Fortesque says.

Jones chuckles instinctively, then, realizing what he's done, clamps his mouth tightly shut.

'Have I said something funny, Private Jones?' Fortesque asks angrily.

'No, sir. Sorry, sir,' Jones mumbles. 'I didn't mean to laugh, but of course your life's in danger. All our lives are in danger. We're all in the middle of a bloody war.'

Fortesque relaxes a little. 'I apologize for not explaining myself more clearly. What I meant to say was that my life is in danger from someone in these trenches.'

Clay and Jones could not be more shocked if a German shell had landed just behind them.

'Who'd want to kill you, sir?' Clay asks.

And there, he would have had a problem, Blackstone thought. All the training he has received – all the assumptions he holds dear – tell him that he cannot criticize a brother officer to an enlisted man.

'I can't tell you who's threatening me – not now,' Fortesque says. 'But I'd like you to watch my back for me, and if you see someone

about to take my life, then for God's sake step in – whoever that
someone might be. Will you do that for me?'
  'Of course we will, sir,' Jones and Clay say in unison.

Somehow, Maude finds out about the meeting, Blackstone
thought. And when he does, he realizes that he will have to find
a way to have the two privates removed if the plan is ever to be
put into effect.

'There was an offensive the next day. Did Clay and Jones
survive it?' he asked Mick hopefully.

The young soldier shook his head. 'I'm afraid not.'

Of course they hadn't. It would be *far* too easy if they had!

But maybe there was still a way to prove a link – and to tie
that link to Maude and his pals.

'Ask the other lads if they noticed Clay and Jones talking to
Lieutenant Fortesque shortly before their arrest,' he said.

'Officers don't talk to enlisted men,' Mick pointed out.

'Ask anyway,' Blackstone said firmly.

'Is that it?' Mick asked, disappointedly.

'No,' Blackstone told him. 'The other thing I want you to do
is build up a picture of what life was like in that trench in those
last few hours before Fortesque was murdered.'

'It will have been like any other night in the trenches, won't
it?' Mick asked, puzzled.

'Mostly, it will,' Blackstone agreed. 'But there will have been
things that happened that didn't ordinarily happen, and I want
you to find out about *them*, because they just might be connected
to the murder.'

Enlightenment dawned on Mick's face.

'Before I met you, I thought that all coppers were good at was
beating a confession out of lads like me, but you've got a real
head on your shoulders,' he said, with frank admiration.

Blackstone smiled at him. 'Thanks, Mick.'

'I'll be back with everything you need to know in an hour,'
Mick said, enthusiastically.

Too soon! Far too soon!

'I don't want you going at it like a bull in a china shop, Mick,'
Blackstone warned. 'I want you to be a little subtler than that.'

'Subtler?' Mick repeated. 'How do you mean?'

'Don't ask the lads directly if anything unusual happened,'

Blackstone explained. 'Get them talking in general terms, and if anything strikes you as not quite right, say something like, "That's odd." Do you see what I'm getting at?'

'I think so,' Mick said, unconvincingly.

'The real trick to getting the right answers to important questions is to seem as if you're not actually asking any questions at all,' Blackstone amplified.

'Oh, you mean I should be sneaky.'

'Exactly.'

Mick grinned. 'Well, why didn't you just say that in the first place?'

Blackstone grinned back – it was hard not to.

'You're quite right,' he admitted. 'That's just what I should have done.'

'But say, even being very sneaky and very careful, I do find out something that could be important in the next hour or so, I should come to you straight away, shouldn't I?' Mick asked, bubbling over with enthusiasm again.

'You won't discover anything important in an hour,' Blackstone said. 'If you go about it in the right way, it could take you days before you come up with anything.'

'But say I did,' Mick persisted.

'There'd be no point in coming back even if you'd solved the whole mystery – because I won't be here,' Blackstone said firmly.

'Then I'll go wherever you are, and—'

'You won't be able to do that, because I'll be out of reach.'

Mick looked very disappointed. 'Oh, where will you be, then?'

'I'm off on a trip to the seaside,' Blackstone told him.

FIFTEEN

The band – playing loud and strident military music – could be heard long before it could be seen, and a shiver of anticipation was already running through the waiting crowd.

Archie Patterson, standing in that waiting crowd, rocked on his heels in perfect contentment.

It would have been criminal to have visited the royal town of Windsor without watching the ceremonial changing of the guard at the castle, he thought – and anyway, as a loyal subject of His Majesty the King, it was virtually almost his *duty* to grasp the opportunity when it was presented to him.

The military band appeared further down the street – tall men made even taller by the high bearskin hats they all wore, marching in perfect step, and with perfect resolution.

The American tourist who was standing next to Patterson gasped at the spectacle, and Patterson himself experienced a sudden surge of full-blown patriotic pride.

Behind the band came the New Guard, led by a captain with his sword drawn and pointing to the sky.

'Gee, they really know how to do things over here in England,' the American woman said to her husband.

'It's just a show, honey,' the husband growled back. 'It doesn't actually *mean* anything.'

Patterson chuckled to himself.

The disgruntled husband sounded just like Sam Blackstone, who might have admired the discipline on display, but would have had no time for pomp and ceremony, he thought.

The New Guard entered the castle grounds, and was met by the Old Guard. The two captains approached each other, then touched left hands, which was symbolic of handing over both the keys and the responsibility for guarding the monarch.

Sam Blackstone didn't have much time for the royal family, either, Patterson reflected – which was ironic when you considered that he had once risked his own life in order to save that of the Queen.

The New Guard had taken up its position, and the Old Guard began its march back to its barracks.

Patterson turned his back on the castle, and crossed the bridge which led into Eton. The changing of the guard, as impressive as it had been, was only an appetizer, he told himself with relish – the real treat of the day was yet to come.

Ahead of him, he could see the towers and crenellations of Eton College. The college had been founded when most of the London that he knew was still countryside. Fifteen British prime ministers – and many of the young officers now serving on the Western Front – had been educated there. It had stood on the same spot for nearly six hundred years – and if someone had assured Patterson it would still be there in another thousand, he would have accepted the assurance readily.

The closer he drew to the college, the more the 'natives' were in evidence – and a strange tribe they were! The boys were all wearing black tailcoats, waistcoats and pinstriped trousers, but some wore a black gown as well.

The wheels in Patterson's encyclopaedic mind whirred and clicked.

The ones in the gowns are King's Scholars – the brightest of the bunch, he told himself. Nicknamed *tugs*, from the Latin, *togati* – wearers of cloaks.

What else did he know?

He knew that all the older boys had one of the younger boys assigned to him as a fag – or personal servant.

He knew that when one of the senior boys – for some reason called a Library member – wanted some errand running, he simply called out 'Boy, Up,' and every first year boy within earshot was obliged to come running.

He knew that members of Sixth Form Select were allowed to wear silver buttons on their waistcoats, and that House Captains could wear a mottled-grey waistcoat.

And though he didn't like to admit it, he was starting to see some point to Sam Blackstone's disdain for pomp and ceremony.

He grinned to himself. He loved meeting people who had an unjustifiably high opinion of themselves, he thought. They were so much fun to play with.

General Fortesque sat at his desk, deep in troubled thought. He was wondering if he had been open enough with the chubby detective from Scotland Yard, or if he should have told him more.

'You don't *know* any more,' he said aloud. 'You do no more than *suspect* – and even that's putting things too strongly.'

Besides, suspicion, if it was to be of any value, must have a firm foundation of expert knowledge, he argued to himself – just as it had always done in his soldiering days.

He thought back to a time – long ago – when he'd been in command of a small company of cavalry men, out on a routine reconnaissance mission in the high Hindu Kush.

Military intelligence had assured him before he set out that
there were no hostiles in the area. His scouts had reported the
same. But the enemy were not the only people not in evidence.
There was no sign of the caravans of traders, bringing goods
from British India across the mountain passes, either. And not a
single villager had come to the camp he had established,
attempting to sell dried fruits and 'good clean girls' to his men.
They knew something – those traders and villagers – and he
needed to know what that *something* was.

The tribesmen were planning a surprise attack, he decided. It
was the only possible explanation. But where would the attack
come from?

He had made a detailed study of the tactics they had used in
the past, and had discussed those tactics with friendly tribal
leaders, and looking round him now, he fixed his attention on a
ridge in the near distance.

The enemy were behind the ridge at that very moment. He
could sense it. But he knew that since it was the eve of Friday,
they would never think of attacking before their holy day was
over.

He deployed his men under the cover of darkness, and as
dawn broke on Friday, he was ready to launch his own attack.
He had still not known, even an hour before the attack, whether,
by the end of the morning, he would be regarded as a hero or
a fool.

'It turned out that my suspicions were right,' he told his study
wall. 'But I would never have had them if I hadn't already known
something about the way the Afghans thought and acted.'

So whichever way he looked at it, suspicion without knowledge
was no suspicion at all. It was mere whimsy – a fancifulness
quite unsuited to a military man.

He had argued his case well, and he should have been both
satisfied and calmed by the conclusion he'd reached.

And yet a nagging doubt still persisted.

Perhaps, if he'd confided his suspicions – or whimsy, or fancy
– to the fat sergeant, it might have helped Sam Blackstone to
find his grandson's murderer, he thought.

Perhaps, by keeping them to himself, he was sending Blackstone
into battle without the covering fire he was entitled to expect.

He looked out of the window, and saw his head gardener

walking around in the sort of dazed condition which he now seemed to inhabit almost permanently.

He really should pension the old man off, he thought.

Yet, was he any better himself? he wondered – suddenly remembering that there was a task he'd been meaning to complete all morning, but which had completely slipped his mind until he saw the gardener.

He reached for a piece of paper, picked up his pen and began to write.

> *Dear Captain Carstairs,*
>
> *I must thank you for your kind words when informing me of my grandson's death. You say that he was an outstanding soldier who was an inspiration to his men, and though these are standard phrases which flow from the pen on such occasions, I think I can detect a real sincerity when you apply them to Charlie.*
>
> *As you no doubt know, Charlie's body disappeared en route to England. Such things happen in wartime, and I blame no one, especially his company commander who, I am sure, treated the dear boy's remains with all due respect while they were still in his charge.*
>
> *Thus, what I am about to ask of you should not be seen in any way as giving you the opportunity to discharge a debt, since there is no such debt to discharge. Rather I would like you to view it as a humble request from an old soldier who has debts of his own to pay.*

The General put down his pen.

'If all you have is suspicion without knowledge, then why the devil are you even *writing* this letter?' he asked himself angrily.

The housemaster, Edward Harrington Cardew, was in his fifties, and had the arrogant eyes and haughty expression of a man who firmly believed that the world was divided up into gentlemen and others. He did not inform his visitor that he'd been a pupil at Eton himself, but Patterson – who never started digging a hole before he was sure his spade was in perfect working order – did not need to be informed, because he already knew it as a fact.

The interview took place in Cardew's study, a room which

smelled of ancient leather-bound books and was garlanded
throughout with sporting trophies. The housemaster asked the
detective to sit down – though in a tone which suggested he
was bestowing an honour on Patterson which they both knew
he was clearly not worthy of.

'I would not usually agree to see a member of the constabulary
– especially such a low-ranking one,' he said in a drawling voice,
'but since the request for an interview came from General
Fortesque – who is himself a distinguished old boy of this school
– I'm prepared to grant you fifteen minutes of my time.'

Patterson settled back in his chair and rubbed his stomach.
'Oh, I think it will take considerably longer than that,' he said,
easily.

'I beg your pardon!' Cardew exclaimed.

'There's no need to,' Patterson replied. 'I wanted to ask you
about some of your former pupils—'

'I know,' Cardew interrupted him. 'Fortesque, Maude and
Soames – all of them outstanding young men.'

'And Hatfield,' Patterson said.

'Ah, yes, and Hatfield,' Cardew agreed, with considerably less
enthusiasm.

'Isn't *he* an "outstanding young man"?' Patterson wondered.

'Hatfield started out with certain disadvantages,' Cardew said.

'Meaning he's not quite from the top drawer?' Patterson
suggested.

'You may phrase it in that manner if you wish. I would prefer
to say that he has had to learn, by diligent effort, what came
naturally to the other three. But, for all that, he was a reasonably
pleasant boy and very earnest in his approach to his work – though
he had a certain need for approval which I, personally, found
rather irritating.'

'What about Fortesque?' Patterson asked.

'He was the President of Pop,' Cardew said. A thin, unfriendly
smile came to his lips. 'Need I say more?'

'No,' Patterson replied. 'I don't think so.'

Cardew looked distinctly disappointed, and Patterson chuckled.

'What is so amusing?' Cardew asked.

'I find it funny that you seem to think you can make me feel
inadequate by throwing words at me that I can't possibly be
expected to understand,' Patterson told him.

'And I, for my part, find it funny that you so obviously feel the need to pretend that you *do* understand them, even though you clearly do not,' the housemaster countered.

Patterson's grin broadened. 'Pop is more properly known as the Eton Society,' he said. 'Its members are entitled to wear checked spongebag trousers – though why anybody would want to is beyond me – and design their own waistcoats. They're allowed to administer beatings to younger boys – which we'll probably come back to later. They're the only members of the college who can furl their umbrellas within school grounds or sit on the wall in the Long Walk. It's every boy's ambition to be a member of Pop, or, to put it another way, they spend their entire school lives striving to earn privileges that no one in their right mind would want in the first place. Have I got that about right?'

'I can't say I care for your attitude, but you've certainly done your research,' Cardew admitted. 'At any rate, now that I've made it clear to you what splendid chaps they all are, I think we can draw this interview to a close.'

'In case you've forgotten, I'm conducting a criminal investigation,' Patterson said. 'I don't need to be told what it is about these particular boys which makes them such "splendid chaps". I'd rather hear about the sides of their characters that make them complete bloody bounders.'

'A bounder would not last a *week* in this college!' Cardew said, outraged. 'In fact, in EHC, my house, he would not last a *day*!'

'Ah, *your* house!' Patterson exclaimed. 'Am I right in thinking that when parents apply to Eton, they put their son's name down for a specific house?'

'You are.'

'And should I assume that there is some competition to be admitted into your house.'

'*Considerable* competition,' Cardew said, complacently.

'The better the raw material, the better the end product,' Patterson mused, 'You measure your own worth by the quality of the splendid chaps you turn out, don't you?'

'To a certain extent,' Cardew agreed, cautiously. 'What schoolmaster does not?'

'And if they do well in life, some of that glory is reflected on you?'

'Yes, and that is just as it should be. I mould them. Half of what they become is a result of my efforts'

'But what if they *don't* do well? Is some of the opprobrium then reflected on you?'

'The question simply does not arise.'

Patterson chuckled again. 'Of course it does. What about Hadley Featherington Gore?'

Cardew paled. 'Who?'

'Good try,' Patterson told him, 'but not quite good enough. You said I'd done my research well – and so I have. Featherington Gore was in your house from 1903 to 1910. And now, as a result of him trying to pass off one bad cheque too many, he's in quite another kind of house – one with bars on the windows.'

'One bad apple,' Cardew said miserably. 'One bad apple in a whole life dedicated to excellence.'

'Is it time for me to make my threat now, do you think?' Patterson asked casually.

'Threat?' Cardew repeated. 'You dare sit there and say you're going to *threaten* me?'

'Well, I suppose I could call it something nicer, if that would make you any happier,' Patterson conceded. 'I could say it was an inducement. Or perhaps an incentive.' He shook his head. 'No, on the whole, I think threat would be by far the most appropriate word.'

'You can't seriously expect—' Cardew began.

'I want you to be quite frank about the little weaknesses of the boys I'm interested in,' Patterson interrupted. 'And if you're not prepared to cooperate, then I'll dig up all the dirt I can on every other boy who's passed through EHC. It wouldn't take much to make your name mud – I'd only have to come up with a few sordid disclosures before parents start putting their boys' names down for every other house but yours.'

'This is outrageous,' Cardew said.

'Ain't it, though,' Patterson agreed.

Cardew gulped. 'Some of the boys thought Fortesque was too soft to be considered a great President of Pop,' he said. 'Is that . . . is that the sort of thing you're interested in?'

'It may be,' Patterson said. '*Why* did they think he was soft?'

'I suppose it was mainly because he never held a Pop-Tanning during his whole term of office.'

'Pop-Tanning,' Patterson repeated, rolling the word slowly around in his mouth. 'Now, I have to admit, that *is* a new one on me. What exactly is a Pop-Tanning?'

'It's a beating which the President is permitted to inflict on a miscreant from lower in the school,' Cardew said.

'Oh, it's a bare-arsed tanning, is it?' Patterson asked.

'Of course not,' Cardew said disdainfully. 'Only masters are allowed to thrash naked buttocks. In a Pop-Tanning, the boy is told to report to Pop wearing an old pair of trousers.'

'Why's that?'

'Isn't it obvious?' Cardew asked, slightly shiftily.

'No, but I expect it will be once you've explained it to me,' Patterson said firmly.

'The boy wears old trousers because, during the course of the beating, the trousers will become shredded.'

'It'll shred the trousers, will it?' Patterson said thoughtfully. 'If there's enough force behind it for that, it'll cut through the flesh and make his buttocks bleed as well, don't you think?'

'Most probably.'

'And Fortesque disapproved of it?'

'Of course he did not disapprove of it! He respected our traditions as much as the next boy. He merely chose not to enact one of them.'

'He disapproved of it,' Patterson insisted.

'In many ways, he was a rather gentle boy,' Cardew admitted reluctantly. 'Not on the rugby field – there, he was a lion who would crush anyone who got in his way – but certainly when he was not playing sports . . .'

'What about the others?' Patterson asked.

'Soames was all for giving a boy a good beating when he deserved it. He thought it would make a man of him – and so it does.'

'Maude?'

'Maude went through his whole school career without being beaten once himself. I believe that may make him unique.'

'But did he enjoy seeing other boys beaten?'

'He certainly did not shrink away from observing it.'

'And Hatfield?'

'If the others thought something was a good idea, so did he. If they were against something, he opposed it. Since his friends were divided on the question of beating, he tried to sit on the fence – which is typical of his class! He was never truly respected here, you know. Even his own fag despised him.'

'Did Fortesque and Soames ever argue about their different attitudes to beating?' Patterson asked.

'Never. They were always the very best of friends.'

'Did Soames resent the fact that Fortesque was elected President of Pop, rather than him?'

'Not at all. He thought that Fortesque truly deserved the honour, and would have been most distressed if he *hadn't* been elected.'

'So, as far as you understand the situation, Soames had no reason at all for hating Charles Fortesque?'

'For hating him?' Cardew repeated, with an incredulity which Patterson was sure was entirely genuine. 'Soames didn't hate Fortesque. Quite the contrary – he admired him tremendously, and would have laid down his life for him without a moment's thought.'

SIXTEEN

They stood there, side by side, in front of Calais Town Hall. Their heads were shaved, and – to make the executioner's job easier – they had already placed nooses around their own necks.

They really *had* expected to die, Blackstone thought, examining the bronze statue first from one angle and then from another. It was obvious, not just from the expressions on their faces, but from the tension in their muscles and the tightness of their chests. These Six Burghers of Calais had accepted that someone would have to pay the price for resisting the siege, imposed by Edward the Third of England, for eleven long months. And when they walked through the city gates – barefoot, and naked except for their long simple shirts – they were praying that their deaths alone would be enough to satisfy King Edward, and that their city might yet be spared.

At the last moment, they'd been saved. Touched by their willingness to sacrifice themselves for the greater good of their town,

Philippa of Hanault, Edward's queen, had interceded with her husband on their behalf, and Edward had proved willing to forego what he saw as his just revenge.

It was sacrifice that *this* war was all about, too, Blackstone thought, as he turned away from the statue – not conquests or spoils, or any of the other things that war was normally concerned with – but sacrifice. The young men at the front were being asked to throw away their own lives in order that their country – as they knew it – might go on living.

And as much as he might personally despise the three lieutenants who Patterson had called the three musketeers – as much as it would give him satisfaction to see them swinging from the end of a rope – he had no doubt that they were just as willing to make the sacrifice as the Six Burghers of Calais had been.

'Mr Blackstone!' said a voice behind him. 'What a great pleasure it is to see you, sir.'

Blackstone turned, and shook the hand of the new arrival. 'It's good to see you, Bob,' he said.

'Did you have a comfortable journey, sir?' the corporal asked.

'It was *tedious*,' Blackstone replied. 'I lost track of the number of times we were shunted into the sidings in order to let another train through. And two or three times – for some inexplicable reason – we actually went into reverse. As a result, it took me nearly twenty-four hours to complete a journey that probably wouldn't have taken more than four or five by road.'

'Well, that's the war for you,' Baker said. 'You should have asked for a car and driver.'

Good idea – at least on paper – Blackstone thought.

But he doubted that Captain Carstairs would have been at all receptive to the request. Besides, just making the request would have meant telling the captain where he was going – and why he was going there – and he suspected that Carstairs wouldn't have liked that one bit.

'Well, well, well,' Baker said, enthusiastically, 'who would ever have thought that, after all this time, you and me would end up meeting like this, in the centre of Calais.'

The enthusiasm seemed forced, and was perhaps being used to mask anxiety, Blackstone thought.

But *why* was Baker anxious? It was true that a body had gone missing, but that neither explained his nervousness now, nor his unwillingness to talk about it over the phone.

'Yes, it's certainly funny the way things turn out,' Baker said, more to fill the silence than for any other reason.

'You're making it sound like a *chance* meeting, Bob,' Blackstone said. 'But it isn't, is it? We're not just two old mates getting together for a drink – we're here for a purpose.'

Baker gave up all pretence of jollity, and his face immediately darkened.

'Yes, I suppose, in a way, we are here for a purpose,' he admitted.

'And we both know what that purpose is,' Blackstone prodded.

Baker glanced over his shoulder, and – for a moment – Blackstone thought he was about to run away.

Then the corporal took a deep breath, and said, 'Shall we go for a stroll, Mr Blackstone? I think I might find this a lot easier if we were on the move.'

The two men walked along the sea front. Across the water – a mere twenty-one miles away – Blackstone could see the White Cliffs of Dover, and found himself wishing that instead of seeing England from France, he was seeing France from England.

They paused to light a cigarette.

'So what's this information you've got for me?' Blackstone asked.

Baker looked worried again. 'You have to promise that if I tell you what *really* happened to Lieutenant Fortesque's body, you won't let anybody know that you got it from me,' he said.

'What *really* happened to it?' Blackstone repeated, quizzically. 'What really *happened* to it?'

'Promise,' Baker said urgently. 'You have to promise.'

'I promise.'

'We didn't lose it,' Baker said, in a rush. 'It wasn't like that at all.'

'So what *was* it like?'

'The coffin arrived here too late to catch the last sailing of the day, so it was taken to the main warehouse, which is where we keep the supplies for the troops on the front line,' Baker said. 'Now, that warehouse is crammed with all kinds of good stuff that the Frog wide-boys would just love to nick and sell on the black market, so there's always a sentry posted outside at night, and . . . and on this particular night, it was me.'

'Go on,' Blackstone said.

'I was patrolling the perimeter, like I was supposed to, and at around midnight this bloke came up to me, and asked me for a light. Well, like a fool, I reached for my matches – and that's when his mate hit me from behind.'

'You don't strike me as the kind of man who'd be as careless as to be taken in by a simple trick like that,' Blackstone said.

'You're right, I normally wouldn't be,' Baker agreed, 'but, you see, the bloke who asked me for a light was wearing an officer's uniform.'

'Was he, by God!'

'Anyway, I was out cold for at least half an hour. When I came to again, I had a bump on the back of my skull as big as a duck egg. I had a massive headache, too, but I knew that the first thing I had to do was check the warehouse – and that's when I discovered that the coffin was gone.'

'It was stolen?' Blackstone asked incredulously.

'It was,' Baker confirmed.

'Did the thieves take anything else?'

'Not a bloody thing.'

Blackstone's head was reeling. 'But if what happened to the coffin was that it was stolen,' he said, speaking slowly and carefully, to make sure he got it exactly right, 'why was General Fortesque told it had simply disappeared?'

'The CO said that was to spare the old man's feelings,' Baker said weakly. 'The way he argued it, it would be a blow to the General to learn we'd *lost* his grandson, but it would have been even worse for him to find out that somebody had snatched him. Besides, he said, we had our own reputation to think of – you don't end up looking very clever if you *lose* a coffin, but if you have it taken from right under your nose, you look like a complete bloody *idiot.* '

There was something about his tone which was not quite right – not quite genuine – Blackstone thought.

'You're happy with your CO's explanation, are you, Bob?' he asked.

Baker hesitated again.

'Yes,' he said, unconvincingly. 'I mean, it makes sense, doesn't it? We're policemen – that sort of thing's not supposed to happen to us.'

'What do you *really* think?' Blackstone persisted.

Baker looked down at the ground.

'I think the CO was just feeding us a load of old bollocks,' he mumbled.

'So what was the true reason that he wanted the lid kept on what had really happened?'

'I . . . I think he did it to protect the thieves.'

'And why would he want to do that?'

'Can't you work that out for yourself?' Baker asked plaintively.

'I'd rather hear it from you,' Blackstone said.

Baker sighed. 'I think he was worried in case it turned out that the robbers weren't just *dressed* like officers . . .'

'. . . but were exposed as actually having *been* officers!' Blackstone said, completing the thought.

Baker nodded. 'Officers are like gods. They can do no wrong. *Whatever* they do has to be *right* – simply because they're the ones that have done it.'

'Unless they do something so *horribly* wrong that no amount of doubletalk will ever make it seem right,' Blackstone said. 'And stealing Lieutenant Fortesque's coffin was so horribly wrong that, whatever happens, it can never be admitted that the thief was an officer.'

It just had to be the work of the three musketeers, he told himself – it was the only reasonable explanation – but what possible reason could even *they* have had for wanting the body?

Blackstone paced furiously up and down for several minutes. He did not look across the water at his beloved England again. He did not even seem to notice the other pedestrians, who had to jump out of their way to avoid him.

Why would they have done it? his quick brain demanded. Why, why, bloody why?

He came to a sudden halt.

Perhaps they hadn't stolen the body at all – because there'd been no body to steal, he thought.

Perhaps there'd been something else in the coffin – something which, if it was discovered by anyone else, would ruin them all!

'I think I'd like to see the warehouse where the incident occurred,' he told Baker.

'I was afraid you'd say that,' the corporal replied gloomily.

New experiences were raining down on Lieutenant Warren with such force and regularity that he felt he was in an almost permanent state of confusion.

Only a few months earlier, he had been one of the golden boys of his minor public school. He had been head of his house and the captain of cricket. The world had seemed simple, clear and predictable.

Then, suddenly, he was not a boy at all, but a man. And, as if that were not a big enough jump to make, he was an officer – and there could be no doubt about that, because the pip on his epaulette said so.

Now he was in France, amid a scarred and battered landscape which seemed a million miles from the immaculate green cricket pitch on which he felt so at home. He was billeted with officers who drank like fishes, and talked of doing to women things that he considered both revolting and near impossible. And he was in daily contact – though usually that contact was mediated through an NCO – with the enlisted men who made up his platoon.

He did not understand the common soldiers at all. They appeared to view everything through very different eyes to his own – to embrace a reality which was quite alien to the one he had long accepted as indisputable.

And if that was true of the English soldiers, it was even more extreme in these four Welshmen, who he was leading along the trench.

They were short, heavy, dark men. They moved with their heads slightly bowed, and in a manner which suggested they were passing between close invisible walls. Occasionally, one would whisper to the others in an incomprehensible language, but apart from that, they were silent.

When they reached the large white X which had been marked on the wall of the trench, Warren called a halt.

'This is where I want you to dig,' he said.

The Welshmen made no reply.

'Did you hear what I said?' Warren asked.

'This is where you wants us to dig, sir,' said one of the men, who Warren had heard the others call Dai.

'I want you to keep the tunnel at this level, and proceed in a straight line,' the lieutenant said. 'Do you think you can manage that, Private Thomas?'

Dai Thomas poked the earth with his thick stubby index finger. 'Shouldn't be a problem,' he said.

'It will be quite a long tunnel,' Warren cautioned. 'I don't know quite *how* long, but it could be at least a hundred and fifty yards.'

'We have dug five tunnels under the German lines,' Thomas said. He turned to one of his companions. 'How long was the longest, Alun?'

'Must have been five hundred yards,' the other man replied.

'See, sir, when you're born in the Valleys, you come out of the womb with a pick in your hand,' Thomas explained.

'That's why all our mams find giving birth so painful, like,' said Alun – and all the others laughed.

Warren frowned, unsure of whether they were being deliberately overfamiliar with an officer and a gentleman – or whether they just couldn't help themselves.

The problem was, he decided, that though he had not yet learned how to gauge the responses of the ordinary men, he was even further away from knowing how to deal with the Welsh. And these men were not even really soldiers – they were coal miners in soldiers' uniforms.

He really should have brought an NCO along to translate, he thought, but he'd been keen to show he could do this on his own.

One of the other miners nudged Thomas in the ribs with his elbow.

'Tell the lieutenant about that German tunnel,' he suggested.

Thomas chuckled. 'This'll make you laugh, sir. We was digging this tunnel towards enemy lines when we heard this scraping ahead of us. "They's digging a tunnel towards us," I tells Alun. "That they is," Alun agreed. "I'll tell you what we'll do," I says. "We'll go lower." And that's what we did. We dug lower, then we stopped digging and we waited. And sure enough, the next day we heard the noise of them digging above our heads.'

'This is the funny bit,' Alun said.

'Well, we'd already got our tunnel packed with explosives, so we went back to the trench, and set them off,' Thomas said. 'There was the big bang that made a crater five yards wide—'

'Closer to seven,' Alun interrupted him.

'It was five yards wide,' Thomas said firmly. 'And there was bits of Germans flying all over the place – arms, legs, even a head. Well, talk about laugh – we nearly wet ourselves.'

Warren shuddered. This really wasn't cricket, he thought.

'The point is, we don't think we's'll have any trouble with this little tunnel of yours, sir,' Alun said.

'Your main difficulty is the lack of precision actually attached to your instructions,' Warren said, in his best crisp officer tones. 'I told you it was a hundred and fifty yards, but that's only an approximation. And whilst we believe that what you'll be looking for is in a straight line from here, it could well be a little to the right or a little to the left.'

'Come again?' Thomas said.

'The officer thinks that we's going to have to root around a bit, Dai,' Alun explained.

'No problem, sir,' Thomas said. 'We once had this pit disaster in the valleys where there was bodies all over the place. Took us two weeks, but we got them all out, right enough – some of them bit by bit.'

The Welshmen were approaching this whole mission far too casually, Warren thought.

'You should be aware that though I'm the one who's briefing you, the orders come from much higher up,' he said. 'In fact, I don't think there's any harm in you knowing that this whole operation is being mounted at the personal request of General Fortesque. And the War Office takes that request so seriously that it had his letter specially couriered out – by airplane.'

The Welshmen did not look over-impressed.

'We'd have used a pigeon in the valleys,' Alun said. 'They's more reliable than airplanes. Why, I once had one that—'

'Yes, well, I'm sure the War Office knows more than you do about carrying messages,' Warren interrupted him. 'Are there any more questions – and I mean relevant questions – before you start work?'

The four miners looked at each other, then Thomas said, 'Who did you say we was digging this tunnel for, sir?'

'It is at General Fortesque's request,' Warren repeated, laying emphasis on the words 'General Fortesque', in case the Welsh ears had not quite picked up the significance of them.

The Welshmen stared blankly at him.

'You've surely heard of him, haven't you?' Warren asked, exasperatedly. 'He was one of the heroes of the Afghan Campaign.'

'Where's Afghan?' Alun asked.

'Don't show your ignorance,' Dai Thomas said scornfully. 'It'll be somewhere in England, look you.'

Lieutenants Hatfield and Maude were observing the scene with the miners from the other end of the trench.

'Do you think they'll find him?' Hatfield asked, worriedly.

'Probably,' Maude replied. 'Those Welsh are like greedy ferrets – they'd dig for weeks in search of a farthing. But what does it matter if they *do* find him? It's not as if they're going to learn anything from it, is it? There are no clues for that grubby little detective, Blackstone, to latch on to.'

'How can you be so sure of that?' Hatfield demanded. 'You're not a detective, are you?'

'Of course I'm not a detective,' Maude said contemptuously. 'I don't *look* like a workman, do I?'

'You should have done something to prevent things ever going this far,' Lieutenant Hatfield said. 'You should have stepped in, right at the beginning, and put a stop to it.'

'Should I?' Maude asked. 'And exactly how would I have gone about doing that?'

'You could have talked to Captain Carstairs. Or even someone higher up the chain of command. You're always saying you've got influence.'

'And so I have. But what would I have said? Would you have liked to explain the real reason we don't want this tunnel dug?'

'Of course not.'

'Then what other story could I possibly have come up with?'

'I don't know.'

'Problems rarely come from what happens – they come from how we *react* to what happens,' Maude said. He held out his hand, palm down. 'Look at that. It's as steady as a rock, isn't it?'

'Yes.'

'That's because one of the marks of a true English gentleman is that he is able to keep his head in all sorts of difficult situations. And if you ever wish to be taken for a gentleman yourself, Hatfield, that is something that you will simply have to learn how to master.'

'I know.'

'If you keep calm, they'll never be able to touch us,' Maude said, in a soothing voice. 'If you keep calm, we'll all be perfectly safe.'

SEVENTEEN

The British Expeditionary Force warehouse was located near the edge of the main dock. It was distinguished from the other warehouses which surrounded it only by the fact that it had a large sign mounted on the wall.

Blackstone examined the sign, looking first at the imperial crown which stood proudly at the top, and then at the words, '**HM Government Property. Keep Out**', which were written underneath.

They might as well have put up a sign saying, 'Want to nick some British Army stuff? You'll find it here,' he thought.

But as tempting as the goods inside might be, breaking in wouldn't be an easy job, because it was a formidable building, with stone walls, small barred windows and a door constructed of solid oak.

'How long did you say you were out cold after you were attacked?' Blackstone asked Corporal Baker.

'It was probably around half an hour.'

'And the first thing you did when you came round again was to check the contents of the warehouse?'

'Yes.'

'How did you get in?'

'Through the door,' Baker said, as if that should be obvious to anyone.

'So you had your own keys?'

'No, only the clerk-in-charge has the keys, but I didn't need a key, because the door was open.'

Blackstone bent down to examine the lock. It was probably a few years old, but since it was a Firbank and Bains' MB 5-2 – one of the finest locks ever made by one of the best locksmiths in London – its age didn't really matter.

'There are probably only a couple of dozen men in the whole of England who could have opened this lock,' he told Baker. 'And out of that couple of dozen, I doubt there's more than three or four who could have done it without damaging the lock itself. So what do you think the chances are that one of those three or four men was here in Calais the other night?'

'Slim,' Baker said.

'*Very* slim,' Blackstone replied.

The front half of the warehouse was crammed with packing cases containing bully beef, tins of baked beans, powdered milk and jugs of rum. Blankets, uniforms, picks and shovels and all the other necessities of trench life, were stored in the rear.

The clerk-corporal in charge of this little empire was called Hoskins. He was a small man, and wore glasses which had lenses as thick as jam jar bottoms.

'The coffin was delivered by lorry,' he told Blackstone. 'It wasn't anything fancy to look at. In fact, you might have mistaken it for an ordinary packing case, if it hadn't been for the shape, and the Union Flag draped over it. I expect they'd have taken him out of it, and put him in a much fancier one, once he was safely back in Blighty.'

'Yes,' Blackstone agreed. 'I expect they would have.'

And then the boy would have been carried to the family vault with due ceremony and full military honours, and laid to rest with his ancestors, he thought.

It would have been some consolation to poor old General Fortesque to see such a fitting interment – but now the consolation had been denied him.

'To tell you the truth, I didn't really fancy having a rotting corpse in my warehouse at all,' the clerk continued, 'but what else were they going to do with it? And anyway, I figured out that it wouldn't really start to stink until all the ice had melted . . .'

'What ice?'

'Didn't I say? The body was packed with ice.'

'How did you know that?' Blackstone asked sharply.

'I'm not sure, now you ask. I think the blokes who delivered it must have told me.'

'You didn't look yourself?'

'Course not! That would have been really morbid,' the clerk said dismissively. 'And anyway,' he added, 'the lid was screwed down and sealed.'

A wise precaution, if what the casket actually contained was something other than Lieutenant Fortesque's remains, Blackstone thought.

'What did you do with the coffin?' he asked.

'I had them put it over in that corner, where it's nice and cool.'

'And then?'

'And then I closed up shop for the night, and went back to my billet.' The clerk turned to look at Baker for confirmation. 'You saw me leaving, didn't you, Corp?'

'That's right, I did,' Baker confirmed.

'Did you go *straight* back to your billet?' Blackstone asked.

'I most certainly did. I was really knackered, you see, so all I wanted to do was get my head down.'

'So if I question the men who share the billet with you, they'll confirm that, will they?'

'Why would you want to go and do that?' Hoskins asked uneasily.

'They'll confirm it, will they?' Blackstone repeated stonily.

'Now I think about it, I did actually go for a walk before I turned in,' the clerk said unconvincingly.

'Even though you were really knackered?'

'Yes, I . . . er . . . wanted to make sure that once I was in bed, I really did fall asleep.'

'There's something that's bothering me about this whole business,' Blackstone said. 'Would you like me to tell you what it is?'

'Yes, I suppose so . . . if you want to,' Hoskins replied, without much enthusiasm.

'It bothers me that the thieves found it so easy to break in,' Blackstone told him. 'In fact, strictly speaking, they didn't *break in* at all – they simply came through the door. And how did they manage to open that door?'

'They must have picked the lock.'

'They didn't. If they had, I'd be able to tell.'

'Then I don't know *how* they did it,' Hoskins said sullenly.

'Of course you do! They opened it with the key that *you* gave them!'

'Now look here—' Hoskins protested.

'If you tell me how it really happened that night, Corporal Baker will be willing to overlook the fact that everyone involved in the robbery is equally responsible for him being knocked unconscious,' Blackstone said. 'Isn't that right, Corporal Baker?'

'Since you ask – and since I'm in your debt – I suppose I'll have to,' Baker agreed.

'I'll also overlook the fact that looting is an offence which is punishable by death,' Blackstone continued. 'On the other hand, if you make me go to all the trouble of digging up the proof myself, I'll personally organize your firing squad.'

'I . . . I . . .' Hoskins stuttered.

'They come for you at dawn,' Blackstone said. 'They tie your hands behind your back, take you into a courtyard, and stand you against a wall.'

'There's no need . . .' Hoskins said weakly.

'A chill runs through you, though you're not sure if that's due to the temperature or your own fear. They offer you one last cigarette. You accept it, not because you want to smoke – your mouth feels too dry for that – but because it will put off the moment when the order to fire is given.'

'Enough!' Hoskins sobbed.

'Sometimes you're killed immediately, but sometimes you're not, and you lie there on the ground – in agony – waiting for the officer to come across and finish you off with a bullet to the head . . .'

'I didn't know they were going to hit you, Corporal Baker,' Hoskins babbled. 'I'd never have agreed to it if I'd known they were going to do that.'

'Perhaps you'd better tell us exactly what it was you *did* agree to,' Blackstone suggested.

The men have been following Hoskins since he left the warehouse, but it is not until he is sitting down in the seedy bar – a glass of absinthe in front of him – that he notices them.

There are three of them. One is sharp-faced, the second chunky, and the third slim and nervous-looking.

Hoskins' first panic-stricken thought is that the sharp-faced one has bought up his gambling debts, and the chunky one is there to break his bones if he does not pay up immediately.

Then he relaxes, because though the men are in civilian clothes, they are not the kind of civilian clothes that a third-rate French gangster would wear. No, these men are English – and probably gentlemen.

The men sit down at the table – surrounding him.

'And that's when they offered you the bribe?' Blackstone asked.

'Not a bribe, exactly,' Hoskins said, uncomfortably.

'Then what *did* they offer you?'

'They said they had a bit of a problem, and that if I'd be kind enough to help them sort it out, it might be worth a couple of drinks.'

'We have a business proposition to make to you,' the thin-faced one says.

'What kind of business proposition?' Hoskins asks suspiciously.

'A very simple one. If you lend us the keys to the warehouse for half an hour, we will give you one hundred pounds.'

Hoskins' fear has been receding slightly, but now, once he has heard the size of the bribe, it comes back stronger than ever.

'They shoot you for stealing government property,' he says.

'It's not government property we're after,' the sharp-featured one tells him. 'The only thing we're interested in is the coffin – and that belongs to the family of the dead man.'

It's wrong – Hoskins knows it's wrong – but when the sharp-faced one starts counting out the big white banknotes on the table, he feels himself weakening.

With a hundred pounds, he could pay off all his gambling debts and make a fresh start in life, he tells himself.

'There's a sentry outside the warehouse,' he says, in a desperate attempt to save himself from making a big mistake.

The sharp-faced one smiles. 'You've got your uniform in the vehicle, haven't you?' he asks the tall nervous one.

'Yes, but . . .' the tall nervous one replies.

'The sentry shouldn't be much of a problem,' the sharp-featured one tells Hoskins.

'And when he said that, I thought he meant they could get in without hurting you,' Hoskins told Baker.

'And how did you think they'd manage that?' Baker asked angrily. 'By offering *me* a bribe, too?'

'Well, yes. They seemed to have plenty of money on them, and—'

'Not everybody's like you, you dirty little scumbag,' Baker growled. 'Some of us have a sense of honour and decency that can't be bought.'

A minute later, the keys and the money have been exchanged, and the deal is done.

They'll return the keys in half an hour – maybe even less than that – the sharp-faced one promises, and nobody will be any the wiser.

Hoskins watches them leave the bar, knowing that – even now – he could probably call it off if he wanted to. But he needs to pay his gambling debts, and maybe, once he has paid them and his credit is good again, he'll have one last flutter for old-times' sake.

'They never said they were going to *steal* the coffin, you see, only that they were *interested* in it,' Hoskins whined.

What the hell *was* in the coffin, Blackstone wondered.

It couldn't have been anything small, or they'd simply have removed it, and left the coffin where it was.

'You say they came in a vehicle?' he demanded.

'That's right. The tall thin one said that was where he'd left his uniform.'

'You're sure that he said a *vehicle* – not a motor *car*?'

'Yes.'

It would be a lorry, then, Blackstone thought.

'How heavy was the coffin?' he asked.

'I don't know. I didn't weigh it,' the clerk replied. And then, seeing Baker glowering at him, he quickly added, 'But it must have been quite heavy, 'cos it took four blokes to carry it in.'

'And you didn't think it was just a little odd that a body should have weighed so much?'

'Maybe he was a big bloke. And anyway, the ice would have weighed quite a lot, wouldn't it?'

Yes, it would, Blackstone thought. If there had *been* ice in the box. If there had been a *body* in the box.

What else would be heavy enough to need four men to carry it? It had to be something that would make three young men from privileged backgrounds risk everything they had to steal it.

Gold! Blackstone thought suddenly.

Gold was heavy.

Gold had such a magic attached to it that, throughout history, fabulously wealthy despots had gambled their whole empires on the chance of acquiring more of it.

Gold was portable wealth which, in times of war, was often moved around – and often went missing.

Yes, it was perfectly possible that the young officers – even Lieutenant Fortesque – had been seduced by the thought of gold.

But it was still *only* a possibility, Blackstone thought, reining in his rampant speculation – one possibility of many.

'How much did the three men you met in the bar *really* pay you?' he asked Hoskins.

'I told you,' the clerk replied shiftily.

'Then tell me again.'

'They bought me a couple of drinks.'

Blackstone mimed raising a rifle, pointed the imaginary rifle at Hoskins, and said 'Bang!'

'They paid me a hundred quid,' Corporal Hoskins muttered, looking down at the floor.

That was a lot of money, even for wealthy young men like the three musketeers, Blackstone thought. *Whatever* was in the coffin, they must have wanted it very badly indeed.

'And where's the money now?' he asked.

'Gone,' Hoskins told him. 'I . . . I got into a game of cards, and I was very unlucky.'

Corporal Baker threw the punch with a speed which impressed even a veteran street fighter like Blackstone. And it was not only fast, it was well-aimed, catching Hoskins squarely in the middle of his face.

The force of the punch lifted the clerk off the ground for a second, then he collapsed in a heap on the floor.

Blackstone, looking on, said nothing.

Hoskins gently felt his injured face, and winced.

'You've broken my nose,' he sobbed.

'Good,' Baker replied. 'So maybe the next time you're entrusted with the care of the dead, you'll show them a little more respect.'

A fair point, Blackstone thought, and maybe next time Hoskins would do just that – but it was by no means certain that he had been entrusted with the care of the dead *this time*.

EIGHTEEN

Returning to the front line was, if anything, even slower and more frustrating than the journey to Calais had been, and it was late afternoon – more than twenty-four hours after he had met Baker in front of the statue of the Six Burghers – when Blackstone finally found himself back in St Denis.

He was as exhausted as he could ever remember being, and the prospect of going straight to his billet and getting his head down was almost irresistible. But resist it he must, he told himself, squaring his shoulders. There were too many questions still unanswered – too many opportunities still available to the three musketeers that would allow them to wriggle off his hook – for him to even think about sleeping. And so, with a heavy sigh, he turned his back on the village and began to walk towards the chateau which it shared its name with.

If the size of the stable block in the grounds of the Chateau St Denis was anything to go by, then the count who had ordered its construction must have been a real enthusiast of equine pastimes, Blackstone mused.

And it was not just *large*, it was also highly elaborate, with gargoyles and crenellations aplenty. It was almost, in fact, a small chateau in its own right, and it must have cast a long shadow over the hovels of those peasants whose back-breaking work had financed it.

Blackstone wondered what had eventually happened to the extravagant, horse-loving count. The date set in the brickwork of the stable – 1777 – made it more than likely that he had ended his life in the Place de la Revolution in Paris – his body knelt before the guillotine, and his head in a basket below, looking up at it. And if that was what *had* actually happened, then he really had no one to blame but himself.

There were no horses in the stables now. The British Army had taken over the whole estate, assigning the chateau itself to those high-ranking officers who could not reasonably be expected to endure the grubby conditions of trench life, and converting the stable block into a garage.

And a busy garage this was, Blackstone saw. All around him, corporal-mechanics were hard at work – tinkering with the engine of a militarized Rolls-Royce Silver Ghost, welding new steel plates on to the side of a Lanchester armoured car, changing the tyres on a supply lorry . . .

Yes, it was a very busy place – and it had probably been equally as busy when the three musketeers had appeared in search of a vehicle which would take them to Calais.

A sergeant – slightly plump and in his mid-twenties – appeared in the stable doorway, walked over to the Lanchester, and looked down at the work the welder had been doing.

'Well, if I was a betting man, I'd definitely put my money on you winning the prize, Corporal Philips,' he said.

The corporal looked up. 'What prize, Sarge?'

'The prize for the prettiest armoured car in the whole of northern France, of course.'

'I didn't know there was a prize for that,' the corporal replied.

The sergeant emitted a dramatic, theatrical sigh. 'That's because I just made it up, you bleeding halfwit.'

'Oh,' the corporal said, clearly confused.

'You see, lad, the idea behind an armoured car isn't that it looks nice – it's that it's bloody *armoured*,' the sergeant explained. 'So I'm not really interested in how *neat* your welding looks – all that concerns me is that when it hits a bump in the road, the bloody steel plate doesn't fall off. Got that?'

'Yes, Sarge,' Philips said miserably.

'Then let's have a little less delicacy and a little more strength,' the sergeant said. He turned to face Blackstone. 'Can I help you?'

'I'd like to ask you a few questions,' Blackstone said, producing his warrant card.

'A copper, are you?' the sergeant asked. 'My dad was a copper, God rest his soul.' He held out his hand. 'Winfield's the name – Ted Winfield..

'Are you related to the sergeant who runs the telegraphy office?' asked Blackstone, shaking the hand.

'That's my brother, Wally – the black sheep of the family.'

Blackstone grinned. 'What makes him the black sheep?'

'He put in his papers to be an officer, didn't he? Think of that – Wally Winfield, an officer and a gentleman! I laughed like a drain when they turned him down. It would have had our poor old dad turning over in his grave. Still, he's not a bad bloke – in his own way.'

'And he's a dab hand at transmitting Shakespeare,' Blackstone said.

'Told you about that, has he?' the sergeant said drily. 'Well, I suppose he would have – if you'd been talking to him for more than a couple of minutes.'

'About my questions . . .' Blackstone said.

'Would you mind asking them in my office?' Winfield asked. 'It's not as noisy as it is out here – and anyway, I've got this bottle of very fine French brandy that's screaming out to be opened, and I've been told it's bad luck to open it when you're alone.'

'I've heard that, too,' Blackstone said.

Though the room to which Winfield led Blackstone was less of an office and more of a storeroom for spare parts, it did have a table and chairs, and there was indeed a bottle of good French brandy sitting on the table.

'I was on easy street when the war broke out,' the sergeant said, pouring out two generous shots of the cognac. 'I was the foreman at one of the biggest garages in the West End.' His eyes went misty at the memory of it. 'You should have seen the cars that came into that garage – Rolls-Royce, Hispano-Suiza, Mercedes . . .' He paused. 'I've not been back to Blighty recently, but I'll be willing to bet you don't see too many Mercedes being driven around London nowadays – not with them being German. People don't even dare walk their dachshund dogs any longer, for fear that some bugger will kick the shit out of them. And I believe they've even changed the name of the German shepherd, and have started calling it an Alsatian.'

'That's right, they have.'

Winfield shook his head. 'Mad! As if it was the poor mutt's fault what it was called. Anyway, as I was going to say, it was a good business, that garage, and what with the inducements and everything, I was starting to build up a nice little nest-egg for myself.'

'Inducements?' Blackstone said.

'Some chauffeur would bring in his boss's Lanchester, and take me over to a quiet corner. "Now look here, my man, there's something I want to ask you," he'd say."' Winfield grinned. '"My man"! That's what they'd call me, these ponces who thought that being dressed up in livery made them better than me. "Look here, my man, Lord Toffee-Nose wants his vehicle back as soon as possible, and if you're prepared to move it to the head of the queue, there could be a couple of pounds in it for you." And, naturally, I'd say I'd see what I could do.'

'And *did* you move it to the head of the queue?'

'Course not, but I always told them I had – which meant me and the lads had a couple of quid to share between us. I saw myself as a bit of a Robin Hood – taking from the rich and giving to the poor.'

'And that's exactly what you were,' Blackstone said.

'Anyway the war broke out, and the posters started to appear – "Your Country Needs You", "What Did You Do In The War, Daddy?" – all that kind of guff – and my lady-friend started nagging me into joining up.'

And she wouldn't have been alone in that, Blackstone thought, remembering one poster with the banner 'Women of Britain Say Go!', in which a woman and her children were standing at the window and watching soldiers march away.

Winfield reached over and poured them both a second glass of brandy.

'Effie – that's her name – said that when she got married, she wanted it to be to a hero, and there wasn't much heroic about taking internal combustion engines to pieces,' he continued. 'Well, you can't argue with a woman who's right, can you? Come to that, you can't argue with a woman who's wrong, either – so I went and enlisted! And then, of course, my brother Wally had to do the same.'

Blackstone laughed.

'As a matter of fact, once I'd signed up, I did begin to think that maybe I *could* be quite heroic if push came to shove,' Winfield told him. 'I started picturing myself storming the Hun trenches, and then getting a medal pinned on me by the King himself. And what happened instead?'

'Somebody told the powers that be what a bloody good mechanic you were?' Blackstone suggested.

'Exactly,' Winfield confirmed. 'So here I am, doing just the same job as I'd be doing back in London, but without any of the home comforts.'

They had drained their glasses, and Sergeant Winfield filled them up for a third time.

'I want to ask you about some officers who might have requisitioned a vehicle from you,' Blackstone said.

'Don't talk to me about officers requisitioning vehicles,' Winfield said. 'They make me sick – the lot of them. They turn up, looking all serious and high-minded, and say they need a car. So I ask for the paperwork, and they tell me that it hasn't come through yet, but they still need the car immediately, because they're on important official business. And what kind of important official business is it, do you think? It's the kind that involves them writhing around between the legs of a high-class whore in the nearest big town!'

'So what do you do in that situation?' Blackstone asked.

Winfield shrugged. 'I give them the car – because something that officers have in common with women is that they're right even when they're wrong, and while their commanding officer might know full well they were pulling a fast one, it's me that would get the rocket if I put in a complaint.'

'Do you remember three officers asking you for a vehicle a few days ago?' Blackstone asked.

'Skinny, Beefy and Sly?' Winfield replied, without hesitation. 'Oh yes, I remember them, all right. But they didn't want a car – they wanted a lorry. I asked them why it had to be a lorry, and Sly told me not to be so impertinent. Me! Impertinent! I've got a few years on the snot-nosed young bastard – and, as you may have noticed, I'm not exactly built like Jack Johnson – but if him and me ever got into an altercation outside a pub on the Mile End Road on a Saturday night, I reckon I could still beat the crap out of him.'

'I'm sure you could,' Blackstone agreed. 'You did give them the lorry, though, didn't you?'

'I did not,' Winfield said, 'but only,' he continued, slightly shamefacedly, 'because I didn't have one.'

They wouldn't have liked that, Blackstone thought – they *needed* a lorry, because they were about to steal a coffin.

'So what happened next?' he asked aloud.

'Beefy started blustering about how, if I didn't come up with a lorry in the next five minutes, he'd have my stripes. So I told him that none of the lorries I had in the garage would be road-worthy for at least three or four hours – which was quite true. And that made him really hit the roof.'

It would have, Blackstone thought, because Soames knew – as did the other two – that if they lost three or four hours, the coffin might well be on a ship bound for England by the time they reached Calais.

'While Beefy was throwing a fit, Sly was looking around him,' Winfield continued, 'and that's when he noticed the ambulance. "Is that roadworthy?" he asked, and when I told him it was, he said, "Fine, we'll take that." Skinny didn't like the idea at all. He said they couldn't take the ambulance, because it might be needed for injured men. But Sly just smiled, in a nasty way, and said that given what they wanted to use it for, an ambulance would be perfect.'

And so it had been, Blackstone mused – because who would have thought twice about seeing them load the coffin into an ambulance?

'So you let them take the ambulance?' he said.

'I did,' Winfield admitted. 'And, thank God, it wasn't needed for anything else while they were using it.'

'Would you be prepared to sign a statement outlining what you've just told me?' Blackstone asked.

Winfield's bonhomie melted away immediately.

'No, I'm not sure I would,' he confessed. 'It's one thing to chew the fat with a like-minded soul over a couple of brandies, but it's quite another to put what we've been talking about down in writing.'

'You don't seem like the kind of man who'd want to see someone get away with murder,' Blackstone said.

'Is one of *them* a murderer?'

'Yes.'

Winfield nodded. 'It'll be Beefy,' he said.

'Why do you say that?' Blackstone wondered.

'Because Skinny's too frightened to kill anybody, and while Sly might *want* somebody dead, he's too smart to do it himself.'

'*Are* you the kind of man who'd want to see a murderer get away with it?' Blackstone asked.

Winfield shrugged again. 'If you'd said that to me a year ago, back in England, I'd have been insulted that you even needed to ask. But life's a lot cheaper out here, isn't it? Every Tommy mowed down by machine-gun fire is being murdered – and not by the bloke firing the gun, but by the General who sent him out to certain death. And that General's never going to pay for his crime, now is he?'

'No,' Blackstone agreed. 'He isn't.'

'Besides, if Beefy killed somebody, Beefy will get away with it – because he's an officer.'

'It was an officer he killed,' Blackstone said.

'You think he was the one that topped that Lieutenant Fortesque?' Winfield gasped.

'Yes, I do.'

'Well, you could knock me over with a feather,' Winfield said. 'I'd never have thought he'd have murdered one of his own kind.' He fell silent for a whole minute. 'But, when you think about it, it doesn't really make any difference if it *was* a brother officer he killed, does it? He could have wiped out half a dozen of them, and his regiment still wouldn't admit he was guilty – because that would mean admitting that he wasn't exactly the paragon of virtue that all officers are supposed to be.'

'It's more than likely that you're right,' Blackstone conceded reluctantly, 'but there's just a chance it will turn out differently this time – and isn't that worth taking a gamble on?'

'Maybe for you,' Winfield told him. 'But I've got my girl waiting for me back home – and even if I can't walk down the aisle a hero, I do at least want to walk down the aisle.'

'Once you've made your statement to me, you'll be safe,' Blackstone promised him.

'If I make a statement to you, you'll use it as part of your case against Beefy,' Winfield said. 'And when your case falls apart – and it will – you'll go home, and I'll still be here.'

'You'll be safe,' Blackstone repeated. 'Whatever happens to my case, you'll be safe.'

'Oh, they won't kill me, if that's what you're talking about,' Winfield agreed. 'But they'll find some way to punish me – they'll have to, if only as an example to the rest of the poor bloody infantry of what happens when you cross the officer class. So they'll trump up some charge against me, and I'll spend the next ten years of my life in the glasshouse.'

'It doesn't have to happen that way,' Blackstone said stubbornly.

'That's just how it *will* happen,' Winfield insisted. He looked Blackstone squarely in the eyes. 'Here's what I'll remember of this little meeting of ours if I'm asked: I'll say you wanted to know if I remembered three officers asking me for a vehicle of some sort, and that I told you that it was strictly against regulations for any officer to take a vehicle without official permission.'

'Even though everybody knows it happens?'

'Even though everybody knows it happens! And I'll add – if I'm pushed – that I considered it an insult to all the officers serving on the Western Front that you'd even ask the question, because they're fine upstanding men who would never even think of doing such a thing.' Winfield shook his head, sadly, from side to side. 'Sorry, Mr Blackstone, but that's the way things are.'

NINETEEN

There were only two sorts of people he kept coming up against in this investigation, Blackstone thought dispiritedly, as he walked back to the village.

On the one hand, there were those who believed that it was impossible for an officer to have been a killer – and that included not just the officers themselves, but also those outside the officer class, like Corporal Johnson, who had fully accepted the ruling class myth.

And on the other hand, there were people like Sergeant Winfield, who could be persuaded to accept that such a thing might just be possible, but had embraced another, equally damaging, myth – that officers were above the laws which applied to ordinary folk like him.

'But officers are as likely to commit a murder as anybody else, and they'll swing from a rope as well as the next man,' Blackstone said aloud – and with fresh resolve. 'I *know* that for a fact – and I'll prove it, if it's the last thing I do.'

As he approached his billet, he was not in the least surprised to see the young soldier waiting impatiently outside his door. It would, in fact, have been a surprise if – fired up with enthusiasm for the investigation as he was – he *hadn't* been there.

'You've been gone a long time,' Mick complained, as the policeman approached him.

Blackstone grinned. 'Well, you know what it's like once you're at the seaside – you find it difficult to tear yourself away.'

'I wouldn't know about that. I've never been to the seaside myself,' Mick replied, perhaps a little sadly.

Of course he hadn't. The chances were that, before he'd come to France, he'd never wandered more than three or four miles away from the house in which he was born.

Blackstone glanced quickly up and down the street. There was no one else in sight – no witnesses to report what the Scotland Yard man and the private soldier did next.

'You'd better come inside,' he said.

Once they were through the door, he was expecting Mick to immediately start babbling out the gossip he had picked up from the other members of his platoon, but instead, when the boy did start talking, it was about himself.

'My old mum used to do a bit of cleaning for this lady called Mrs Robertson, who lived in this big house north of the river,' Mick said. 'Once, when I was a nipper, and the whole Robertson family was out for the day, she took me to see the house. I couldn't believe it when I walked through the front door. It was like stepping into a palace. I'd never dreamed that anybody could be so rich.'

The young man's obvious naivety brought an involuntary smile to Blackstone's face.

Despite what Mick might believe, this Mrs Robertson hadn't really been rich at all, he thought. If she'd been rich, she wouldn't have employed Mick's mum to pop in now and again and char for her, she'd have had a permanent staff – butler, maids, footmen – waiting on her hand and foot. And her house couldn't really have been a palace, either – it had only *seemed* like one to a lad brought up in the slums.

'Have I said something funny?' the boy demanded, with a suspicion which was bordering on anger. 'Are you laughing at me, Mr Blackstone?'

'No,' Blackstone said hastily, feeling thoroughly ashamed. 'I was just remembering something amusing that happened yesterday.'

'Are you sure about that?' Mick asked.

'I'm sure,' Blackstone lied. 'Carry on with what you were saying.'

'Well, this Mrs Robertson used to give my mum all the stuff she didn't want any more – clothes and things. She told mum she could cut the clothes up, and use them for floor rags, but mum would never have done that.'

'Of course she wouldn't,' Blackstone agreed. 'So what *did* she do with them – wear them herself, or sell them to a stall on the New Cut Market?'

'Sometimes one, sometimes the other,' Mick said. 'Anyway, this once, it wasn't clothes she gave her – it was a jigsaw puzzle. Do you know what a jigsaw puzzle is, Mr Blackstone?'

'Yes,' Blackstone said. 'I do.'

'This particular jigsaw was a big heavy wooden thing. It had a picture of a windmill on it. And I suppose you know what one them is, and all.'

Blackstone smiled again – and this time he was smiling *with* Mick.

'Big pointy thing with sails on it?' he suggested.

Mick smiled back. It was a good-natured smile, and his earlier animosity was obviously quite forgotten.

'You know just about everything, don't you, Mr Blackstone?' he said. 'There's no wonder you're a detective.'

I wish I *did* know everything, Blackstone thought. I wish I knew why three apparently normal young men had decided to cold-bloodedly murder another young man who they had been friends with for most of their lives.

'The picture was peeling off that jigsaw a bit,' Mick continued. 'To tell you the truth, there was some pieces that had no picture left on them at all. But I thought it was a bloody marvellous thing. I used to spend hours working at it. My pals all called me a proper Mary Ellen for wasting my time, but I didn't care. I loved that puzzle.' A tear ran down the corner of his eye. 'It was the first real toy I ever had.'

Blackstone nodded. 'I know what it's like to be without toys,' he said, thinking back to his days in the orphanage.

Mick took a deep breath and squared his shoulders. 'But that's neither here nor there,' he said, matter-of-factly. 'The only reason that I mentioned it at all was because, when you first gave me this job, I had no idea what it was you wanted me to do, did I?'

'Well, you couldn't have been expected to grasp the whole thing right away,' Blackstone said tactfully.

'Not an idea in the world,' Mick said firmly. 'Not a bleeding clue. And then I began to think about it like it was that jigsaw puzzle, and suddenly it all started to make sense. See, you collect a little piece of information here, and a little piece of information there, and then you try to fit them together to make a picture.' He looked at Blackstone uncertainly, as if he was suddenly afraid he'd made a fool of himself. 'It is a *bit* like that, isn't it?' he pleaded.

Blackstone beamed at him. 'It's a *lot* like that,' he said. 'You'd make a fine detective.'

'Really?' Mick asked.

'Really,' Blackstone confirmed. 'Now let's hear about the bits of puzzle you've found.'

'Well, the first thing that any of the lads remembers as being unusual . . .' He paused. 'You did *ask* me to find out what was unusual, didn't you?'

'Yes, I did,' Blackstone assured him.

'The first thing that was unusual was Lieutenant Soames taking a couple of lads out on night patrol,' Mick said. He paused for a second time. 'No, that's not quite right. It wasn't the patrol that was unusual at all – because there are patrols every night.'

He shook his head in frustration. 'I need to get the story straight in my head. I need to be able to tell it properly.'

'Take your time,' Blackstone said soothingly. 'We've got all the time you need.'

'The thing about these patrols is, they're not as dangerous as they might seem,' Mick continued. 'Even if the patrol stumbles across a few Fritzes – doing the same thing as they are – nobody usually gets killed.'

'So what *do* they do when that happens? Ignore each other?'

'That's right. It'd be certain death not to.'

Of course it would, Blackstone thought. One flash from a weapon in No Man's Land, and both sides would open fire from the trenches.

'Anyway, that night, one of Lieutenant Soames' patrol *did* get killed, and another got wounded,' Mick continued. 'Nobody's quite sure how it happened. It was probably just bad luck – some Fritz sentry fancied firing a couple of shots into the dark, and by pure chance he hit our lads.'

'I think I've already heard part of this story,' Blackstone said. 'Lieutenant Soames dragged the wounded man back to our trench, didn't he?'

'That's right, he did,' Mick agreed. 'And that's where we come to the *next* unusual bit of the story. When he got back to his dugout, Lieutenant Maude and Lieutenant Hatfield were there waiting for him.'

'What was strange about that?'

'They weren't on front-line duty that night, so you might have expected them to stay in the reserve trench, and catch up on a bit of sleep. That's what most officers do when they get the chance. Course, there's no law that says an officer can't go to the front line if he feels like it – but there's never any real reason to.'

But there *was* a reason that night, Blackstone thought – the three musketeers needed to get together to put the final touches to the plan to murder Lieutenant Fortesque.

'Anyway, the next funny thing – and that makes three funny things, you know.'

Blackstone smiled again. 'I do know,' he agreed. 'I'm counting.'

'The next funny thing was that Maude left the other two, and went to visit Fortesque in *his* dugout, further along the trench.'

Now that *was* strange, Blackstone told himself.

Since Soames was the one nominated to actually commit the murder, he would obviously have to chance being spotted near the scene of the crime. But there was no need for either of the other two to run such a risk. Quite the contrary – it would have been no more than prudent for them to keep well away from Fortesque in the hours before his impending death.

Yet Maude *had been* to see Fortesque! Now why would a man like him – who otherwise hadn't put a foot wrong so far – even think of doing that?

'What time was it that Lieutenant Maude visited Lieutenant Fortesque?' Blackstone asked Mick.

'Nobody's quite sure. Apart from the ones who are on sentry duty, none of the lads pay much attention to time down in the trenches. But as near as any of them can tell, it was a couple of hours before dawn.'

Perhaps the reason that Maude had visited Fortesque was to make one last attempt to talk some sense into him. Perhaps he'd still hoped that he could convince Fortesque to change his mind, because if he *could be* persuaded, there would no longer be any need to kill him.

'Are you still listening to me, Mr Blackstone?' Mick asked.

'I'm still listening,' Blackstone said. 'Carry on with your tale.'

'Maude stayed with Fortesque for about ten minutes, and when he left, he went back to Soames' dugout. And then, maybe half an hour before dawn, Lieutenant *Soames* paid a visit to Lieutenant Fortesque.'

Maude's efforts at persuasion having so obviously failed, Soames is sent to deliver the killing blow, Blackstone thought. He finds Fortesque alone, as he expected to . . .

He felt a sudden chill run through him, as he began to see a hitherto unsuspected flaw in his own logic.

Soames would have had no real basis for believing that he would find Fortesque alone!

None at all!

At that time of day – just before the morning stand-to and the inspection which followed it – what would have been more natural than that Fortesque would ask his servant to make him a cup of tea and cook him some breakfast?

As it happened – *as things turned out* – Fortesque *had been* alone, because he had sent Blenkinsop to the reserve trench for more whisky – but Soames couldn't possibly have *known* that he would do that.

Hell, even Fortesque himself couldn't have known, with any degree of certainty, when the whisky would run out.

And that was where the theory broke down, wasn't it? The three musketeers *couldn't* have been planning to kill Fortesque that morning – because there were far too many imponderables.

Wind it back, Blackstone ordered himself. Start again.

The plan had been for Fortesque to die sometime later – perhaps when they were all back in St Denis. But then Soames – hot-headed, impulsive Soames – had taken a spur of the moment decision!

Blackstone pictured the scene in his mind.

Fortesque is sitting at his table when Soames enters the dugout.

'Have you thought about what Maude had to say to you, Charlie?' Soames asks.

'I have,' Fortesque replies.

'And what conclusion have you reached?'

'I've examined my conscience, and I now see, more clearly than ever, that while it will be damaging to all of you, I really have no choice but to come clean.'

But come clean about what? Blackstone asked himself.

About bloody *what* – for God's sake?

Had they come across a stash of abandoned gold – or something almost equally valuable – and decided between them to keep it for themselves? Had Fortesque changed his mind about it, leaving the others with no choice – in their own minds, at least – but to kill him? And had those gold bars been in the coffin that Maude, Soames and Hatfield had stolen from the warehouse in Calais?

Or was that all just wild speculation – a fantasy he had dreamed up himself to explain away something which simply couldn't be explained?

Blackstone forced all these speculations to the back of his mind, and focussed, instead, on what might possibly have happened in the dugout.

*   *   *

'I've examined my conscience, and I now see, more clearly than ever, that while it will be damaging to all of you, I really have no choice but to come clean,' Lieutenant Fortesque says.

Soames is not a complicated man. He has been brought up with a simple set of rules and a simple set of prejudices which are perfectly adequate to carry a chap through life, and, as far as he is concerned, a conscience is quite unnecessary. Besides, he has just lost a man – and nearly been killed himself – and his nerves are worn ragged.

'I can't allow you to do it,' he says.

'I'm sorry, but you can't stop me,' Fortesque replies.

But that's just where Fortesque is wrong. There is a way to stop him – just one – and this is the way that the three musketeers have been discussing among themselves for some time. And it is the way Soames takes now – well ahead of the planned schedule – when he picks up the nearest blunt object and smashes it down on his friend's skull.

He probably panics when he realizes what he's done, but then his instinct for self-preservation takes control.

If he walks away now, it will be obvious he killed Fortesque, he argues. But if he leaves it for half an hour, and then 'discovers' the body, he might have just muddied the waters enough to get away with it.

'I'm assuming that Soames then left the section, and came back later for the dawn inspection,' Blackstone said.

'No,' Mick replied. 'He didn't come out of the dugout again until the Morning Hate started.'

Then what was left of the theory was crumbling before his eyes, Blackstone thought.

Because if Soames had killed Fortesque, there would have been absolutely no way to avoid getting blood spattered all over his uniform.

And if he'd had blood all over his uniform, the men he was inspecting would have noticed it!

'What's the matter?' Mick asked.

'I'm thinking,' Blackstone said, more sharply than he'd intended.

And he was – thinking furiously, in a desperate attempt to square the circle.

Perhaps Soames had taken all his clothes off before he'd attacked Fortesque – but if anything could have put Fortesque on his guard, it would have been the sight of his friend stripping naked.

Perhaps Soames had covered himself with a blanket or a sheet before launching the attack – but smashing in a man's skull is a very messy business, and however careful he was, there would have been some blood on his uniform.

There was really only one way Soames *could have* done it without drenching himself in blood, Blackstone realized.

And in accepting that, he was forced to accept that all the assumptions he had made so far were completely – grotesquely – wrong.

TWENTY

I f there was one point in the day that the Tommy could usually call his own, then it was the time between late afternoon and early evening.

All his routine tasks had been completed. He had cleaned his rifle and his bayonet. He had refilled the sandbags that had to be refilled. He had shored up the crumbling sections of the trench which needed shoring up, and had repaired the duckboards which needed repairing. Thus, until dusk began to fall and he was called to evening stand-to, he was at perfect liberty to do whatever he wished – as long as what he wished to do was no more than write a few letters home, catch up on sleep, or play cards.

Yet even this small luxury was being interrupted in that particular section of the trench on that particular afternoon, because Captain Carstairs would be visiting the section, and though he seemed completely oblivious to their presence, they had been ordered by their sergeant to stand at attention until he had passed by.

Carstairs was not alone. As well as the sergeant, he was accompanied by a tall thin civilian in a shabby brown suit.

And just why *am* I here? Blackstone wondered, as they progressed along the trench.

The most straightforward answer to the question was that he was there because he had been told – or rather, *ordered* – to be there.

But why would Captain Carstairs – who plainly couldn't stand the sight of him – want to see him at all, unless it was to give him a rocket for some minor infringement of military etiquette?

And if he was to be given a rocket, why should it be delivered in the trench, rather than in the company's command dugout?

'I've been trying to contact you for at least the last forty-eight hours, Blackstone,' Carstairs said as they walked. 'I would like to know where the hell you have been all that time.'

'I've been pursuing my inquiries,' Blackstone replied.

Captain Carstairs snorted. 'That may be enough of an answer for some of the people you normally rub shoulders with, but I am a captain in His Majesty's Armed Forces, and I consider it highly unsatisfactory,' he said.

If he told Carstairs the truth – if he admitted he'd been tracking the movements of the three musketeers in Calais – then the captain would do everything within his power to sabotage the investigation, Blackstone thought.

'I've been investigating the possibility that, from the very start, you may have been right – and I may have been wrong,' he said aloud.

'What are you talking about?' Carstairs demanded.

'You think it was one of the enlisted men who killed Lieutenant Fortesque, and, as a result of my investigations, I'm inclined to agree with you,' Blackstone lied. 'Now, if you'd like more details of those investigations . . .'

'No, no, I'm perfectly happy to leave it in your hands,' Carstairs replied, sounding both pleased and relieved. 'But the moment you have tracked down the guilty party, I shall, of course, expect to be informed.'

'Naturally,' Blackstone agreed.

They came to a halt at the mouth of a tunnel which was being dug in the side of the trench. One stocky Welshman, inside the tunnel, was passing a basket of earth to another stocky Welshman who was outside of it. They seemed unaware that Carstairs was there – or indeed, of anything beyond the task in hand.

The sergeant coughed, and the two miners looked up briefly, and then returned to their work.

'You are in the presence of an officer, Sapper Thomas,' the sergeant barked. 'Show the proper respect!'

'Oh, sorry, sir,' the Welshman inside the tunnel said to Carstairs, before giving what was probably as smart a salute as the confined space allowed. 'We thought you was in a hurry to get the tunnel finished, see, and every time we stops to salute you, that's another shovel-full of earth we hasn't shifted.'

'Do not address an officer directly,' the sergeant screamed.

'Oh, sorry again, Sergeant,' the Welshman said. 'We thought the captain was in a hurry to get the tunnel finished, see, and—'

'You've already said that,' the sergeant told him.

'Yes, but look you, the first time I said it, it was to the officer, then you told me I'm not allowed to—'

'Silence!' the sergeant shouted.

'Ask him how the work is progressing,' Carstairs said to the sergeant.

'How is the work progressing?' the sergeant asked Thomas.

'We's gone maybe ten yards,' the Welshman replied.

Carstairs frowned. 'That doesn't seem very far.'

'You's never dug a tunnel yourself, has you, sir?' Thomas asked.

'Do not address an officer directly,' the sergeant roared.

'I thought he was addressing me, like,' Thomas said, completely unperturbed. 'Anyway, I was only asking him if he have ever dug a tunnel himself, and it's obvious that he haven't.'

'Ask him how long it will take him to complete the tunnel,' Carstairs said to the sergeant.

'Save your breath, Sarge, 'cos I've already heard,' Thomas said. He raised his hand, and scratched his head with a dirt-encrusted finger. 'To be honest with you, it's hard to say exactly. There's all sorts of things what have to be taken into account with a tunnel, look you. But don't you go worrying yourself, sir, we's'll get there in the end.'

'Do not—' the sergeant began.

'Forget it, Sergeant,' Carstairs told him, with evident weariness in his voice. 'Blackstone and I are leaving now, but I want you to stay here and watch these men work, just to make certain there's no shirking.'

'We doesn't—' Thomas said.

'Silence!' the sergeant commanded.

Carstairs turned, signalled Blackstone to follow him, and walked a little way down the trench.

'They're barbarians, these Welshmen,' the captain complained. 'They have no idea of proper military discipline, and if they weren't the best tunnellers we've got – by far – I wouldn't tolerate having them anywhere near my men.'

An awkward silence followed, in which it was plain that Carstairs was expecting Blackstone to say something, and Blackstone himself had determined to say nothing at all until he had a clearer idea of what lay behind this little expedition down into the trenches.

Finally, after perhaps a minute, Carstairs said, 'Well?'

'Well, what?' Blackstone replied.

'What do you think?' Carstairs asked, pointing back towards the tunnel.

'I think it's a tunnel,' Blackstone said.

'Yes, it's a tunnel!' Carstairs said exasperatedly. 'And . . . ?'

'And as far as I can tell, it's pretty much like every other tunnel I've seen,' Blackstone said. 'It's got two walls, a floor and a ceiling – and I really can't think of much more to say about it.'

'You do *know* why I've brought you to see it, don't you?'

'As a matter of fact, I don't.'

Carstairs sighed at the detective's obvious stupidity.

'I wanted you to see it,' he said, speaking slowly, to make sure Blackstone got the point, 'so that when you report back to General Fortesque, as I've no doubt you will, you can tell him that we on the front line have done everything possible to comply with his wishes.'

'I have no idea what you're talking about,' Blackstone admitted.

'The General hasn't told you of his request?'

'No.'

Carstairs smirked. 'Then perhaps you are not quite as much in his confidence as you would like to think you are.'

'Maybe I'm not,' Blackstone agreed.

'Would you like to hear now what that request was?'

Yes, he did want to know, Blackstone thought, because whatever the General's request had been, it was probably relevant to the investigation. But after Captain Carstairs had been so bloody supercilious, he was damned if he was going to ask him.

'I'm not particularly interested,' he said, 'but since you seem so desperate for the General to be told what a good boy you've been, I should imagine you want to give me all the details.'

'Don't push me too far, Blackstone,' Carstairs growled.

'I'll tell you what, why don't we just forget the whole thing?' Blackstone suggested.

'I have the greatest possible respect for General Fortesque, and, because of that, I would like him to think well of me,' Carstairs said, through clenched teeth. 'And that is the reason – and the *only* reason – that I am prepared to tolerate your insolence on this occasion.'

Blackstone grinned. 'In other words, I'm a bit like the Welsh miners – you might not *like* me, but you *need* me.'

Carstairs cleared his throat. 'General Fortesque has asked us to recover the body of a Private Danvers, who was killed – and subsequently buried – in No Man's Land, a few days ago,' he began, as if the last few unpleasant exchanges had never occurred. 'Since it was already planned to build a new sap listening post, which would, of course, be connected to this trench by a tunnel, I decided that the best idea would be to combine the two operations. The tunnel will first be used to recover the body – undoubtedly the *safest* way to do it – and then will be converted into part of our defences.'

Blackstone had stopped listening after the first sentence.

Danvers!

Where had he heard that name before?

Of course!

Danvers was the man who Lieutenant Fortesque had been planning to make his servant, before he changed his mind and appointed Blenkinsop.

Danvers was the soldier who had not just been *killed* in No Man's Land, but had been killed on a patrol led by *Lieutenant Soames* – and only hours before Lieutenant Fortesque was murdered.

'But why should the General *want* the body recovered?' he asked Captain Carstairs.

'It is an old man's privilege to be slightly eccentric,' Carstairs said, 'and when that old man happens to be as distinguished as General Fortesque, it is our duty to respect those eccentricities.

The regiment would not have the reputation it undoubtedly has today without men like the Hero of Afghanistan.'

Sod the regiment! Blackstone thought.

'What I want to know is how the General even found out that Danvers was dead,' he persisted. 'After all, he was nothing but a common soldier – one of scores of thousands who've been killed since this bloody war started.'

'Oh, that,' Carstairs said, offhandedly. 'It seems that Private Danvers was the General's head gardener's grandson, and that, before the war, he had been training to be a gardener himself.'

'So Lieutenant Fortesque already knew Private Danvers, *before* they served together?' Blackstone said.

'Knew him?' Carstairs repeated incredulously. 'A gentleman does not *know* members of the labouring classes. But I expect he will have ridden past while the boy was working in the gardens, so it's perfectly possible that he knew *of* him.'

Oh no, it was more than that, Blackstone told himself – *much* more than that.

It was suddenly all clicking into place for him, and now he could not only see that he had been entirely wrong about almost everything, but *why* he had been wrong about it.

It was not Fortesque's threat to expose their racket that the three musketeers had thought would ruin them – because there had *been* no racket.

And it was not some kind of contraband – perhaps gold – that they had been trying to get their hands on when they stole the coffin from the warehouse in Calais, because the box had contained exactly what it was supposed to contain – the corpse of Lieutenant Fortesque.

He had speculated about why there was no blood on Soames' uniform when he had emerged from Fortesque's dugout to carry out the inspection – and reached a conclusion which he was now almost certain had been correct.

All he needed, he told himself, was a single confirmation with which to frame all the pieces, and then he would have the whole investigation wrapped up.

'There was another soldier with Fortesque and Danvers on the night that Danvers was killed, wasn't there?' he asked Captain Carstairs.

'Yes, there was. As I believe I told you, Lieutenant Soames risked his own life to drag the man back to our trench.'

'And what happened to him?'

'Happened to him?'

'Once he was back in the trenches.'

'I expect that if the bullet was still in his body, it was removed in the dressing station, and that after that extraction, the wound was dressed.'

Blackstone was managing to resist the urge to grab Carstairs by the shoulders and shake him until his teeth rattled – but only just.

'What happened after the wound was dressed?' he asked. 'Was the man invalided out – or is he still here?'

'Good God, you can't expect me to be aware of mundane little details like that. I have a whole company under my command.'

And maybe if you did *know* those mundane details, you might command it better than you do now, Blackstone thought. Maybe if you'd paid a little more attention to what was going on around you, both Private Danvers and Lieutenant Fortesque would still be alive.

'Who will know what happened to the man who was wounded?' he asked.

'Ask Lieutenant Soames' sergeant,' Carstairs said. 'He's *bound* to know.'

TWENTY-ONE

The cavernous dugout was located in the reserve trench. It was an outpost – or perhaps a sub-branch – of the quartermaster's store, and it was where Blenkinsop, the hapless servant, had been waiting for the bottles of whisky to be delivered on the morning that Lieutenant Fortesque had died.

Blackstone had no idea who had been in charge of the store on that fateful morning, but the man who was running it now was a young private with his right arm in a sling, who went by the name of Mitchell.

'I thought this might have bought me my papers back to

Blighty,' Mitchell told him, pointing with his left hand at the sling. 'But when the Doc examined me, he said it wasn't serious enough for that, and I suppose he was right.'

Had the decision that Private Mitchell should stay in France really been a medical one?

Blackstone didn't think so.

What was much more likely was that he was still there because the three musketeers *wanted* him there – where they could keep an eye on him – and that they had put some kind of pressure on the doctor to pronounce the man fit to continue his military service.

'You must have been quite disappointed when you were first told you wouldn't be going home,' Blackstone said.

'I was,' Mitchell admitted. 'But I've no complaints now, because this job is a really cushy number, just like I was pro—'

His mouth slammed shut, trapping the dangerous words which had been just about to escape from it.

'What were you about to say?' Blackstone asked.

Mitchell looked down at the counter.

'Nothing,' he mumbled.

'That's not true,' Blackstone countered. 'You were going to say you'd been given a cushy job *just like you were promised.* Isn't that right?'

A look of indecision crossed Mitchell's face as he debated whether to simply deny the obvious truth, or to tell an outright lie.

'That's right,' he said finally, plumping for the lie. 'That is what I was going to say. It was the doctor who promised it me, you see. He said he'd make sure I wasn't given any heavy work.'

'How did you feel about going out on patrol, that night you got shot?' Blackstone asked, changing tack.

'What do you mean?' Mitchell asked, suspiciously.

'When your sergeant came up to you, and told you that Lieutenant Soames had selected you to go out on patrol with him, what were your feelings?'

'I didn't really have any feelings, one way or the other,' Mitchell said, avoiding what he probably thought was one trap, and stepping right into the middle of another one.

'So it *was* Lieutenant Soames – rather than the sergeant – who chose you,' Blackstone said.

'I suppose so.'

'When an officer makes the selection, he usually picks a man he thinks he can rely on, doesn't he?'

'I wouldn't know. The sergeant doesn't tell you *why* you've got to do something – he just tells you to bloody well do it.'

'But it makes sense that the officer would think that way, doesn't it?' Blackstone insisted. 'No Man's Land's a dangerous place, and any officer worth his salt would want good men – men he could trust – covering his back.'

'Maybe,' Mitchell said, non-committally.

'So if you're a good man – and we've already both agreed that you are – Danvers, who was the third person on that patrol, must have been a good man, too, mustn't he?'

'Yes,' Mitchell replied – far too quickly.

'Listen,' Blackstone said, 'I'm not trying to blame you or the lieutenant for Danvers' death – we all know that it was just a bit of bad luck that he was killed, and that it could have happened to anybody – but I really would like to know just what kind of soldier he was.'

Mitchell hesitated for quite a while, then said, 'Well, to be honest with you, I was a bit surprised when the lieutenant chose him for the patrol.'

'And why was that?'

'I don't really know.'

'Yes, you do.'

'Danvers hadn't been in our platoon long. He was transferred from Lieutenant Fortesque's platoon.'

'I know.'

'And from the moment he arrived, Lieutenant Soames seemed to take a dislike to him. He was always picking on the poor lad, and telling him how completely bloody useless he was.'

'You said *he* told Danvers how bloody useless he was.'

'That's right.'

'He told him *personally* – it didn't come from the sergeant?'

'No.'

'And did Lieutenant Soames speak to any of the other Tommies in the trench directly?'

'I don't think so.'

'*Did* he – or *didn't* he?'

'He didn't.'

Now wasn't that interesting, Blackstone thought.

'*Was* Danvers completely bloody useless?' he asked.

'If I had to have somebody covering my back, Danvers wouldn't have been my first choice,' Mitchell admitted. 'He was a bit too soft for my liking.'

'Soft?'

'Say you've got Fritz charging at you with a fixed bayonet, your first thought would be to stop him – to stab him in the guts – wouldn't it?'

'It would,' Blackstone agreed. 'And are you saying that that wouldn't have been Danvers' first thought?'

'I know this might sound loony, but I don't think it would have been,' Mitchell said. 'Danvers would have been more likely to look the bloke in the face, and start wondering if he had a wife and kids back home. Course, he'd *eventually* start worrying about himself . . .'

'But by then it would be too late.'

'By then he'd be bloody well dead!' Mitchell paused for a second. 'Still, he wasn't a bad soldier, in his own way, and he certainly didn't deserve the sort of treatment Lieutenant Soames meted out to him,' he concluded.

'Tell me what happened out in No Man's Land,' Blackstone suggested.

Mitchell looked suddenly wary again.

'Danvers got shot, and I got shot, and Lieutenant Soames dragged me back to the trench,' he said.

'What position were you in when you got shot?'

'I don't know what you mean,' Mitchell said – though it was perfectly plain that he did.

'Were you on your knees?' Blackstone asked. 'Were you bent over in a crouch?'

'We were flat-out on our bellies. That's how you always cross No Man's Land.'

Blackstone took a step back, and examined Mitchell.

'The wound's at the bottom of your left shoulder, isn't it?' he asked.

'That's right,' Mitchell agreed, uneasily.

'I don't see how you could have got shot there if you'd been lying on the ground.'

Mitchell gave a half-shrug, which was all that his injured shoulder would allow him.

'Funny things happen in war,' he said. 'You know that yourself.'

'I'm investigating a murder,' Blackstone said, with a new harshness entering his voice. 'If anybody gets in the way of that, I'll see to it that they're punished with the full rigour of the law – and since it's *military* law out here, that will probably mean the firing squad.'

'But I don't see what Lieutenant Fortesque's murder could have to do with what happened out there in No Man's Land,' Mitchell said, in a voice so weak that it was almost a whimper.

'Who said we were talking about *Lieutenant Fortesque's* murder?' Blackstone asked. 'Tell me exactly what happened – while you've still got the chance.'

There is only one way to cross No Man's Land, and that is on your belly. It's easy at first – so easy that you feel you could keep going forever. But after a while, each extra few yards become an effort. And then it is every single *yard you are struggling to cover, until you reach the point at which you feel that even one additional foot would be too much.*

'But you have to go on,' Mitchell tells himself.

Because that's what you've been ordered to do by your officer, and because you don't want to admit – even to yourself – that you might not be as tough as the next man.

This night, the three of them – Lieutenant Soames, Private Danvers and himself – have only gone a hundred yards or so when Soames says, 'I'm heartily sick of this!'

Mitchell feels a surge of relief.

Soames has had enough, he tells himself. He's going to call it a night, and turn back.

But he soon learns that that is not what the lieutenant means at all.

'Why should we crawl around like animals?' Soames asks. 'We're men. We should walk on two legs, as God intended.'

Mitchell feels his stomach turn to water. 'We'll be bigger targets if we stand up, sir,' he says.

'Bigger targets?' Soames repeats. 'It's the middle of the night, and it's pitch black out there. We could be dancing around a bloody maypole, and they still wouldn't see us.'

'But, sir . . .' Mitchell protests.

And then he is aware that the dark shape to his left – which is Lieutenant Soames – is suddenly upright.

'Stand up, Private Mitchell,' Soames says. 'You, too, Danvers. And that's an order.'

If he stands up, there is a chance a random shot in the dark will pick him off, Mitchell thinks, but if he disobeys a direct order, there is a certainty that he will be facing a firing squad by the end of the week.

He stands up, and, from the noises he hears next to him, knows that Danvers is doing the same.

That's when the flare goes off – a terrible crimson light, arcing through the sky.

The next moment, Mitchell feels a thud to his shoulder – as if he has been hit by the largest, heaviest sledgehammer that had ever been made. And then he is down on the ground.

'Where was the flare fired from?' Blackstone asked.

'It's hard to say,' Mitchell admits – and he is being honest, rather than evasive. 'I didn't know anything about it until it was overhead.'

'But once it's reached its zenith, it starts to fall to earth again, doesn't it?' Blackstone asked.

'Its zenith?' Mitchell repeated.

'Once it has gone as high as it's going,' Blackstone explained. 'When it's reached that point, it comes down again, doesn't it?'

'Yes.'

'So which way was it falling? Was it going to land close to the enemy's trenches, or was it going to land close to ours.'

'I wasn't really thinking about that,' Mitchell said. 'I was much more interested in the fact that I'd been shot in the bloody shoulder.'

'If you had to choose one or the other, which one would it be?' Blackstone persisted. 'Come on, man – think!'

'It was falling towards the Fritzes' trenches,' Mitchell said reluctantly.

It would have to have been, Blackstone thought. Given the timing, it would have been too much of a coincidence for it not to have been.

'Tell me what happened next,' he said.

*   *   *

It feels as if a giant has taken hold of his arm, and is attempting to wrench it out of its socket, but at least there is some consolation to be drawn from the pain, because as long as he is hurting – and God, he is hurting – he is not dead.

Madness has broken out over No Man's Land, with the troops in both lines firing wildly into the darkness. And soon, when the two sides are organized enough, there will be machine-gun fire raking the ground – because while no one knows exactly what is out here, everyone knows it needs killing.

Through the pain, Mitchell becomes aware that someone is talking to him.

'Are you hit, Mitchell?'

The speaker is Lieutenant Soames, now no longer standing like a man, but flat out on the ground next to him.

'I asked you if you'd been hit,' Soames repeats.

'Shoulder,' Mitchell grunts.

'Can you make it back to the trench unaided?'

'Don't think so, sir.'

A pause.

'I'm going to have to drag you,' Soames says. 'It'll hurt like hell, but it's better than leaving you out here.'

'It *did* hurt like hell,' Mitchell told Blackstone. 'It took three times as long to get back to the trenches as it had taken to get into No Man's Land, and every inch was pure bloody agony.'

Blackstone nodded curtly. It was a nod which said that he might eventually show Mitchell some sympathy – but he was not going to show it yet.

'Who was it who had a quiet word with you when you were back in the trench?' he asked.

'I don't know what—' Mitchell began.

'Was it Lieutenant Maude?' Blackstone demanded.

'Yes, it was Maude,' Mitchell admitted.

'You look like you could use some fresh air,' Maude says to the two orderlies in the dressing station.

The orderlies look at each other, and then at the officer.

'We're supposed to be watching the patient, in case there are any complications, sir,' one of them says.

'Did you hear me?' Maude barks. 'I said you could use some fresh air. And you could use it right it now!'

Reluctantly, the orderlies step out into the trench, and the moment they have gone, Maude sits down opposite Mitchell.

A smile comes to the lieutenant's face, though it is totally devoid of either warmth or sympathy.

'You've had a bit of a rough time,' he says.

'Yes, sir,' Mitchell agrees.

'Would you like a cigarette? I'll light it for you, if you can't manage yourself.'

'Thank you, sir.'

Maude lights the cigarette, and hands it to Mitchell.

'You do realize that Lieutenant Soames saved your life out there, don't you?' Maude asks.

So he did, Mitchell agrees silently, but if he hadn't made me stand up, he wouldn't have bloody needed to!

'I can read what you're thinking,' Maude says.

'Can you, sir?'

'Yes, and you're quite right. If we were being totally honest with each other, we'd both have to admit that what Lieutenant Soames did out there was a big mistake, wouldn't we?'

'It's not my place to say, sir,' Mitchell replies cautiously.

'A big mistake,' Maude repeats. 'But you will also admit, won't you, that despite that mistake, he remains a courageous and gallant officer?'

There is only one permissible answer, and Mitchell gives it.

'Yes, sir.'

'Private Danvers is dead, and there's nothing we can do to bring him back to life, however much we might wish to,' Maude continues, 'so it's the living we have to consider now. You wouldn't want to see the career of a fine officer ruined by one momentary misjudgement, would you?'

'No, sir.'

Maude nodded, sagely. 'And neither would I,' he says. 'So if anyone asks you what happened out in No Man's Land – and it doesn't matter whether that person is an officer or whether he is just an enlisted man – it might be wise not to mention the fact you were standing up when you were shot. Do you understand what I'm saying? What I've just done is give you my permission to lie to an officer. You do understand that, don't you?'

'*Yes, sir.*'

'*Good,*' Maude says. '*And in return for your cooperation, I will see to it personally that, for the remainder of the war, you are given a cushy billet, and never have to go out on the front line again.*'

'*Thank you, sir.*'

Maude walks to the door, then turns around again.

'*You will remember what I said about telling no one what really happened, won't you?*'

'*Yes, sir.*'

'*That applies* particularly *to Lieutenant Fortesque. If he questions you – and he is almost bound to – you are to be* especially *careful with your answer. Understood?*'

'*Understood, sir.*'

'He had a point though, that Lieutenant Maude, didn't he?' Mitchell asked Blackstone, defensively. 'Everybody's entitled to one little mistake, and it would have been a shame if it ruined Lieutenant Soames' career.'

'Besides, you were frightened about what might happen if you didn't cooperate, weren't you?' Blackstone asked.

'It's never a good idea to cross an officer,' Mitchell admitted, 'specially a cold bastard like Lieutenant Maude.'

'And the idea of a cushy number really appealed to you, because you saw it as your chance to get through this whole bloody war in one piece.'

'There's that as well,' Mitchell agreed.

'So you agreed to lie.'

'What would you have done in my place?' Mitchell demanded.

'I'd like to think that I would have refused,' Blackstone said. 'But I can't be absolutely certain that I wouldn't have acted in exactly the same way as you did.'

The reserve trench zigzagged, in much the same way as the front-line trench did, and it was not until Blackstone had turned the first corner beyond the quartermaster's outpost that he saw Lieutenant Maude.

The young lieutenant was standing in the very centre of the trench, waiting for him. He had no weapon in his hand at that moment, but he was far enough away to have easily drawn his pistol by the time Blackstone reached him.

'I was rather hoping it wouldn't come to this,' Maude said.

They'd been watching Mitchell, Blackstone thought.

He should have considered that possibility.

He should have taken more care.

'When you're already in a hole, the best thing to do is to stop digging,' he advised Maude.

The lieutenant laughed. '*Au contraire*,' he said, 'the best thing to do is *keep on* digging, so you'll have plenty of space to bury your mistakes.'

'It's over,' Blackstone said.

'Indeed it is,' Maude agreed, looking beyond the other man's shoulder.

And as Blackstone realized that what he should have been wondering was where Soames was, Soames himself swung a sock full of sand and hit the inspector squarely on the back of the head.

TWENTY-TWO

H is return to consciousness was slow, erratic and uncertain – like a fire which is catching hold, but may still yet die back.

At first, all he could focus on was the angry buzz which was coming from somewhere in the back of his brain.

Next, he became aware of himself as a physical presence – a presence which, moreover, was sitting down, and did not seem to be able to move either its arms or its legs.

A minute passed, and the angry buzz transformed itself into what he recognized was a stream of words, though each word followed on so rapidly from the one which preceded it that they still meant nothing to him.

Another minute ticked by, and the words – spoken from the bottom of a deep metal jug – began to make sense.

'*What are we going to do with him?*'

'*What we* have *to do!*'

And what they have to do is kill me, he thought. Now they've gone this far, they have no choice.

He kept his eyes closed, knowing that the moment they realized he was back with them, they would rob him of what little freedom he still had.

'*We* can't *kill him. Not like this – not in cold blood!'*

Hatfield!

'*Of course we can. He's nothing – a piece of working-class scum, who thinks that just because he's employed by Scotland Yard, he has the right to ride roughshod over his betters – and if it comes to it, I'll crush him in much the same way I might crush a cockroach.'*

Soames!

'*When you talk about the honour of the regiment, Benjamin, it's just words, isn't it? I suppose we shouldn't expect any more of you. I, on the other hand, am prepared to do whatever it takes to avoid tarnishing its proud reputation.'*

Maude!

They were all there – the three musketeers.

But exactly where *was* there?

Even though his head had cleared, the three men's words still had a slightly hollow sound, which would suggest that they were in a small, enclosed space.

A dugout – probably in a trench which had long since been abandoned, and thus was the perfect place to commit a murder!

His hopes of survival were slim, Blackstone told himself, but if he could find a way to turn the musketeers against each other, there was still a small chance that he might come out of all this alive.

He opened his eyes. Just as he had suspected, he was in a dugout, and was tied to a chair.

And there they all were, revealed in the flickering light of an oil lamp – Maude sitting across the table from him; Soames standing behind Maude; and Hatfield uncertainly hovering near the entrance to the dugout, as if he would rather not be there at all.

'Welcome back, Inspector Blackstone,' Maude said sardonically. 'It was rather inconsiderate of you to keep us waiting for quite so long.'

'If you didn't want me to keep you waiting, then you shouldn't have hit me quite so bloody hard, should you?' Blackstone replied.

Maude laughed. 'That was Lieutenant Soames' doing, I'm

afraid. He's a fine chap, our Roger – but he can be a little heavy-handed sometimes.' He paused. 'Would you like a drink of water?'

'If it's no trouble,' Blackstone said.

'It's absolutely no trouble at all,' Maude said graciously. 'Give him a drink, Hatfield.'

Hatfield crossed the dugout, picked up the jug which was easily within Maude's reach, poured some water into a tin cup, and held the cup up to Blackstone's lips.

'Is that better?' Maude asked.

'Yes.'

Maude nodded. 'Good – because, before we've finished, you have a lot of talking to do.'

'Is that right?'

'Indeed it is. Before we've finished, you're going to tell us exactly what it is that you know.'

'I know a great deal,' Blackstone told Maude.

'A great deal, you say. Would you care to give me an example of that knowledge?'

'I know, for one thing, that I've been on the wrong track for most of this investigation, and that the three of you *didn't* kill Lieutenant Fortesque.'

'Are you . . . are you prepared to swear to that?' Hatfield gasped.

'Yes,' Blackstone said.

'Oh, for God's sake, does it matter whether he's willing to swear to it or not?' Soames asked exasperatedly. 'He's not a gentleman – his word is not worth the breath it takes to give it.'

'He doesn't have to be a gentleman if he's willing to swear to it with his hand on the Bible,' Hatfield said desperately. 'And if he really doesn't believe we killed Charlie, we can let him go.'

'And give him the opportunity to file charges against us for assault?' Soames asked. 'Have a worthless creature like him appearing as a witness against us at our court martial? I'd rather die.'

'But if he was *also* willing to promise that he'll say nothing about what happened here today . . .'

'He'll promise anything that you want him to promise,' Soames said, with obvious disgust. 'Don't you see that? He'll tell any amount of lies in order to save his own miserable life.'

'They're fools, aren't they, Blackstone?' Maude asked mildly.

'Complete bloody idiots.' He turned to his two friends – if they *were* his friends, if his huge ego had ever been capable of encompassing friendship – and continued, 'The reason that Blackstone has reached the conclusion that we didn't kill Charlie is because he knows what we really *did*.'

'Do you, Blackstone!' Hatfield screamed. 'Do you?'

'As I told you earlier, I know a great deal,' Blackstone replied. 'I know why you put those two privates – Clay and Jones – on a charge, Lieutenant Hatfield, even though you knew that by doing so you were making yourself look weak and incompetent.' He grinned. 'It was *always* going to be you who was going to put them on the charge, wasn't it? There was never really any question of it being Soames or Maude?'

'There . . . there were good reasons why I was the one chosen to do it,' Hatfield said.

'I'm sure they *sounded* good, when Maude explained them to you,' Blackstone replied. 'We both know how persuasive he can be. But whatever he said to you, it simply wasn't true. The *real* reason you were chosen was that you were the one with the least amount of honour to lose – and deep down inside yourself, you know that.'

'You're wrong,' Hatfield protested. 'We discussed it, and we decided that I should . . .'

'All right, all right, have it your own way,' Blackstone said dismissively. 'What else do I know? I know why Maude went to see Fortesque shortly before he died. I know why Soames smashed in Fortesque's skull half an hour before stand-to, and I know why you felt it was vital to steal the coffin from the warehouse in Calais.' He paused for a second. 'I also know, Lieutenant Hatfield, why Maude ordered you to attack me with the tent peg mallet.'

'He *didn't* order me to attack you,' Hatfield said angrily. 'It was something we all decided on.'

'Of course it was,' Blackstone agreed. 'And what exactly *were* your instructions?'

'Shut up, you bastard!' Hatfield said. He turned to Maude. 'Make him shut up, William.'

'Since the whole purpose of this interrogation is to find out what he knows, making him shut up would be rather pointless, don't you think?' Maude asked coldly. 'Besides, I find the whole way he's chosen to handle this situation absolutely fascinating.'

'Fascinating!' Hatfield repeated. 'For the love of God, what's *fascinating* about it?'

'Most men in Blackstone's position would either be begging for mercy by now, or doing all they could to ingratiate themselves with us. He's chosen quite a different approach, and I'd be most interested to see where that leads.' Maude turned his attention back to Blackstone. 'You may continue, Inspector.'

'At the time, I thought you'd been sent to kill me, Lieutenant Hatfield, and had simply made a mess of it,' Blackstone said. 'I see now that that wasn't the case at all. If you'd wanted me dead, you'd have been going for my skull, and you wouldn't have switched your flashlight on until you'd reached the head of the bed – but since you'd only been told to hurt me, you switched the light on when you were no more than halfway there, level with my trunk. And what I'm wondering at this moment, Lieutenant Hatfield, is if you even know *why* you were told to attack me.'

'Of course I know why I attacked you!' Hatfield said angrily. 'Maude thought – I mean, we *all* thought – that you were getting too close to the truth. We knew we couldn't kill you, because though you're only a lowly policeman, you are still *a* policeman, and Scotland Yard would feel duty-bound to send more officers over to investigate your death.'

'So the plan – as you saw it – was to take me out of action for at least a week or so?'

'Exactly.'

Blackstone laughed. 'You're not even close to the truth,' he said. 'Maude didn't particularly want me out of action, because he was rather enjoying playing games with me.'

'That's not true,' Hatfield protested. 'We all agreed . . .'

'Ask yourself one question,' Blackstone suggested. 'If Maude had really wanted me thoroughly worked over, why didn't he send Soames instead? Soames wouldn't have run like a scared rabbit the moment something went wrong. He would have stayed and finished the job. But the whole point of the exercise was never to hurt me – it was to muddy the waters a little.'

'I don't understand,' Hatfield said.

'Of course you don't,' Blackstone agreed. 'What Maude

wanted was to link the two crimes firmly together in my mind. I'd been attacked with a mallet, so I'd naturally think it was the same mallet which had been used to kill Fortesque. And the reason that would have muddied the waters is because Fortesque *wasn't* killed with a mallet at all – he wasn't even killed by a blow to the head!' He paused for a moment. 'Maude didn't explain that particular line of thought to you, did he? But then why should he have done? You weren't his co-conspirator – you were nothing more than an instrument.'

'I . . . we . . .' Hatfield stuttered.

'Don't you see, you've *always* been Maude's dupe?' Blackstone asked. 'Why, even back in your schooldays, in good old Eton College—'

'That's enough!' Maude said, suddenly.

Blackstone laughed again. 'Well, well, well, whoever would have thought it?' he asked. 'I've frightened you, haven't I, William? Here I am, tied up in a chair, and completely helpless, and I've still succeeded in frightening you.'

A look of black anger crossed Maude's face, and then was quickly replaced by his customary sardonic smile.

'You don't frighten me, Blackstone,' he said. 'A man like you could never frighten me.'

'Prove it,' Blackstone challenged.

For an instant, caution fought out a battle with arrogance on Maude's face, but then – as Blackstone had known it would – arrogance won a decisive and overwhelming victory.

'All right,' the young lieutenant agreed. 'You carry on with your clever little speech, Blackstone – and then you'll see for yourself just how little good it does you in the end.'

'You must have felt unworthy from the first day you set foot in the hallowed grounds of Eton College,' Blackstone told Hatfield. 'What right had you to be there, you asked yourself – a tradesman's grandson, rubbing shoulders with the descendants of men who fought with William the Conqueror? But despite feeling unworthy, you still desperately wanted to fit in, didn't you? You would have done anything to turn these wonderful people into your friends. You weren't to know – how could you? – that all your attempts were doomed to failure, right from the start.'

'That shows just how little you know,' Hatfield said, in a voice which probably even he didn't find convincing. 'I . . . I made some very good friends at Eton. And you're in this dugout with two of them now.'

'You didn't have *friends* then, and you don't have *friends* now,' Blackstone countered. 'All you've ever had is people who were prepared to *use* you for their own convenience, in much the same way as they might have used a groom – or a whore.'

'You're wrong. I—'

'When you were at Eton, did you take the blame for things you hadn't done?' Blackstone ploughed on, remorselessly. 'Were you ever given beatings that should rightfully have been administered to your "friend" Maude?'

'I don't remember.'

'Of course you do!'

'It's the kind of thing that friends do for one another,' Hatfield said. 'If you can spare a friend by taking the punishment on yourself, you do it without a second's thought.'

'And did Maude take any beatings for you, in return?'

'I . . . he may have done.'

'He didn't! My sergeant talked to your old housemaster – Edward Harrington Cardew – and Cardew told him that Maude was never beaten the whole time he was at Eton.'

'He . . . he was lucky.'

'No, he wasn't. He avoided punishment by using you as his whipping boy,' Blackstone said. 'And it didn't stop once you'd left your schooldays behind you, did it? Here in France, you did something for him that was far worse than anything you'd ever done for him before – you shot down a man in cold blood.'

'I did it for the honour of the regiment.'

'You might tell yourself that now, but the real reason you did it was simply because Maude asked you to,' Blackstone said harshly. 'You did it because you thought it might make him like you a little more. But it hasn't. If anything, it's only increased the depth of his contempt for you.'

'That's not true!' Hatfield protested.

'Not true! Look at his face, and tell me it's not true!'

Hatfield was so desperate for reassurance that it would have taken only the slightest effort on Maude's part – the smallest expression of insincere approval – to convince the tradesman's grandson that the man who he admired so much admired him in return.

But it was never going to happen. Maude's pride would not let it happen – especially with Blackstone looking on – and the expression that both the policeman and the young lieutenant saw on his face was one of open contempt.

Hatfield turned as pale as death. 'I . . . I have to go outside,' he gasped. 'I need some air.'

He rushed to the doorway, and stepped out into the trench. Once he was there, they could hear him retching.

'I was wrong in what I said earlier,' Maude told Blackstone. 'Your clever little speech *has* had some effect, after all. But, if I were you, I would draw no comfort from that.'

'Wouldn't you?'

'Most certainly not. By holding up a mirror to Hatfield – and letting him see himself as I have *always* seen him – you have caused me some little inconvenience. And I will not easily forgive you for that.'

'So what are you going to do about it?' Blackstone asked. 'Kill me? That was always your intention anyway.'

'Yes, it was,' Maude agreed. 'But perhaps now I might not make your death as merciful as it could otherwise have been.'

Blackstone fought off the urge to look at the door.

Hatfield had finished being sick. He was now completely silent, and was probably trying to work out, in his turmoil of a mind, what he should do next.

If he decided to come back into the dugout, the inspector told himself, then the game was as good as over.

But if Hatfield didn't come back, then he himself still had a small chance of emerging from this dugout alive.

TWENTY-THREE

A minute passed – a long, drawn-out minute, in which each second felt as momentous and heavy as a tent peg mallet being smashed down on an unsuspecting skull.

And when that minute did finally end, another followed on, beginning the same slow journey into a future of its own making.

Tick-tock . . . tick-tock . . .

Blackstone was still resisting the urge to look towards the door, though Soames had glanced in that direction several times.

Maude, for his part, was looking vaguely into the middle distance, with the sort of expression on his face that he might have worn if he'd been umpiring a rather boring cricket match.

It was Maude who finally broke the silence, as they'd all expected that it would be.

'Well,' he said, 'since Hatfield has obviously gone off to find a hole to crawl into, I suppose we'd better continue the interrogation without him.'

'What did you do with Charlie Fortesque's coffin once you'd stolen it from the warehouse?' Blackstone asked. 'Did you throw it into the sea? Or did you make a nice big bonfire out of it?'

'Those are monstrous suggestions!' Soames said angrily. 'Of course we didn't do anything like that. We buried it.'

A tear – so small that Blackstone might not even have noticed if he hadn't been looking for it – ran slowly down Soames' right cheek.

'We dug a grave – or, at least, Hatfield did – in some rather thick woods near Calais,' Maude said. 'I can tell you that, because even if you had the chance to search for it – which you won't – you'd never find it.'

'We couldn't give him a headstone,' Soames said. 'We didn't dare take the risk. But I said a few words over the grave and –' he sniffed – 'and it was as close to a Christian burial as we could manage.'

'That was such a touching little speech, Roger,' Maude said. 'Maybe later, you could write it down, and when we get back home, I'll have it set to music for you. But in the meantime,' he continued harshly, 'we still have the problem of this troublesome policeman to deal with.'

'Charlie Fortesque was a very bad President of Pop, wasn't he, Lieutenant Maude?' Blackstone said. 'He didn't hold a single Pop-Tanning all the time he was in charge.'

'How do you know all this?' Soames asked.

Because I got a very long telegraph from Sergeant Patterson, expertly decoded by Wally, the black sheep of the Winfield family, Blackstone thought.

'I'm ordering you to tell me how you know all these personal details of our private lives,' Soames raged.

'You wouldn't have held back on the beatings if you'd been in Fortesque's place, would you, William?' Blackstone asked, ignoring Soames, and speaking directly to Maude. 'You'd have held as many of them as you thought you could get away with. And you wouldn't have done it because you enjoy inflicting physical pain – I suspect that's more Soames' idea of fun – you'd have done it because you had the *power* to do it. And what's the point of having power if you don't use it?'

Maude smiled. 'I could use my power right now – by killing you where you sit,' he said.

'But you won't,' Blackstone told him, 'because before you can do that, you need to find out to what extent I'll be a danger to you even when I'm dead. You need to know what evidence I've collected, and where it is.'

'You have a good brain, and a strong nerve – I'll give you that,' Maude admitted. 'Not that either of those will save you, of course.'

'Of course not,' Blackstone agreed.

'So how do you think this whole unpleasant business started?' Maude asked, almost conversationally.

'It started with Charlie Fortesque,' Blackstone said. 'He was a gentle boy, by nature. We already know he wouldn't organize floggings at Eton, but there is much more evidence of his gentleness than that. He made an incompetent soldier called Blenkinsop his servant, in order to save him from being bullied – even though he had probably already half-promised the job to Danvers.'

'That shows just how little you *do* actually know,' Soames said scornfully. 'It wasn't Charlie who decided that Danvers would not be appointed his servant – it was us. We made it quite plain to him that it simply wouldn't do, and then we arranged for Danvers to be transferred to my platoon.'

'Which means that at that point you still thought you could contain the damage,' Blackstone said, unperturbed. 'But it had quite the reverse effect, didn't it? It only succeeded in bringing matters to a head.'

'Yes, you're quite right about that,' Maude admitted. 'It did bring matters to a head.'

'Would it really have ruined you – have tarnished the reputation of the regiment *so* much – if Charlie Fortesque had lived long enough to do what he so desperately wanted to do?' Blackstone asked.

'Of course it would!' Soames blustered. 'We'd have been the laughing stock of the whole army.'

'And there was his family's reputation to think of, too,' Maude added. 'How would old General Fortesque have felt if he'd known the truth?'

'Charlie wouldn't have been the first officer ever to be a homosexual, you know,' Blackstone pointed out. 'There's a long history of it – stretching right back to Alexander the Great.'

'*He* was a foreigner!' Soames said, with disgust.

'It wasn't so much what Charlie *did* – because you're right, and all armies have had their share of nancy boys,' Maude said. 'No, the problem with Charlie was that he had a conscience about it. He wanted to come clean about his sordid little affair, resign his commission on medical grounds, and set up a little love nest with Danvers.'

'With *Danvers*!' Soames exploded. 'With a common soldier – a peasant.'

'Yes, you must have thought that was *terribly* wrong of him, Lieutenant Soames,' Blackstone said.

'Damn right, I did!' Soames agreed.

'Especially when you consider that he could have had *you* instead – simply by asking!'

'You bastard!' Soames screamed. He appealed to Maude. 'I swear I never touched him – or any man.'

Maude smiled sadistically. 'I'm sure that's quite true, Roger' he said. 'But, let's be honest – we both know you've always wanted to.' He turned back to Blackstone. 'Do carry on with your narrative, Inspector.'

'You tried to persuade Fortesque to keep his secret, but he wouldn't, because – I suspect – he really *did* love Danvers. So what could you do? Well, you could remove the *reason* for the secret – by removing Danvers.'

*   *   *

'We can't just kill him,' Hatfield says.

'Have you got a better plan?' Maude counters.

'How would we do it, William?' asks Soames, who seems to have no qualms about the murder. 'Could we stick a rifle barrel in his mouth, and make it look like he killed himself?'

Maude gives him one of those looks he has grown accustomed to over the years, and now more or less accepts – a look which says he has the brain of an ant, and that he'd be better leaving the thinking to someone better equipped for it.

'And how do you propose to fake this suicide, in a trench full of witnesses?' Maude asks. 'Or do you perhaps plan to ask all the other Tommies to leave before we do the deed?'

'No, that wouldn't work,' Soames says.

'And besides, Charlie would never believe that his "lady friend" had killed himself – not when they were both so looking forward to their happy little life together,' Maude continues. 'It would be better if it looked like he'd been killed by Fritz. You could take him out on night patrol, Roger, and make sure he doesn't come back.'

'You want me to kill him personally?' Soames says.

'Would you have any objection to that?'

'No.'

'I thought not. But having you kill him wouldn't solve the problem at all,' Maude says.

'Why not?' Soames asks. 'What kind of problem could there be, once he was bloody well dead?'

'The problem is that Charlie would suspect we were behind it – just as he would suspect we were behind a suicide. And God alone knows what he might do then.' Maude thinks for a moment. 'No, what we need is an independent witness to Danvers' death – a witness who could swear that you had absolutely nothing to do with it.'

'How's that possible?' Soames asks.

'You don't just take Danvers out on patrol – you take another of your men as well. And the other man will be a witness to the fact that Danvers was shot down by Fritz.'

Soames looks troubled. 'I don't see how we'd ever manage that,' he tells Maude. 'The only way to ensure Fritz fires on us is to expose ourselves – and if we expose ourselves, the chances are that all three of us will be killed.' He pauses. 'Or is that the

*plan? We all three get killed?' He squares his shoulders. 'Well,
anything's better than having it known that not only is one of
our officers a nancy boy, but he's not even ashamed of it – so
for the good of the regiment, I'm prepared to make the
sacrifice.'*

*'You're not thinking – though that comes as no particular
surprise to anybody,' Maude says. 'I wouldn't send you out to
your death – not unless it was absolutely necessary. Besides, if
you remember, I said that the other Tommy with you had to come
back in one piece, so he can tell Charlie what happened.'*

Soames frowned. 'Then I don't see . . .'

*'It won't be Fritz who actually shoots down Danvers – it will
be Hatfield and myself.'*

'That was why, on the day that Danvers died, Hatfield came up
with a spurious reason for putting the two privates – Jones and
Clay – under arrest,' Blackstone said.

'Balderdash!' Soames said, though he was now the only one
in the dugout who thought there was any point to denial.

'Officers are issued with revolvers,' Blackstone said. 'You
needed rifles to kill Danvers, and arresting the two privates was
the best way to get your hands on a couple without raising any
suspicion.' He paused for a moment. 'That's right, isn't it,
Lieutenant Maude?'

'Indeed it is,' Maude replied.

'Apart from meeting the obvious need to get rid of Danvers,
the plan held a bonus for each of you,' Blackstone said. 'It
gave you, Maude, the chance to scheme and manipulate. It gave
Hatfield the opportunity to do something really appalling, and
thus demonstrate just how much your friendships meant to him.
And it gave you, Soames, the chance to lead to his death a man
who you were so jealous of that you hated him more than you'd
ever hated anyone before.'

'You swine! You filthy swine!' Soames screamed, as he lashed
out and slapped Blackstone hard across the face.

'Control yourself, Roger – there'll be plenty of time for that
later,' Maude said.

Blackstone rolled his head, in an attempt to shake off the
grogginess that came with the blow.

'Do you want me to carry on with my story – or would you

prefer to knock me about a little more first?' he asked Soames.

'Soames would like you to carry on,' Maude said. 'He is fascinated to learn how the mind of a common man works, aren't you, Roger?'

Soames said nothing.

'*Aren't you, Roger?*' Maude repeated.

'Yes,' Soames agreed grudgingly.

'It all went according to plan,' Blackstone said. 'It's true that because you, Maude, can't shoot straight, the other soldier, Private Mitchell, was wounded . . .'

'How do you know that I was the one who shot Mitchell?' Lieutenant Maude interrupted.

'Because it would have been Hatfield's job to shoot Danvers,' Blackstone replied.

'Are you saying I didn't have the nerve to kill Danvers?' Maude asked, and for the first time there was a hint of anger in his voice.

'Of course I'm not saying that,' Blackstone replied. 'You'd kill anybody or anything that got in your way, without a second's thought – but you get much more pleasure out of compelling others to do something than you'd ever get from doing it yourself.'

Maude nodded. 'Very clever,' he said. 'Do carry on.'

'Mitchell was wounded,' Blackstone continued, 'but that was all to the good, because it gave Soames the chance to play the hero – and who would ever suspect a hero of being a cold-blooded killer?'

'No one,' Maude said. 'Do you know, I wish that I'd have thought of that myself, and shot Mitchell deliberately.'

'It's as well you didn't,' Blackstone countered. 'With your degree of marksmanship, you'd probably have killed him. But, to get back to the story, we now move on to the next phase of the plan. You, Maude, went to see Fortesque a couple of hours before he died. At one time, I thought that you did that because you wanted to make one last appeal to Fortesque not to ruin you all. But it wasn't that at all – what you were actually doing was breaking the bad news.'

The moment Maude appears at the door to his dugout, Fortesque knows that something has gone very wrong.

'I'm so sorry to have to tell you this,' Maude says, 'but Private Danvers is dead.'

'How . . . how did it happen?' Fortesque gasps.

'A Fritz sniper, out in No Man's Land.'

'But . . .'

'These things happen in a war, Charlie,' Maude says. He advances into the dugout, and puts his hand on Fortesque's shoulder. 'I didn't approve of what was going on between the two of you, you know that, but you're my friend, and if you're hurt, then I'm hurt, too.'

'Thank you, old chap,' Fortesque says.

'Would you like me to stay with you for a while?' Maude asks. Fortesque shakes his head.

'Perhaps you're right,' Maude tells him. 'A man is better handling these matters on his own.'

'You could have insisted on staying, but you didn't,' Blackstone said. 'Instead, you decided to leave Charlie Fortesque alone with his grief, and – what was probably worse – his guilt,' Blackstone said.

'His guilt!' Soames exclaimed. 'Why should Charlie have felt guilty? He had nothing at all to do with Danvers' death.'

'Ah, but you see, he did – at least in his own mind,' Blackstone said. 'He could have made Danvers his servant, but he caved in under your pressure, and appointed Blenkinsop instead. Worse still, he allowed Danvers to be transferred to your platoon, Lieutenant Soames. And he knew that if he hadn't given way on those two things – and especially the latter one – Danvers would not have been out in No Man's Land that night. So whose fault was it that Danvers was dead? It was his!'

'So that's why he did it,' Soames said, almost choking on the words. 'That's why he . . .'

'Yes, I think so,' Blackstone said.

It is an hour before dawn when Soames reaches Fortesque's dugout. He has not come because Maude told him to – though Maude has – but because Charlie is his friend, and he loves him.

When he enters the dugout, Fortesque is sitting with his head on the table, and for a moment Soames thinks he must simply have collapsed from nervous exhaustion.

And then he sees the gun in his hand.

A great wave of anguish sweeps over him. He cannot believe that Charlie – beautiful, intelligent Charlie – would have done this to himself. He cannot accept that the one person he really cared about in the whole world is dead. He feels his legs give way under him, and when he hits the ground, his body curls up into a ball. And he is sobbing, weeping salt tears on to the packed earth floor.

Slowly, the grief abates a little, like a briefly retreating wave, and he can think – if only fracturedly – again.

Questions will be asked about Charlie's suicide – they are bound to be.

There are officers serving on the front line whose deaths could be put down to a loss of nerve – a cowardice which led them to believe that certain death now was preferable to the constant worry about possible death in the future. But anyone who had known brave, courageous Charlie Fortesque would not believe that of him for a moment.

So why, they would ask themselves, had he taken his own life?

And then it would all come out.

They would learn of the dirty disgusting things that he and Danvers had done together.

They would tie that in with the death of Danvers – and suddenly that death wouldn't seem as straightforward as it once had.

Disgrace would descend on the Fortesque family, and ridicule would be heaped on the regiment.

'How can I stop that happening?' asks Soames, still on the ground, still in the foetal position. 'What can I do?'

He wishes Maude was there to advise him. But Maude is not there – and he dare not go to look for him in case someone else happens to discover the body in the meantime.

As he is climbing to his feet – eyes stinging and mucus running down his chin – he has an idea.

If, instead of committing suicide, Charlie had been murdered, then an entirely different set of questions – the wrong questions – would be asked about his death. And if the wrong questions were asked, the right answers would never emerge.

He sees a hammer hanging on the wall, and lifts it off its hook. He walks over to the table, and stands there for a moment, looking down at his dead friend. His free hand lifts, almost of its own

volition, and gently strokes the dead man's cheek. Then he
removes the hand, steps back, and swings the hammer.

As it strikes the point at which the bullet entered Fortesque's
brain, he is sobbing again.

'I wondered how you could inflict so much damage and yet not
be covered with his blood,' Blackstone said. 'And then, of course,
I reached the only conclusion it was possible to reach – there
was so little blood because the heart had already stopped beating
before your attack began.'

'There was blood enough,' Soames said with a shudder. 'Blood
and bone and gristle. God, it was truly awful.'

'And then you left the body and carried out an inspection,
before returning to the dugout and "discovering" it again,'
Blackstone said. 'I must admit, I admire you for that. There can't
be many men who could have held themselves together after
what you'd been through.'

'Having survived Eton, you're prepared for anything,' Soames
said, almost mournfully. Then a sudden anger entered his voice,
and he added, 'Don't you *dare* say you admire me – I don't want
admiration from a man like you.'

'You must have panicked when you learned the body was
being sent back home,' Blackstone said, 'because while whoever
examined Fortesque here might have accepted that he'd been
battered to death, it wouldn't have taken long for a good police
surgeon in England to work out that he'd been shot. So you
dashed to Calais and stole the body.'

'Is that it?' Maude asked.

'Why would you want more?' Blackstone countered. 'There's
ample evidence there.'

'So there is,' Maude agreed. 'More than enough. But, you see,
it's all *circumstantial* evidence.'

'Even so, it would get you convicted in any court in England,'
Blackstone said, 'and at a court martial – which requires a lesser
burden of proof – it will be a cakewalk for whoever's prosecuting
you.'

'Not if you're not there to provide it.'

'I've written down everything I've just told you,' Blackstone
lied, 'and in the event of my death, it will be handed over to the
authorities.'

'Do you know, I don't believe you,' Maude said. 'But it doesn't really matter, anyway. If you're lying, your death will mean we'll get away with it. And if you're not lying, we're as good as dead anyway.' He reached into his belt and produced a long wicked-looking knife. 'So why should I let *you* live?'

'Didn't they teach you the difference between right and wrong at Eton, Lieutenant Soames?' Blackstone asked.

'Of course they did,' Soames replied.

'Then you know what's about to happen is wrong,' Blackstone said. 'And not just wrong – it's dishonourable.'

'I . . . I . . .' Soames said, his mouth opening and closing like a fish's.

'Be your own man for once,' Blackstone urged. 'Don't do what Maude wants you to do – do what you *should* do! Stop him before it's too late.'

Maude smiled. 'Well, what's it to be, Roger?' he asked. 'Do I kill him – or do I let him live?'

'I . . . I . . .' Soames repeated, his mouth once more doing a fish impression. He turned, suddenly, so that his back was to them. 'Do what you want,' he said, over his shoulder.

Well, you tried, Sam, Blackstone told himself. You did the best you could, and you failed. Now it's time to prepare yourself for the end.

There was a sound of footfalls in the trench outside.

Maude lurched across the table, and placed the point of his knife against Blackstone's throat.

'If you make a sound now, I'll kill you!' he hissed.

The door opened, and two men – one of them carrying an oil lamp – stepped into the dugout. The one with the lamp was Lieutenant Hatfield, and the one without one was Captain Carstairs.

Maude dropped the knife, and sprang to his feet.

'You went running straight to the beak, did you, Benjamin?' he sneered at Hatfield. 'Well, I suppose that's all I should have expected from a man of your background.'

'You will not speak in my presence without my express permission!' Captain Carstairs barked.

Maude came to attention. 'I apologize, sir,' he said.

'As you have rightly surmised, Lieutenant Maude, Lieutenant Hatfield came to me and told me all about this unfortunate affair,'

Carstairs said. 'It was the right thing to do – it was no more than his duty – and I will not have him criticized for it. Is that understood?'

'Yes, sir,' Maude said.

Carstairs nodded. 'Good. And now I would like you all to follow me, gentlemen.'

He turned smartly, and left the dugout. He had not looked at Blackstone once, in all the time he was there.

TWENTY-FOUR

Whatever the time of year, it always felt as if there was a slight chill in the trench in the hour before dawn. That morning, the chill seemed more intense than usual. It clung to the sandbags, and wafted along the duckboards. It enveloped the Tommies who were queuing up for their ration of rum. And it appeared to have frozen the three lieutenants – standing apart from their men – into the sort of statues that would later be seen mounted on war memorials in country churchyards.

Mick had had two fears pressing down heavily on him. The first – more immediate one – had been that the rum would run out before he reached the front of the line, but now he had his tin cup of rum firmly in his hand, it was time for the second fear to come into its own.

'I've never been into battle before,' he told the man standing next to him.

'I can tell that, just by looking at you,' the other soldier replied, then took a small, careful sip of his rum.

'Yes, this is my first time,' Mick said, 'and to tell you the truth, I'm a little bit scared.'

The other man laughed. 'You don't want to waste your precious time being scared,' he said.

'Don't I?'

'Of course you don't. Look at this way – if you survive the assault, you've nothing to worry about, have you?'

'No, I suppose not.'

'And if you're killed by Fritz – well, then you *really* have nothing to worry about.'

Mick took a sip of his rum, and felt it burn, strangely comfortingly, deep down in his stomach.

'If I live there's no problem, and if I die there's no problem,' he mused. 'I've never thought about it that way before.'

'*Someone* needs to say *something*,' one of the officer statues – Soames – told the other two.

'I've nothing *to* say,' replied the second, Maude. 'Not to you, and certainly not to this Judas.'

'I'm so sorry,' Hatfield said.

'For God's sake, has Eton taught you nothing!' Soames exploded. 'You *never* – under any circumstances – apologize!'

Hatfield nodded, acknowledging the truth of the statement, then took a deep breath.

'I did the right thing,' he said firmly. 'We were all caught up in a cycle of madness, and killing wasn't just the *easy* answer – it was the *natural* one. Somebody had to put a stop to it.'

'Typical bourgeois thinking,' Maude sneered. 'You're nothing but a costermonger in a bespoke uniform.'

'That's enough!' Soames said forcefully.

'Enough?' Maude repeated, surprised.

'That's what I said. Whatever happened in the past is over and done with. You and Hatfield are comrades who are going into battle together. You will shake hands, and you will wish each other good luck. And you will do it now!'

Maude hesitated for a moment, then held out his hand. 'Good luck, Hatfield, old chap,' he said. 'See you in Berlin.'

And as Hatfield took the hand, they heard the sound of a whistle blowing – and knew it was time to climb the ladder and step out into a living hell.

The oil in the lamp had run out shortly after Soames, Maude, Hatfield and Carstairs had left, and the dugout had been plunged into darkness.

Blackstone did not know how long he had been there. His aching body screamed that it must be at least half a lifetime, but his mind told him it could not be more than a few hours.

Initially, he had tried to escape, but whoever had tied him to the chair – probably Soames – had made an excellent job of it, and after a while, he had simply given up.

As he sat there, with only the sound of the occasionally muffled explosion to distract him, he thought about his life – the women he had loved and the friends he had seen die. He wondered why his successes seemed to him so modest, and his failures so monumental.

He did not think about the future – he was not sure he had one.

When he heard the footsteps in the trench, he knew that matters would soon be resolved, but he was not sure what that resolution would be – even once the door was opened – because the light which flooded in temporarily blinded him.

'How are you, Inspector Blackstone?' asked a voice.

'As well as can be expected, Captain Carstairs,' Blackstone replied, as his vision returned.

Carstairs produced a knife. It may well have been the same knife that Maude had threatened him with earlier.

'We'll have you free in a moment,' he said, cutting through the rope which bound Blackstone's wrists and ankles to the chair, 'and by tomorrow you should be back in England, with all this unpleasantness left behind you.'

Blackstone stood up, and began to walk around. The first few steps were painful, but then the pain eased as his circulation improved.

'So you think all this "unpleasantness" will be behind me, do you, Captain?' he asked.

'Oh, yes,' Carstairs said confidently.

'Then you seem to be forgetting that there's still the small matter of a murder that I have to clear up.'

'You'll never find out who killed Lieutenant Fortesque,' Carstairs said. 'No one will.'

'Fortesque committed suicide,' Blackstone replied. 'It's the murder of Private Danvers I'm talking about.'

'Danvers was killed by Fritz, and Fortesque was murdered by person or persons unknown,' Carstairs said flatly.

'Lieutenant Hatfield will confess,' Blackstone told him. 'It might take a while, but, in the end, he'll spill the whole story.'

'Unfortunately, Lieutenant Hatfield is dead, as are Lieutenants Soames and Maude,' Carstairs said.

'What!'

'They all died bravely, defending the country that they love. They were heroes.'

'You sent them out on a suicide mission,' Blackstone accused.

'I sent them to capture a German machine-gun position, and – after their deaths – some of the men they had been leading succeeded in doing just that.'

'How many of our men lost their lives in capturing that position?'

'I believe it was fifteen.'

'You *believe* it was fifteen? You don't *know*?'

'In the confusion of war, it's often some time before we have accurate casualty figures.'

'And will the men who survived – the ones who captured the machine-gun nest – be able to hold it?' Blackstone asked.

'Possibly not.'

'So they'll die too?'

'This is war, Mr Blackstone,' Carstairs said. 'Men die.'

'So you've sacrificed perhaps thirty men – though it could be more, because you won't have the accurate casualty figures for some time – in order to save the reputations of three public schoolboys,' Blackstone said angrily.

'Sooner or later, all those men would have died anyway,' Carstairs said, indifferently. 'Most of the men who are currently serving with me will die before the war is over – myself included. But the regiment itself, though stained with the blood of its fallen, will emerge from the war with its reputation intact – and I will be able to go to my own death knowing that.'

'You're insane,' Blackstone said.

'Perhaps I am,' Carstairs agreed. 'But it is just that kind of insanity which has transformed a small wet country, on the edge of Europe, into the mightiest nation on earth.' He paused for a moment. 'You have got what you came for, Mr Blackstone.'

'Have I?'

'Indeed you have. You wanted three men, who you might choose to call murderers, to be punished for their crime – and so they have been. They are as dead now as they would have been if they'd been hanged or marched before a firing squad. You should be well satisfied with your work here.' He paused again. 'But *are you* satisfied, Inspector Blackstone?'

'No,' Blackstone admitted, 'I'm not.'

'Of course you're not,' Carstairs agreed. 'And why aren't you? Because we both know that yours is a mere tactical victory – that seen in terms of the wider history, you have lost, and the regiment has won.' He shook his head, almost pityingly, from side to side. 'So go back to England, Inspector Blackstone – because you can do nothing more here.'

TWENTY-FIVE

The White Cliffs of Dover had been visible ever since they set sail from Calais, but that had not stopped the enlisted men from crowding on to the lower deck to watch them getting ever-closer. There was some pushing and shoving for a better position as the voyage progressed, it was true – there was even a little shouting and complaining – but, on the whole, it was all good-natured.

And why wouldn't the soldiers be good-natured when, after enduring all the horror of the trenches, they were finally going home on leave? Blackstone asked himself.

He pictured them turning up at their own front doors, and being embraced by wives and sweethearts.

He could almost hear them telling those same wives and sweethearts that though this *was* only a leave, and they would soon be going back to France, there was nothing to worry about, because the war would soon be over.

Perhaps they would even believe these assurances themselves, Blackstone thought.

But he had seen quite enough – on his own short visit to the front line – to know that they could repeat the words a thousand times, and it still wouldn't make them true.

The two sides were too evenly matched – and too equally supplied – for a quick victory. The war would drag on until everyone, even the high-ranking officers sitting in their comfortable chateaux miles from the front line, was heartily sick of bloodshed – and then it would drag on a little while longer.

He looked up, and watched the officers – almost all of them

young second lieutenants – strolling around the comfortably empty upper deck. He did not begrudge them this moment of luxury, for while it was probably true that many of the enlisted men on this boat would eventually die in action, it was almost certain that most of these officers would.

He went below deck, to visit those men who would not be going back to France – men who had lost arms or legs (and sometimes both); men who had half their faces blown off; men who lay on stretchers, groaning and holding their stomachs, as if that would take away the pain.

He lit cigarettes for those men who could not light their own, and chatted to those who wished to talk.

'Was it like this when you were soldiering in India?' asked one of the soldiers who had lost a leg.

'No,' Blackstone said, 'it was quite different.'

'Was it as terrible as this?' the soldier wanted to know.

'All wars are terrible.'

'But was it as terrible *as this*?' the soldier insisted.

The man had lost a limb defending his country, and deserved an honest answer, Blackstone decided.

'No,' he said, 'if only by the sheer scale of the carnage, no war has *ever* been as terrible as this – and I hope to God that no war ever is again.'

Behind him – and amidst all this misery and suffering – he heard someone singing. He recognized the song. It was a ditty which was very popular in the music halls, and told the story of a patriotic young woman, who, furious at seeing a young man standing alone, marches up to him, and demands to know why he is not 'fighting for your country as it's fighting for you?'

Blackstone turned around. The singer was sitting alone in the corner. He had only a stump where his right arm had once been, and it was this stump that he was serenading.

He had reached the point in the song at which the young man answers the young woman's question.

'I would if I'd the chance,' he crooned, in a cracked voice, 'but my right arm's in France; I'm one of England's broken dolls.'

As Blackstone took the stairs back up to the deck, he resolved to track down the writer of that sickly, sentimental song and give him just a little idea of what real pain was like by bloodying his nose for him.

The White Cliffs of Dover had drawn much closer while he'd been below deck, and the boat would soon be docking in the port.

There were two very important things he had to do as soon as he got back to England, he reminded himself, and it was only when he *had* done them that this bloody episode in his life would finally be over.

They were in General Fortesque's study, looking out on to the gardens and watching an old man examining a hoe and wondering what he should do with it.

'I've failed you, General,' Blackstone said. 'I can tell you that your grandson was a fine officer and that his men would have followed him anywhere, but I can't tell you who killed him.'

'Can't?' the General asked sharply. 'Or won't?'

It came to the same thing, Blackstone thought. The old man had already suffered enough, without heaping any further heartbreak on him.

'I'm not sure I understand what you mean,' he said aloud.

'Was my grandson a homosexual?' the General demanded.

'Why would you ask that?'

'Charlie used to play with Danvers' grandson when he was a boy. The rest of the family disapproved – including his parents – but I didn't want him growing up believing that the working man is nothing but scum, and so I overruled them.' He smiled wistfully. 'I could do that, you know – I was the head of the family.'

Blackstone returned his smile. 'And the head of the family is always right,' he said.

'I thought so at the time, and sometimes I still think it,' General Fortesque said. 'But then I also thought that as the two boys grew older, they would also grow apart. Yet even once Charlie had gone to Eton – and had a wide circle of friends drawn from his own class – he still found time for young Danvers. Of course, I never allowed myself to even contemplate the notion that there was anything improper or unnatural in their relationship. In fact, if you'd asked me only a few days ago, I would still have said that though it was a somewhat unusual friendship, that was still all that it was – a friendship. I would have said it, and I would have believed it – or, at least, I would have *believed* that I believed it.'

'But you're not so sure now that you *did* believe it?'

'No, I am not.'

'So what happened?' Blackstone asked gently.

The General sighed. 'I caught myself writing a letter to young Charlie's commanding officer, asking him to see to it that young Danvers' body was repatriated,' he said.

'I know about that letter,' Blackstone told him.

'I may not have been to the front myself, but I have some idea of what it's like out there,' the General continued. 'I knew that recovering Danvers' body from No Man's Land would be a hazardous business, and that men might be injured – or even killed – in the process. I myself had no particular wish to see the body returned to England – and as for old Danvers, he's reached the point now where he probably doesn't even remember *having* a grandson. Yet I sent the letter anyway. Why was that, Sam?'

There was no point in pretending any longer.

'Because you knew, deep inside, that that's what Charlie would have wanted you to do,' Blackstone said.

'Because I knew, deep inside, that that's what Charlie would have wanted me to do,' the General agreed. 'So I'll ask you again, Inspector Blackstone, was my grandson a homosexual?'

'Yes, he was.'

'And now we've got that out of the way, perhaps you can tell me why he died – and who killed him.'

Blackstone outlined the whole story, and as it drew to a close, he cautioned, 'But you'll never get anyone in the army to admit that's what actually happened, you know.'

'Of course I won't,' the General agreed. 'Nor would I even try. The Soames, Maude and Hatfield families have all lost sons – young men who, whatever else they might have done, did give their lives for their country – and it is not for me to add to the anguish that they are already suffering.'

'I think you're right,' Blackstone agreed.

The General hesitated before speaking again, and when he finally did, he said, 'Was this thing that went on between my Charlie and young Danvers merely an expression of their animal urges, or was there more to it than that?'

'If it had been merely sexual, he would have kept quiet about it,' Blackstone said. 'But he had decided to come clean, even though he knew it would cost him almost everything he had ever held dear. I think you can draw your own conclusions from that.'

'My late wife and I loved each other deeply, but true love doesn't come to every young man,' the General said.

'No, it doesn't,' Blackstone agreed.

'But when it *does* come, it is a glorious gift,' the General continued. 'And that, I think, is true whatever form that love may choose to take.' He paused again. 'Do you agree with me, Sam?'

'I do,' Blackstone told him.

The General looked at him quizzically. 'You can be honest with me. I'm strong enough to take it.'

'I am being honest,' Blackstone said firmly.

'Then there is still the question of the reward I offered you,' the General said, suddenly businesslike. 'It was five thousand pounds, wasn't it?'

'Give the money to Dr Barnardo's Orphanage,' Blackstone said.

'All of it?'

'All of it.'

'Well, if that is your wish . . .'

'It is.'

'And there is nothing at all that you want for yourself?'

'Nothing,' Blackstone said.

And then he suddenly realized that, though he didn't want it for himself, there *was* something he wanted – and wanted quite badly.

The long narrow street, standing in the shadow of a stinking tannery, was lined with terraced houses. The houses themselves were crumbling and neglected, owned by landlords who knew they need do nothing to them, because their tenants had no choice but to put up with the conditions and pay the rent every Friday.

The street was only a mile or so from one the finest parks in London, and not much further from Buckingham Palace itself, but it was in another world – a world which Blackstone knew well, a world he regarded as his own.

He knocked on the front door of No. 16, and a woman answered. She was only in her late-thirties, Blackstone guessed, and must once have been quite pretty, but the hard life she had led meant that she was already old.

'Mrs Flowers?' he asked.

'Yes?'

Blackstone smiled inwardly. Mick had never told him his surname was Flowers, but that was more than understandable. For a hard lad from the slums – a lad whose whole sense of self-esteem was based on being tougher than his mates – the surname must have been a real curse.

'My name's Blackstone. I've come about your son, Mick,' he told the woman.

'Mick's . . . Mick's dead,' Mrs Flowers said. 'He was killed on the Western Front.'

'I know,' Blackstone agreed. 'Do you think I might come in for a few minutes?'

'Of course,' Mrs Flowers said. 'Where *are* my manners?'

She led him into the front parlour. There was not much furniture, but there was a large pile of cardboard sheets in one corner, and a number of cardboard cylinders in the other.

'Sorry about the mess,' she said, indicating he should sit on one of the two chairs. 'I make hat boxes, as you can see for yourself. And when there's no call for them, I make paper flowers or scrubbing brushes. It's what they call a cottage industry, but I just think of it as cheap labour.'

'The money's not very good then?' Blackstone asked, though he already knew the answer.

'You're wrong there,' Mrs Flowers said. She chuckled. 'The money's wonderful – but there's just not much of it.' She sat down opposite Blackstone, then stood up again immediately. 'Would you like a nice cup of tea?'

'I'm fine,' Blackstone assured her. 'Please sit down again.'

Mrs Flowers sat. 'So what do you do for a living, Mr Blackstone?'

'I'm a policeman – a detective inspector from Scotland Yard – but I'm not here on police business.'

'If you were, you wouldn't be the first policeman who's ever been in here for that purpose, you know. They were always calling round about our Mick. Not that I can blame them – I loved him, but even I have to admit he was a bit of a tearaway.'

'He doesn't sound much like the bloke I met in France, then,' Blackstone said. '*That* Mick was a fine young man.'

'Are you sure that it's my Mick you're talking about?' Mrs Flowers asked suspiciously.

'It was your Mick,' Blackstone confirmed. 'He helped me solve a murder – I'd never have been able to do it without his assistance – but he was killed before I had time to thank him, so I'm doing the next best thing, and thanking you.'

'It was good of you to take the trouble to come,' Mrs Flowers said gratefully.

'And that's not the *only* reason I came,' Blackstone said. 'I wanted to inform you that they're going to give Mick a Distinguished Conduct Medal, and you'll probably have to go to Buckingham Palace to collect it.'

'You're not joking, are you?' Mrs Flowers asked, the suspicion back in her voice. 'Because if you was, it would be a very *cruel* joke.'

'I'm not joking,' Blackstone promised her.

'But there's thousands of our poor brave lads die in France every month, and they don't all get medals,' Mrs Flowers said.

'You're right in everything you've just said,' Blackstone agreed. 'They *are* brave lads, they *do* die in their thousands, and they *don't* all get medals – but, by God, they all bloody well should.'

'So what's so special about our Mick?' Mrs Flowers wondered.

'Just before he died, he captured an enemy machine-gun post,' Blackstone said. 'That one action saved the lives of a lot of other lads just like him. He died a hero.'

And maybe it was even true, he thought. *Somebody* had captured the machine-gun post that Carstairs had ordered his men to attack, and it might easily have been Mick. Even if it *hadn't* been him – even if he'd been cut down by a bullet the second he left the trench – he would certainly have had both the character and the courage to have done it if he'd survived. And, if all that was true, why shouldn't his mother have the consolation of a medal, which wouldn't fill the aching void she'd been left with, but was at least better than nothing?

'You're not telling the whole story,' Mrs Flowers said. 'There's something else you've left out.'

Blackstone smiled. 'I told Mick he would have made a good detective – and I can see where he got it from now.'

'Let's have it,' Mrs Flowers said firmly.

'There is an element of influence in him getting the medal,' Blackstone admitted. 'Mick had a very good friend—'

'That would be you,' Mrs Flowers interrupted – though she was clearly finding it hard to believe that her tearaway son could have had a good friend who was a police inspector from New Scotland Yard.

'That would be me,' Blackstone confirmed. 'And not only was I a very good friend of Mick's, but I just happen to know an old man who was once a general – and who still has influence in some very high places.'

ML   2-12